DRAGON FAE CURSE

THE ELUSTRIA CHRONICLES: DRAGON FAE
BOOK TWO

CAETHES FARON

BECOME AN INSIDER

Get sneak peeks and stay up to date on new releases by signing up for the author's Insider Newsletter at

CaethesFaron.com.

_I_ should have known better. Happy endings, vacations, rest, those weren't for people like me. Normal wasn't for people like me.

Deacon laughed at a line in my favorite sitcom. We were supposed to be watching it together, cuddled up on Sybil's sofa, but I was busy watching his reactions.

He caught me looking at him. "You were right, this is funny."

"I'm always right. Better you learn that now." I cuddled even closer into him, relishing the normalcy even as I pushed down the feeling that it was a stolen moment.

After last night, I'd expected things to be awkward with Deacon. In my vulnerable moment of exhaustion, he'd shown care and concern as he washed the blood from me after our mission. I'd welcomed the tenderness of his touch.

Showering after a mission was a ritual for me. It was the end point. I washed away not just the Arizona dust but the mental dirt of the job. When I entered the shower, I was a spy and assassin. When I exited, I was Nadiya.

Letting Deacon into my ritual in such an intimate way was out of character for me. In the light of day, I'd expected to be angry at myself for exposing that kind of vulnerability, for allowing him to care for me. But when I woke and came to Sybil's apartment to see him, anger was the furthest emotion from me.

Another joke on the TV, another laugh from Deacon. Seeing him laugh made me a kind of happy I hadn't been in years, a kind of happy I didn't deserve.

The kind of happiness that would crumble in a second.

The TV turned off with a pop. Sybil stood in front of us, her face paler than any person I'd ever seen. She brought a cold with her that chased away the warmth of the atmosphere. The chill slammed into my chest and settled into my bones.

This was my normal.

"What is it?" I asked, standing in front of her. If she didn't speak soon, I'd shake it out of her.

Sybil's eyes stared into the distance of some unseen plane. "Queen Malev. She's demanding to see you."

The fae queen terrified any sensible person, but what I saw in Sybil's face went deeper than fear.

"She can demand all she likes. I'm not one of her subjects." I didn't feel as confident as I sounded, but I resented the fae queen scaring someone I cared about into sending me a message.

Sybil's blue eyes focused on me with such sharp intensity that it cut through my faux confidence. "She has Alistair."

My stomach dropped to the floor. This shouldn't be possible. Alistair wasn't one of Malev's subjects. That the Circle of Sorcerers, my employers, allowed Malev to take him meant they'd either abandoned us or endorsed her actions. Or Malev had no interest in maintaining good relations with the Circle. In the empty cavern of my gut, anger swirled.

"We have to go," I said before I even came up with a plan. I wasn't one to jump to Queen Malev's command, no matter how much she scared me, but I couldn't leave her waiting if she had Alistair.

Alistair was my handler, the one constant in my life. If anyone should get kidnapped, it was me. He should be safe behind the scenes.

I shouldn't have let him go to Elustria to warn people about the Directorate's attack.

Then again, there would've been no stopping him. His only niece had died during the preliminary attack. No one could have stopped him from doing what he thought necessary. I respected and loved him too much to stand in his way when he'd told me about his plan. He would've felt the same anger I did now. I understood how that fire stoked a person to action.

"Of course we're going to go," Deacon said beside me. "But we need to have some sort of plan. We can't show up blind in the fae court."

The sound of his voice, the feel of him beside me, it sunk into me in a comforting wave. This whole situation was new to me. I was used to putting my life in danger on missions. I was, unfortunately, used to losing partners, but Alistair was different. He was family, and he was taken because of me.

"No, you can't go." I turned in time to see the surprise and a hint of hurt in Deacon's eyes. "It's bad enough that she has Alistair. I can't risk her getting you too."

The people closest to me were always getting hurt by my actions. Alistair's kidnapping had me stretched to my limit. If I worried about Deacon, it would cloud my judgment with Malev. I needed all my senses to spar with her verbally or even physically if it came to it.

"I have no intention of letting her capture me," Deacon said.

"And Alistair did?"

"That's not what I meant."

Deacon's confidence should have bolstered me, but it didn't. "I know, but I need to focus on getting Alistair out. I can't worry about protecting you."

"Has it ever occurred to you that I don't need protecting? That maybe you should let the rest of us protect you for a change?"

In Deacon's eyes, I saw the last week of memories we'd made together. Had it really been so short a time? He'd proven capable. His only blunders had been intentional ones. His competence was one of his most attractive qualities, and I wanted to rely on it now, but I couldn't.

"I don't need protecting here. If Queen Malev wanted to hurt me, there are a thousand better ways to do it. She captured Alistair because she wants something from me. She won't hurt me. But you are another source of leverage over me. She'll do anything she has to in order to get what she wants, including taking a dragon shifter. There's no upside to you going, only risk. I'm not being irrational."

He rolled my words around in his head, and once he was satisfied with their logic, he nodded.

I smiled at him. "Besides, someone's going to have to explain this to Pint." My miniature dragon companion would be quite bent out of shape when he heard this development.

"He's going to kill me when he finds out I let you go without me," Deacon said.

The corners of my lips twitched into something that would be a smile if it weren't so serious an occasion. "Nonsense. Pint knows me well enough to know that no one lets me do anything."

Deacon gave me a grim nod then pulled me into a hug. I sucked in a breath of surprise. Elustrians weren't huggers, except for Sybil, who had seemed to take to the human custom.

Our magics crashed into each other with the same force with which Deacon held me to him. This was why magic folk didn't hug. His magic probed mine, searching for places to intertwine, and when it found them, it hung on tight.

This was more than a hug, though. He seemed to hold me as if he could keep me from leaving or as if his strength could somehow transfer to me. He breathed in the lavender scent of my hair, the scent he had shampooed into it just last night.

"Be safe. I only just found you," he whispered into my hair.

I didn't know if he meant me or if he meant that he'd only just found the Dragon Fae, the woman whom he'd sacrificed his hide to protect. To him, I supposed they were one and the same even though I didn't think of myself that way.

"Don't waste energy worrying over me. I'll be back in no time. Besides, how mad can Malev be? I did what she wanted." I suppressed the shudder that threatened my body at so casually referring to the fae queen. No one used her given name like that.

I didn't believe what I said, but it was important to put on a brave front. Malev wanted me to be the Dragon Fae, but that didn't mean she'd be happy with what I'd done. I'd taken it upon myself to forcefully declare my identity to the world without her, depriving her of control over the narrative.

"I don't think it's wise to keep her waiting any longer," Sybil said. "She's not used to waiting for anything."

I nodded. "Let's go then."

"I'm going to take us right into the court. She'll want to show off that the Dragon Fae appears at her command. Try to show more humility than you did with Drake. She won't be as forgiving as he was. She may want something from you now, but she could just as easily change her mind and kill you."

I wished she hadn't said that around Deacon. I was accustomed to everyone I came in contact with preferring me dead, but he wasn't yet used to the dangers of this job. His face showed only grim determination. It reminded me that he'd spent much of his life on the unforgiving Spineback Mountains protecting the remaining dragons.

Sybil looked more serious than I'd ever seen her. Holding my tongue didn't come naturally. When I'd mouthed off at Drake, the Dragon Prince, it had been instinct. She was right, though, he'd tolerated it because he wanted to be the Dragon Companion.

"I'll do my best. I won't give her a reason to hurt Alistair." I had to give Malev credit. She knew how to get to me. My team's safety was about the only thing that would get me to mind my tongue.

Sybil took my hand. "Then into the fae court we go."

2

The fae court existed in the fae realm, a distinct place separate from Elustria and Earth. It was only accessible to the fae and those they permitted. It was a big part of why Malev could be so cavalier about the world. Elustria and Earth could burn, and she could retreat to her realm.

I'd never known many fae. The few I had known wouldn't have been invited to Malev's court. She only allowed her favorites and the political elite to remain in the fae realm. So nothing could have prepared me for what I saw.

Sybil took us right into the throne room. It seemed like a dream that would dissolve as soon as I moved. The floor beneath my feet looked like pastel stained glass, held together with golden metal vines that were surprisingly flush and smooth with the rest of the floor. The pale pinks and greens shimmered in the light.

Looking around, I couldn't find the source of the light. It seemed to come from the glass walls, floor, and ceiling itself. Above me, glass jutted down like stalactites. Above the glass ceiling there appeared to be grass, as if a garden grew above our heads.

The giant room we stood in was cleared in the center in expectation of our arrival. All around the outskirts of the room were different types of fae. Some big and ugly, others small and pretty like Sybil.

Sybil.

She stood beside me, but the glamour that encompassed her on Earth fell away. A part of me knew that she had to use glamour on Earth. Fae didn't look as human as she did. I supposed I'd let myself be fooled.

Her blonde hair gave way to a dark green. Her eyes were purple here and her ears formed little points. Translucent wings jutted from her back. On Earth, I'd often sped my car down the freeway, trying to fly across the road to release my frustration over not being able to use magic. Sybil, on the other hand, had literally given up flying. I didn't know if I'd be able to do that.

"Ah, the Dragon Fae, come at last to pay homage to this court," the fae queen said from her throne. She wore a circlet of golden flowers atop her head as a crown. Even without it, there'd be no mistaking who she was. A female attendant stood behind her, ready to do her bidding.

Rose-colored hair fell in waves over her shoulders. Her pale green dress seemed to be made out of the same nearly translucent glittery material as her gossamer wings. Her skin was a light pink and white color, like a child with pink skin who got into her mother's powder.

The effect was glorious. She was the most beautiful woman I'd ever seen. I wondered for a moment if she was using glamour. It wouldn't do for the fae queen to be upstaged by one of her subjects. Even her eyes were a pale pink color. Instead of a bloody or demonic look, it came off angelic.

I was so taken in by her that it took me a moment to realize she was waiting for a reply of some sort. I hadn't come here to pay homage, but if that's what it took to get Alistair released, I could put on a show, no matter how much it pained me to do so.

"Your Majesty." I curtsied down to one knee and bowed my head. "As the Dragon Fae, it is only right that I appear at the fae queen's command." I took careful stock of my words. While I still wasn't completely convinced of my supposed fae blood, there had been evidence of it, and a fae could not break their word. They were not bound to honesty the way humans liked to believe, but they are bound by their word. I didn't know if that applied to me or not. I'd have to ask Sybil when we were back home, but now was not the time to test it.

Malev left me kneeling for a moment to let everyone present see the submission of the Dragon Fae. This was all a power play for her. "Rise, Nataliana, or do you prefer Nadiya?"

After all this time, it was jarring to hear someone use both my names in the same conversation. No one was supposed to know them. Until now, Deacon and Sybil had been the only people to do it. Malev having that kind of knowledge about me was unsettling, but I needed to get used to it. After I had the shade announce me as the Dragon Fae using my imprint, I supposed it would be common enough knowledge eventually.

I let the surprise at her comment wash over me before I rose so there'd be no trace of it on my face. The answer to her question required no thought. I may have been Nataliana once before, but no longer. "I prefer Nadiya, Your Majesty."

"Oh, you don't prefer Dragon Fae? Interesting since you took it upon yourself to take that title." A dangerous undertone laced her cheery voice.

So this was the direction this was going. I heard a few snickers from the fae looking on.

Before I could answer, she continued, "But that's a conversation for another place. Come, let me show you around my court."

She descended the few steps from her dais, wiggled her fingers, and we appeared outside the throne room. It'd been so long since I'd been in a magical realm that the casual use of teleportation momentarily threw me. It should feel comfortable, like home, but it didn't.

We stood at the base of a giant oak tree. Light shone beneath my feet between the blades of grass. A closer look revealed that we were standing on top of the throne room we'd just left.

Malev casually walked away, expecting us to follow. "They've seen your display of obedience, no need for them to see how you'll react to the rest of what I have to say."

"Ah, you don't want them to see my anger. Don't want the subjects getting any ideas."

Malev looked over her shoulder at me and cocked an eyebrow. "I can't decide if you're brave or stupid."

"There's no need to choose."

"Hmm." Malev looked away and resumed walking.

Beside me, Sybil whacked my arm and gave me a look that said I needed to be smarter. She wouldn't say anything in front of Malev, but she was worried. I gave her a cocky grin and lengthened my stride to walk by the queen's side.

"You have me here. What is it you want? And why did you feel kidnapping my handler would get a better response than a simple summons?"

Malev glanced at me from the corner of her eye as she walked. The brief glimpse of her eyes showed a hint of admiration at my confident bearing. "It got you here, didn't it? Besides, I didn't want you getting any ideas. Just because you decided to declare yourself the Dragon Fae doesn't make it so. I can still take what's most precious to you."

Her words cut too close to my heart. I may have killed my fair share of people but she'd wielded cruelty to maintain her crown for longer than I'd been alive.

"I didn't decide to be the Dragon Fae. I was told that I was by Chancellor Meilin. She said she acted with your consent."

"Yes, that's the key to all this: my consent. You're not the Dragon Fae yet. I can just as easily pick another young woman to fulfill the prophecy."

"Actually—" we both turned to look at Sybil as she spoke for the first time, "Nadiya has already been anointed. The temple has accepted her as the Dragon Fae."

Malev's eyes flared. "Then I'll kill her, and we'll move to the next coming."

That didn't sound good. I glared at Sybil, urging her to undo whatever this anointing business was.

"Your Majesty, as the Oracle, I must tell you that there will not be another Dragon Fae in my lifetime." Or double down, that's good, Sybil. Better than backpedaling when it came to my life.

"Well then your lifetime might be short indeed."

I could see the effort it took Sybil to not wither beneath Malev's glare. I wanted to cheer her I was so proud, but since I couldn't, I did the next best thing. I moved in front of the queen, breaking her line of sight to Sybil. Distraction was the only remedy I could think of.

"Your Majesty, there's no need for any of this. You've brought me here for something. Let me know how I may be of service to you."

I lowered my eyes from hers in deference. I hated the words as they came out of my mouth, but I wasn't here for me. Sybil, Alistair, even Deacon depended on me handling this situation. Malev's temper would be our ruin. She'd escalate matters out of spite.

"Yes…" She took stock of the situation. "This is actually a bit of good fortune. Your new powers as the Dragon Fae will help you serve my purposes."

New powers? I'd have to ask Sybil about that later, but I couldn't betray my ignorance, so I kept my surprise to myself.

"I have a rival who has setup court on Earth. I don't know who it is. It could even be someone in my own court."

I went into work mode and treated this like any other assignment briefing. "How do you know about it then? Couldn't it just be a rumor?"

"First, no one would dare risk my wrath to simply spread rumors. Second, everyone I've interrogated has refused to give up any information. Whoever it is has either bound their followers with a powerful spell that I'm unable to counter or has managed to instill more fear in their hearts than I have. This is a formidable opponent.

No one is willing to die for rumors. I need to know who they're willing to die for."

All of this for a petty turf war. "I'll need everything you have so far. You can give it to Alistair. He'll process it, and we'll come up with a plan."

"Tsk, tsk, tsk." Malev shook her head. "I'm afraid you'll have to do this one without Alistair."

"I always work with Alistair. We're a team. If you're serious about finding out who your rival is, I need him."

"If I give him to you, you'll disappear on Earth, and I'll be left with nothing. After you've brought me the name of my rival, I'll give you your handler."

I needed to tread carefully. A wrong move could lead to Alistair's death or mine. Malev was hard to read. With her kind of power and long life, there was no telling what motivations would win out. I didn't see any way to convince her to give me Alistair. If I pushed harder, she may decide to try her luck with someone else and be rid of me and Alistair. The only thing I could do was guarantee my work would be rewarded.

"Do I have your word on that?" The only power I had over her was her inability to break her word. That would have to be enough.

Malev pursed her lips into a smirk. "Yes, you have my word that after you give me the name of my rival, I will give you your handler."

"Then I want to see him to make sure he's alive and well."

"Of course." Malev walked away.

3

We descended a stone staircase, deeper and deeper into the damp earth. The farther we went, the more it felt like the walls would collapse in around us. The air seemed to suffocate me. Nausea swirled in my stomach. Looking at Sybil, I could see the same discomfort in her eyes.

The walls weren't physically closing around us, they were choking off our magic. Malev appeared undisturbed. This must be her enchantment at work. Instinctual panic hit me, but I calmed it. Other than the discomfort, I wasn't in a different position than I normally was. I hadn't been able to rely on magic for years.

Alistair, on the other hand, wasn't used to having his magic constrained. Being down here, if the enchantment continued where he was, would be torturous. It would likely be days, maybe even weeks before he'd be released. As far as I knew, Alistair had never had to deal with anything like this. Why would he? As a handler, he was always far away from the action.

The light from the entrance quickly faded to nothing as we descended. What I first assumed were orbs of light were in actuality magical fireflies illuminating our path. They fluttered about unaffected by the enchantment. It would have been pretty if it weren't for the nausea I continually fought.

The stairs ended and we stepped onto what looked like a giant oak tree trunk that had been cut, its age rings too numerous to count beneath our feet. Around us, the dirt walls had no openings or marking of any kind.

Once all three of us were off the stairs, Malev waved a hand, and they disappeared. Had the fae queen intended to trap us down here? If so, how long would it take Deacon to realize something was wrong?

Malev turned away from where the stairs had stood and went to the earthen wall. She sank her hand into the soil and life burst forth. Vines and flowers curled outward from her hand, opening up the wall and revealing a doorway. The sight of such beautiful life streaming from such an evil woman was jarring. I'd expected rotting blooms and dried vines to come from her, not something so pretty.

When we stepped through the doorway, my skin prickled. It was enchanted to only let certain people pass. I may have just walked into a trap. Ordinarily, my internal alarms would be blaring right about now. This was objectively foolish, but the promise of seeing Alistair was too enticing.

Sybil saw him before I did. She shrieked and ran to our left. There Alistair stood in front of a desk he'd been sitting at when we entered. On the desk sat a piece of parchment with script in Alistair's handwriting that was rapidly disappearing. A clever torture giving someone the means to write but erasing their words as quickly as they appeared.

Sybil crashed into him, hugging him tight around the neck. Over her shoulder, his eyes met mine. Guilt pooled in their gray depths. I shook my head. This wasn't his fault. If Malev didn't capture him where she had, she would have found him somewhere else or found another way to get to me. I had no doubt that nothing any of us could have done would have changed the outcome.

"How are you?" Sybil asked.

Alistair pulled away and looked into her eyes. "I'm fine. Really. There's no need to worry about me." He caught my eye again over her shoulder. He should know better than to think I wouldn't worry about him, or at least, I hoped he did.

Alistair appeared unharmed. The small room was cozy and not uncomfortable. It would have made a cute little retreat if not for the enchantment locking him in. With his magic constrained, there was no use for bars or manacles. Even if Alistair could physically overpower Malev, he'd never be able to keep the upper hand with her magic still in play.

Sybil stood back from Alistair and gestured for me to take her place. I stepped closer, but I didn't embrace Alistair. It wasn't our way. Besides, if we were to hug, it would be after I'd gotten him released.

Alistair nodded to me. "That was quite the announcement you made."

It seemed so long ago and ludicrous that I hadn't seen Alistair since then. "You know me. Why do things sensibly when I can have a little fun with it?"

A hint of pride lit his face. "I always knew you'd rescue us, but I didn't think it'd be quite so literal in my case."

"No, you thought I was the irresponsible one, but here you are locked up by the fae queen." The banter came easily between us, but it served another purpose. If Alistair had a message he wanted to pass to me, our code would go unnoticed more easily amid casual chatter.

"I only say you're irresponsible because of all the TV you watch. You really need to stop with the sitcoms." That meant he didn't want me to do whatever Malev had ordered.

"No dice. I like them. Besides, they're not the problem. I've always been this way." He was getting saved whether he liked it or not.

"Yes, yes, it's one happy reunion," Malev said. "But he's not leaving with you. The sooner you get me that name, the sooner he'll be released. Time to go."

The nausea in my stomach intensified, nearly doubling me over.

My eyes instinctually closed against the discomfort. When they opened, we were no longer in the cell with Alistair. We stood in an empty field. The nausea ceased and only then did I recognize it as Malev's magic. She'd ported us outside, which meant she could have ported us to Alistair's cell but chose to have us descend those stairs into the enchanted ground. I wished I'd been able to look at Alistair one last time, to say something to him to help him through the coming days, maybe weeks.

"Sybileen should be able to make a portal back to Earth," Malev said, using Sybil's full name, then turned to leave.

"Wait." I hated calling out to her because it was clearly what she wanted, but I had to swallow my pride in order to get more information. "Do you know anything at all about who your rival is?" I asked.

"No one I interrogated gave up any information. However, one of them, Hectavian, is still alive. After finishing with his comrades, I thought if I let him live, he might lead me to some information."

"How can we find him?"

Malev held out her hand and a viewing portal appeared, the same kind I used to look in on Julien. "Ah, he must be on Earth since he's using his glamour. Lucky for you."

If he'd been in Elustria or the fae realm, we would have seen his fae form, which would make him much harder to track on Earth. As it was, the fae in front of us was stereotypically handsome. A fae high enough in the rankings to be in Malev's court would be vain and unable to resist glamouring himself to be as attractive as possible. He had sexy brown hair that was neatly styled but long enough to show some curl. Light blue eyes peered out from beneath gorgeous long eyelashes and well-shaped eyebrows. He was broad shouldered with a trim waist and fairly tall. Height wasn't something that was as easily changed with glamour, so chances were he was tall as a fae.

"His mind was altered after our talk, so he has no memory of it. This assignment should be simple enough. Just follow him. He'll lead you right to my rival's court."

It couldn't be that easy, otherwise she'd send someone else. She knew very well that Earth was too vast to find a single person with no other information to go on. He also wouldn't go to a rival court without covering his tracks. The high fae weren't stupid, which was why she had to send an outsider. Malev couldn't afford for anyone in her court to know she suspected a coup.

"Is that all you have for us?" Anything at this point would be helpful.

"Yes, that's everything. I'll send word if I discover anything else. However, I should think that's plenty for the Dragon Fae."

What a bitch. She knew every member of her court and couldn't figure it out. "I'll get you your name." I didn't know how, but I didn't have any choice.

"Good girl."

The condescending tone rankled, but at least we were done for now. Malev flew off, her wings fluttering so quickly they were mere flickers of glitter.

I turned to Sybil. "Now's your last chance. Do you want to fly a little before we leave?"

Longing flitted across her eyes, but she shook her head. "No, it'll just make it more difficult. Thank you, though."

I knew too well what it was to have to bind part of yourself up and keep it hidden away. The ache she surely felt being confined to the ground on Earth must be nearly unbearable. I had a new appreciation for the light humor with which she lived her life.

4

When we arrived back in Sybil's apartment, the absence of magic stunned me. In that short amount of time, I had gotten used to its ubiquitous presence. Now I'd have to make my peace with its absence again. I hadn't realized how I'd become used to the ache that replaced magic on Earth.

Deacon waited for us almost exactly as we'd left him on the sofa watching TV, except Pint was curled in his lap. Pint was my miniature dragon companion. A curse had kept him the size of a large chihuahua. He must have been worried if he was acting so affectionate, especially with Deacon. Pint didn't take well to other men in my life. His heart was much too big for his small form, and with that heart came a protective streak a mile wide.

When we appeared, Deacon saw us first, standing so quickly that Pint fell a few inches before he took flight, hovering over Deacon's shoulder.

"That didn't take long. That's a good sign, right?" Pint asked in his gravelly voice. He sounded like a smoker, which I supposed was fair since he'd been able to breathe smoke from birth.

Deacon held my gaze, searching my expression for a hint of how it went. I didn't know what kind of read he could get from me. I barely knew how I felt about the meeting. I'd wanted to return with Alistair, but I also knew that it could have gone much worse. At least Alistair was alive and well. If I just did what Malev wanted, he'd be back with us soon.

Sybil's demeanor completely changed, and she paced frantically. "This will be all right. We just have to fix this. I can fix it."

"What are you talking about?" Deacon asked. He looked to me for answers, but I had no more idea than he did.

She stopped and looked at me, but her eyes were wide. "If I hadn't mentioned that you were anointed, she would have held that over your head instead of Alistair. This is all my fault."

"No, it's not, Sybil." I grabbed her shoulders and looked into her eyes. I needed to get through to her. "We were never going to leave with Alistair today. She knows I'm not power hungry enough for the anointing to be a sufficient motivator. She took Alistair because he's my weakness. Trust me, that woman knows I'm not her equal in the fight for power. She'd kill her own family for it. Probably has."

"Wait, what did she want?" Deacon finally asked.

I walked around him and sat on the sofa. "Apparently she has a rival. She doesn't know who, but they're setting up court here on Earth."

"She wants us to stop them?" Deacon asked as he sat next to me. He took my hand, and it wasn't until I relaxed into its warmth that I realized how casually we had progressed in our relationship. I was not the touchy-feely type. Pint would have something to say about this later.

"No, she just wants the name of whomever it is. Once we get her the name, she'll release Alistair."

"That seems simple enough."

I envied his optimism. Right now, he was working on a one hundred percent success rate.

Sybil spoke up. "We can't do anything until you're both anointed. If Malev finds out I lied to her when I said you already were..." She shuddered. "I can't even think what she'll do. It won't be good."

I didn't know what was involved in anointing me the Dragon Fae, but it sounded too official and sacred for comfort. Yes, I stepped up and said I was the fulfillment of ancient prophecy because it seemed the right thing at the moment, but being anointed? In my heart it felt sacrilegious. I didn't even believe in prophecies and the Dragon Fae, not really, not like some people did. Undergoing a religious ceremony would mock those religious beliefs.

"How would she ever find out, though?" I asked. "I'm not prepared to be anointed as anything. It's one thing for us all to say I'm the Dragon Fae because it's expedient, but it's another to do some sort of sacred ceremony about it."

"Yeah, that's all kinds of icky," Pint said. "Besides, can people who are anointed drink whiskey at six a.m.? Because she does that, you know. That doesn't sound like the behavior of an anointed hero."

He wasn't wrong.

"What do you think?" I asked Deacon. His opinion mattered to me more than I expected.

"I'd rather not share my thoughts on the matter. I don't want to influence your decision. You're right, this does feel like a big step. I'll not pressure you into it."

The tranquil sea of his green eyes showed exactly how sure he was that this was the correct course. No part of him seemed the least bit nervous. For him, the anointing was the next natural step because he knew in his bones that this was our fate. I wished I had that kind of conviction.

I wanted to keep going as we were. I could still do my job, protect the people of Earth and Elustria, without taking this step. I was willing to give people hope, but I didn't want to blaspheme or disrespect people who had a strong religious belief in the Dragon Fae. "I don't see the benefit to it."

"Oh, there are loads of benefits," Sybil said. "There are certain powers that you'll get after you're bonded and anointed."

"We can't bond," Deacon said.

I snapped my head around to see his face stricken. It was the most expressive I'd ever seen him. I knew why I didn't want to bond, but this reaction from him took me aback. He was all duty and sacrificing his life for the cause. I didn't expect this.

"Bonding's out of the question," I told Sybil, focusing my gaze back on her. I didn't want to see Deacon's horror at the thought of bonding to me any longer. "I'm not bonding to someone for what amounts to a mission."

"I agree." Deacon nodded, his face once again composed. "You shouldn't bond to someone unless you're sure you want it."

Before this, I would have taken his comment as supportive, but now it seemed he said it just to get himself off the hook. Had I completely misread his actions in the shower? I thought there was something growing between us, something that would make him willing to bond. After all, he'd willingly given part of his hide to make my cuff when I was still a stranger. I would have thought bonding would be an easy decision for him.

"I'm going to have my hands full convincing the others that you can be anointed without being bonded." Sybil tapped her chin with her pointer finger as she thought.

"The others?" I asked.

Sybil waved away my question. "Don't worry about it. When you're anointed, you'll have powers conferred to you as the Dragon Fae. Deacon too, as the Dragon Companion. They're essential to you fulfilling your mission."

If it would help me get Alistair back, I was for it. "Fine. If you're sure it's necessary, then I'll consent to the anointing."

"Excellent." Sybil clapped her hands. "We need to leave immediately. The sooner this is done, the better."

"Where are we going? You can't do it here?" I asked.

"We need to do it at the temple in Elustria." She grabbed my hand and pulled me up from the sofa. "We're wasting time. I can tell you about it when we get there."

She spoke about me going back to Elustria so casually, as if it was something I could decide to do on a whim without the entirety of the continent hunting me. I pulled my hand from her grasp. "I can't go back to Elustria."

"I agree," Deacon said, standing beside me. "It's too dangerous. Why can't we do whatever the ceremony is here?"

"We can't. The ceremony requires the temple. Besides, we need all the support we can get. The priestesses at the temple are loyal to the Dragon Fae above all. They need to see you anointed."

Going anywhere the Dragon Fae was expected to be didn't seem wise. "Malev is going to have that place crawling with spies."

Sybil shook her head. "No, she won't. The temple is too sacred. It's protected by an ancient magic placed by the previous Dragon Fae. No one with an impure heart can go there. If she did have spies, she would know we were lying about you already being anointed."

"And what if I'm the one with an impure heart?"

Sybil took my hands in hers. "You're the Dragon Fae. Your place is at the temple. It will always be a refuge for you."

For so long, my apartment had been my only refuge. It's why I kept everyone out of it. But damn, I started to believe her.

Pint flew right in the middle of the three of us. "Well, if you're all going, I want to go too. I don't want to miss out on this anointing," Little puffs of smoke curled from his nostrils in indignation. "And I don't want to hear any argument. If it's safe enough for Nadiya to go, it's safe enough for me. I'll not be left out."

"Of course you'll come." I leaned down and kissed the top of his head.

I wished Alistair could be at the anointing. He was the true believer. At least I'd have Pint there, someone who knew me before all this Dragon Fae nonsense entered my life. Ever since the meeting with Meilin that sent me down this Dragon Fae path, I felt like I was losing bits of my identity each day.

Sybil took a few steps back from our group and opened a portal. Nerves assaulted me. This was really going to happen. These were my last moments before officially becoming the Dragon Fae. The weight of Pint's, Sybil's, and Deacon's love and expectations nearly suffocated me in the quiet room.

I wanted to bolt.

Sybil stepped through the portal first, followed by Pint.

"You ready?" Deacon asked, holding his hand out to me.

No, I wasn't, but that had never stopped me before. I nodded, and he pulled me through to Elustria.

5

The wind whipped around me, freezing my ears and nose. My hair blew around my face, obscuring my view. We could be on any mountain anywhere on Earth, but the air hung thick and humid with magic. From the arid heat of Arizona to the chilling magic of Elustria, there couldn't be a more stark difference.

"I brought us in as close as I could. We'll have to go the rest of the way by foot since you've never been," Sybil shouted over the wind. She led the way up the mountain.

"Where are we exactly?" I asked as I walked next to her, eager to move and get the blood flowing to ward off the cold.

The answer came from Deacon, not Sybil. "The Spineback Mountains. This is Subtle Peak." Deacon's voice warmed with nostalgia. This was his home. A serene warmth entered his eyes that I hadn't seen before. "It's the smallest mountain in the range surrounded on all sides by higher peaks, hence the name. It's got nothing to offer and is too close to the dragon caves for anyone to settle here. It's too accessible to be appealing to dragons. No one's ever really been interested in it."

"And that's by design." Sybil picked up where Deacon finished. "The Dragon Fae temple is hidden here. When the first Dragon Fae came, she placed all sorts of enchantments to protect her refuge. This particular peak was used as cover because it's unassuming, worthless, and she used some magic to make sure people kept thinking of it that way."

The dirt beneath out feet was dry, devoid of life unlike the mountains around us that were carpeted in green. The place was uninteresting, but that wasn't due to any magical reason. "I don't feel any mind magic at work here."

"It's subtle," Sybil said. "Again, like the name implies. The mountain itself is thoroughly uninteresting. So when people easily forget it or don't think much of it, it's easy to pass it off as being natural thought."

"So this is where I'm from." Pint flew higher and looked around. It was hard to think about him being from here, but it was true. He'd been part of my life for so long that it was easy to forget the time he'd lived here before me.

"Do you remember which peak you're from?" Deacon asked.

Pint flew back down between me and Deacon so that he was at about eye level. His face dropped, and he shook his head. "I was so young, and it was years ago. I think I'd recognize it if I saw it, but we never really strayed from our cave. When the Circle took me, they teleported me away, so I never saw where we were in relation to the rest of the ridge."

"If you see a familiar sight, I might be able to figure it out for you," Deacon offered.

Pint looked all around but didn't find anything. "Thank you."

It was a nice offer, but the Spineback Mountains were a massive ridge, comparable to the Rockies on Earth. It wasn't likely Pint would find anything.

The hike was easy going, like Deacon said, easily accessible to people. All around us were towering peaks blocking out any part of the outside world. It wasn't a bad position. Anyone who wanted to get here by means other than teleportation would have to travel over several mountains. They were both a difficult land journey and high enough that they'd present problems even to those who could fly.

But if someone knew about this place, it'd be easy enough to catch us here. "Be on the lookout for Malev's spies."

"Pint, you might want to stick to flying low," Deacon said.

Instead of arguing like he usually would when given an order, Pint complied. "Don't worry, last thing I want is for the creepy fae queen to get me." Then, as if realizing he'd exposed fear, he added, "I'd hate to have to melt her face off."

"Yes, that would be dreadful," I said.

The mountains were eerily still. Other than the wind, nothing stirred. No birds squawked, no rodents scurried, nothing. It had to have something to do with the enchantment that kept this small mountain forgettable. It was as if even the animals had forgotten about it.

The walk to the peak was uneventful, so much so that I regretted not taking in more of the joy of being back in my homeland. The Spineback Mountains stood majestic all around us, but I couldn't enjoy the sight of them as every nerve in my body stood on high alert for looming dangers.

It wasn't until we reached the peak that the danger emerged. A giant minotaur stood on the other side of the mountain, steam rising from his nostrils as his eyes narrowed.

6

Two pointed horns curved toward us and glinted in the light of Elustria's two suns. Ruddy hair covered the minotaur's body, only thinning slightly on his chest and abs, revealing rock-hard muscle. He stood with his hooves planted on the ground, looking like a battering ram couldn't move him. His dark brown eyes bore into mine, a challenge.

"So this is her?" he said in a deep voice with a little snort that sent more steam into the air. The giant minotaur stepped toward me. I stood my ground. As he tried to circle me, I turned to prevent this adversary from leaving my sight.

"You can speak directly to me," I said, maintaining eye contact. "If you want to talk to Sybil, look at her and speak with some respect."

A little twinkle entered his eye, admiration for my daring, perhaps.

"Yes, you're her, the one who boldly declared herself the Dragon Fae without so much as notifying this temple."

"Jaygar, they were extreme circumstances," Sybil said from behind him. Jaygar's massive bulk hid her completely from my sight.

"And which one is her companion? The little whelp or the shifter who looks like he wants to murder me?"

"I was her companion long before any of you showed up," Pint said, flying up to look Jaygar in the eye.

"I'm the Dragon Companion." Deacon's voice boomed behind me. "And if you want my murderous intent to stay merely a look, you'll step back."

"So boldness is part of the package deal." Jaygar took a step back.

"Jaygar, leave them alone. She's the real deal. You know I wouldn't be with her otherwise." Sybil moved between me and Jaygar. I started to step forward, but Deacon's hand on my arm stopped me. When I looked back at him, he gave a quick shake of his head. This was Sybil's argument.

For the first time, Jaygar looked at Sybil. "There are rumors that you forsook your calling as the Oracle to work for the Circle of Sorcerers."

Sybil's voice lowered. "I dare anyone to say that to my face. I had to work with the Circle to get to the Dragon Fae. You know my one and only allegiance is to her. I'll go where I have to and associate with whom I need to in order to make sure the prophecy is fulfilled."

The prophecy. Was she more loyal to it or to me? To her, there wasn't a difference, but to me, the distinction was important. I didn't doubt her loyalty, but I didn't know where I ranked in comparison to the prophecy.

Jaygar didn't seem taken aback by Sybil's forcefulness. He must have known her for some time, at least long enough to know that she was more than she appeared. "Well, you better come explain it to the others."

"Is there doubt that I'm the Dragon Fae?" I asked Jaygar.

He focused his gaze on me, and I could see that some of the fight had left his eyes. Sybil had a powerful effect on him. If she could bring him to heel, it boded well for us.

"There are some who see this as quite opportunistic. More than anything, it offends the others that they devoted their lives to the Dragon Fae and when she finally appears, she does so without paying them any respect or care."

"That was not my intention at all."

"And what was your intention?" he asked with skepticism.

"To give hope to the people of Elustria." My answer didn't allay the skepticism, but it was the only one I had. "The fault here is entirely mine. Sybil and Deacon had no idea I was going to do it before I did. I didn't even know."

"The idea just entered your head to declare yourself to the entire world? With your history, I find that hard to believe. It seems, to some, that you are conning your way into this position as a means to return to your homeland from Earth."

I stood stunned for a moment. That thought had never crossed my mind. How could anyone think that? "You think I'm free here? With this damn cuff that restrains my magic? You think it's easy being here where magic is thick in the air, where it fills my lungs with every breath, but I can't partake in it? I can't use it? At least on Earth I'm not surrounded by what I've had to give up."

"Then why?"

I looked to the side, trying to figure out how to answer him. Why had I done it? A ready answer didn't come. "At the moment, it seemed like the right thing to do."

"So you've accepted your role as the Dragon Fae?" Jaygar asked.

For some reason, looking into this mighty minotaur's eyes, I couldn't lie. It wasn't fear holding me back. Despite his size advantage, I had no doubt that I could take him. No, the thing holding me back was respect. "I'm ready to try."

It was the most I could honestly give. The only reason I was ready to be the Dragon Fae was to rescue Alistair. That wasn't a good reason to take on the mantle of prophecy.

Jaygar nodded. "That's an answer I can accept. You'd have to question the wisdom of anyone who said she was ready to be the Dragon Fae. It's not a role I envy." He looked at Sybil. "You did a decent job picking her. Let's go introduce her to the others."

As Jaygar turned and made his way down the mountain into the valley, we got our first clear view of where we were headed. I didn't know if it was the enchantment around the place or if I just hadn't bothered to look earlier, but the valley below took my breath away.

So far our journey had been through barren land full of nothing but rock and shrubbery. Below us, a massive lake shimmered in the sun. The dark blue water swallowed the sunlight, offering no reflection of the sky above. On the banks, green, turquoise, pink, and purple vegetation coated the ground.

In the middle of the lake, a large stone dome supported by vine-covered columns rose from an island. The temple.

All around the perimeter of the lake were little boats bobbing in the water. They reminded me of Viking ships that I'd seen in a documentary with Mr. Harmon except they didn't have sails. As we got closer, I saw that a woman riding on a dragon's back adorned the bow and stern of each ship. They were carved out of light brown and purple wood, the two colors swirling together. We headed to one of those boats.

"After you," Jaygar said, gesturing for me and the rest of my party to precede him.

"Wait, take off your cuff," Sybil said.

She had assured me this was a safe place, and I trusted her, so I removed it. My magic buzzed with freedom.

I stepped in the boat and walked all the way forward, making room for those behind me. Magic encircled the boat, strong but not overpowering. It's weight didn't feel oppressive. It danced lightly across my skin. My own magic leapt in my veins, reaching out to the power surrounding me.

When Deacon stepped onto the boat behind me, the magic danced with excitement again.

"See, I told you," Sybil said, looking back at Jaygar as she boarded the boat behind Deacon. Jaygar grunted in reply.

"Told him what?" I asked Sybil when we were seated.

"The boats are enchanted. They only allow passage to true believers. The first Dragon Fae cast the spell. Surely you felt that surge in the magic when you boarded?" I nodded in reply. "That's her magic reaching out to yours in recognition."

The implication that this was some sign made me uncomfortable. I'd better get used to it though, given that I was headed to an anointing. This whole day was going to be uncomfortable.

Pint took a seat in my lap, and Jaygar was the last to board. Once we were all seated, the boat took off for the island. The leisurely pace meant it would take several minutes to reach our destination.

I wished we sailed faster. I wanted this whole ordeal to be over with so I could get back to my main mission: getting the information I needed to free Alistair. I worried that somehow the acolytes would sense my lack of belief and it would be a problem. The sooner Deacon and I got out of here, the better.

Splashing on my right drew my attention. A porpoise jumped from the water and splashed back under. She jumped again, and this time, she leaned to one side and waved a fin at us. Again she rose into the air, waving a fin and releasing a joyful squeal. I couldn't help myself. The sound was contagious, and I laughed and waved back. On her next jump, she did a flip in the air and then swam ahead.

"She's an acolyte," Jaygar said. "Everyone is quite excited by your appearance."

"Does she live here?" I asked.

"No. Aquatic friends are able to access this lake through an aquifer."

How many more "aquatic friends" could I expect to see? I peered over the side of the boat, but the water was too dark to see anything. A few seconds later, a mermaid broke through the water's surface. She flung her blue hair in an arc as she emerged, creating a marvelous effect as sunlight caught the droplets of water in the air.

The mermaid swam alongside us, meeting my eyes then looking to Sybil and finally to Jaygar. "Is this her?"

"Aye, it's her," Jaygar replied.

The mermaid turned back to me with a giant smile. Without

saying anything, she disappeared under the water. Ahead of us, she jumped and did a flip then sped toward the island.

"Looks like everyone's excited to see you," Deacon said behind me.

I snorted. "That's only because they don't know me."

His hand rested on my back, and it reassured me in a way that words couldn't. I may not have Alistair with me, but at least I had Deacon. I wasn't alone.

When the boat ran ashore, a mass of people waited for us. It was the largest gathering of Elustrian races I'd seen in years, maybe ever. I'd forgotten the beauty of all the diversity in my homeland. On Earth, there were humans to interact with, and that was it. Sure there were animals, but they weren't part of society. Elves, minotaurs, dryads, and other fae all stood before me with emotions ranging from awe to skepticism on their faces. A soft murmur played in the air as those gathered whispered among themselves.

I stepped off the boat and stood to the side so the others could disembark. I'd expected some trial, some obstacle to pass before being permitted onto the island, but there was nothing. When we were all off the boat, Sybil stepped forward to address the crowd. The spectators quieted to let the Oracle speak.

"Friends, it is a happy day. I have brought the Dragon Fae and her companion to you to be anointed." She stepped aside and extended her arm in my direction, presenting me to the crowd.

Everyone went silent as more than a hundred pairs of eyes focused on me. I was wrong. This was my trial to pass: lying to all these people about who I was.

The silence grew. I knew what they expected. They wanted a speech, for me to inspire them or enlighten them or comfort them. I had none of that in me to give.

Pint's sturdy weight landed on my shoulder. He whispered in my ear, soft enough that no one else could hear. "We both know this is bullshit, but you're a bullshitter for a living. This is just another mission. You don't have to be the Dragon Fae, just be Nadiya on a mission as the Dragon Fae."

It was what I needed to hear. Just another assignment. I stepped forward and lifted my chin. "Thank you all for coming. Ever since the Oracle revealed that I am the Dragon Fae, I have wanted to come to this sacred place. I'd hoped to wait until it was safer, but safety seems a long time off. Seeing you all, I am deeply humbled." That part was at least true. "I hope that I can perform my role well and serve you as the Dragon Fae. I ask that you accept me and bear witness to my anointing."

That sounded prophetic-heroine enough, right?

Sybil stepped forward. "I accept you."

Jaygar came to Sybil's side. "I accept you."

The crowd parted. Sybil walked in the path they created toward the temple. I followed, Pint still on my shoulder. Deacon fell in a step behind me. As we approached, the crowd murmured, "I accept you." Then they bowed their heads as we passed.

The weight of their gaze had been heavy, but the weight of their reverence was heavier still. How had I gone from anonymity in an apartment in Arizona to this?

7

The temple was a simple dome, open on all sides, supported by columns. Four cracked and crumbling steps led to the flagstone base, purple and green plants freely spilling over between the stones. In the middle stood a font covered in vines. On either side of the font were two four-foot-tall pillars facing one another. It looked like the temple hadn't been used in centuries.

"I think this is where I leave you," Pint whispered when I climbed the first step. His weight left my shoulder, and he hovered in the air in front of the crowd. I wanted to tell him to stay with me, but I couldn't without people noticing. That level of insecurity may exist in me, but it certainly wasn't in the Dragon Fae.

Pint's presence was replaced by Deacon's. He slipped his hand into mine, giving it a squeeze. When I looked at him, a warm smile greeted me. It slowed my racing heart. I hadn't even realized how nervous I was until he calmed me. As much as I loved Pint, and despite all our history, it was Deacon who was my partner. I wasn't the only one getting anointed today. We climbed the stairs together.

Sybil turned to face us and smiled at our clasped hands, the hint of a smirk playing at the corner of her mouth. She gestured toward the pillars. "Each of you go to one."

"See you when this is over," Deacon said as he let go of my hand.

Up close, the pillar was much more than it appeared from a distance. The vines climbed over decorative etchings. Their meaning, if there was one, eluded me. The top of the pillar was smooth, perhaps it had even been polished hundreds of years ago. It was cut at an angle towards me, with a palm-sized gem in the middle. The gem was perfectly round and set in the stone. Blue, gray, and green colors swirled together in it. I'd never seen anything comparable.

Across from me, I looked at Deacon. How did he do it? He stood with that same easy majesty I'd observed on him when we visited Drake. It was a majesty born of duty and humility that made the power simmering beneath the surface that much more potent.

Instead of looking at me, his head turned toward Sybil, awaiting instructions. She stood behind the empty font and raised her hands to the sky, as if in supplication.

"We are here to present the Dragon Fae and the Dragon Companion to the temple to be anointed. May the original Dragon Fae look on us with favor." She lowered her hands and looked at Deacon and then me. "The presented will now place a palm on the dragon eye."

That's what the stone orb was: dragon eye. I'd never seen one before. They were rare stones, some of the most precious material in Elustria. They were particularly potent at holding and conducting magic.

A split second before I placed my right hand over the stone, I swore I could hear Sybil and the crowd collectively hold their breath. The cool dragon eye touched the skin of my palm, and the world disappeared.

8

The only sound in my ears was the thrumming of my heart. My eyes could only see varying shades of black and white. The temple remained intact. The font and pillar stood exactly as they had been, but Deacon and Sybil were missing. I looked out to the crowd, but they were gone as well. The island stood deserted.

Without Sybil there to instruct me, I removed my hand from the dragon eye, hoping the action would pull me out of this vision.

Nothing changed.

I twirled around, taking a few steps toward the center of the temple. Maybe the temple itself caused this vision. I ran down the steps to the water's edge. Still nothing.

This wasn't a vision. I'd been transported somewhere.

"Deacon!"

"Good," a woman's voice answered inside my mind. Was this some fae trick? Had Malev done this? "I should think not. Malev should fear us, not the other way around."

The voice could hear my thoughts.

"Of course I can. You're in the nether to speak with me. How else could we communicate?"

The nether. The place between life and death where the living could commune with the dead. I knew of its existence, but I'd never expected to experience it. Few could access the nether. It took powerful magic and a certain level of insanity. People had gone mad from spending too much time in the nether.

"Who are you?" I had an idea, but I didn't want to believe it.

"I'm the original Dragon Fae. But you already knew that. You're not a fool, Nadiya. Don't act like one. You got off to such a good start."

"What about this has been good?" Of all the adjectives at my disposal, good wasn't one I'd apply.

"That your first instinct was to call out for Deacon. You could have called for Sybil or Pint or even Alistair out of habit, but you didn't. I've been worried about you since you two decided not to bond."

"He's my partner. It's my responsibility to make sure he's safe. This would be easier without him."

Laughter filled my mind. "In some ways you are more wise to the world than most. In others, you haven't the faintest clue. The worst is yet to come. When it does, it'll be Deacon you lean on. It's not your job to protect him. He can handle himself. He's here to help you."

"I don't need his help." The cuff around my wrist felt heavier then as the memory of Deacon's scar flashed before my eyes. The dragonhide used in its construction came from his chest. "I don't need anything more from him than he's already given."

"That's where you're wrong. The weight you are being asked to bear is impossibly heavy. You can't do it alone, and the other people in your life won't be able to understand."

"No one's ever been able to understand." Some understood more than others. Pint and Alistair were the closest to me, but in the end, I was the one with the responsibility of the mission on her shoulders. I was the one whose actions took life, both guilty and innocent. It was a power I should have never been given.

"You're right, but that's different. The trials that lie ahead of you cannot be conquered alone. Soon, the only person you're going to have is Deacon."

What did she know that I didn't? "Are you saying that Alistair is going to die?"

"Oh, I have no idea. Live or die, Alistair isn't the one who will be there in the end."

"I thought, according to prophecy, no one was going to be with me in the end."

"Ah, yes. That. It's true. You are destined to die alone."

"So what then is the point of getting close to Deacon?"

"He's right about you."

"What?"

"The problem isn't that you care too little, it's that you care too much."

My mind went back to when Deacon had told me that.

"You're scared of hurting him when you die. And you're scared of losing him before then."

There was no point denying it when the woman could read my thoughts. I already had too many people in my life, too many vulnerabilities. I was meant to be alone. "So is that why you brought me here? To order me to bond with him?"

"You do need to bond with him, but that's not the purpose of this visit."

"Then why am I here?"

"So I can give you advice. So you can know that a mistake wasn't made. You are my successor."

The truth was whatever people wanted it to be. All I cared about was getting this over with and back on the hunt for Malev's nemesis.

"You are the Dragon Fae. You do nothing at anyone's behest. The fae queen, the Circle, none of them control you."

"She has Alistair. That's all I care about." I didn't give a shit about the fae queen's politics or the machinations of the Circle. I just wanted my handler back and for life to go back to the way it was. "You said you had advice for me. What is it?"

"That you already have the tools you need to face what's coming. You just need to decide to use them."

"What—"

Before I could complete the thought, color appeared around me, its intensity blinding after the black and white of the nether. I blinked against the brightness and looked down to see my hand over the dragon eye. I hadn't moved. Light emanated from the etchings in the pillar, matching the swirling colors in the dragon eye.

Sybil still stood behind the font. She released a deep breath and relief flooded her face as she smiled at me. Across the way, Deacon appeared as regal as before, but there was something unexpected in his eyes. Had he gone to the nether too? Had the original Dragon Fae spoken with him? Or had he talked with the companion? My questions would have to wait until after the ceremony was over.

"The Origin has given her blessing," Sybil declared. She looked into the font. Oil filled it. "The Dragon Fae and her companion can now come and be anointed with this blessed oil."

Ugh. I hated all this ceremony. It made my disbelief feel that much more disrespectful. Sybil gestured for Deacon and I to stand before her. When I got next to Deacon, I could see it in his eyes. Something had happened. He had traveled to the nether. He hid it well, but the slightest hint of something strange lingered in his eyes.

Standing before Sybil, she sighed and broke into a large grin.

"What's that for?" I asked.

"Nothing." She tried to leave it at that, but I held her gaze, pressing for an answer. "Nothing, it's just that the pillar will only light up for the true Dragon Fae."

Why did that have her worried? "But you've always believed in me."

"Oh, I know. I didn't doubt. Not really. It's just that if an imposter touches the dragon eye, they die."

"What?! You didn't think to mention that first?" It wasn't far off from the truth of what happened. I did travel to the space between life and death.

Sybil shrugged. "I didn't want to worry you."

That was one hell of an answer. "No, of course not." She had a point, though. If I had known beforehand, I probably wouldn't have gone through with it. I may risk my life every time I went on a mission, but voluntarily presenting myself to be struck down? That was an entirely different matter.

I looked at Deacon to see his reaction to Sybil's revelation, but he didn't seem to be paying attention to anything we were saying. He stared straight ahead, his eyes burdened by something. Was it because of the weight of his calling as the Dragon Companion or had something he'd seen in the nether bothered him?

"Deacon, you'll need to remove your shirt," Sybil said.

That drew Deacon's attention back to the present. For the first time it hit me how absurd our attire was. Here we were, about to be anointed as mythical saviors, dressed in casual Earth clothes. Today was supposed to be our day off, a chance to relax together after the last week.

Deacon reached for the hem of his shirt and pulled it up and over his head in one smooth movement then discarded it on the ground. His back was just as well-muscled as the rest of his body. The sight of him was incongruous. All this power at his disposal, ready to be used at the first sign of a threat, yet he stood there calm in the middle of this peaceful temple. He was a warrior without a battle. No matter how much we may want it, people like us were never destined for relaxed days on the sofa.

"Place your hands in front you, palms up," Sybil directed. I focused back on her and the ceremony. Her eyes said she saw my appreciation of Deacon's body, and I wondered if removing his shirt was necessary or if she had merely wanted to show me what I was rejecting by not bonding with him.

Deacon and I followed her orders. His hands dwarfed mine, and I wondered whose had taken more life. He'd spent his days defending dragons, and I'd spent mine defending the interests of the Circle. His way seemed simpler, more honest. Even as I worked to prevent war, sometimes I wished for one, facing my enemies on a battlefield, one giant messy conflict where one side would emerge victorious. A clean victory despite the messiness of the war.

Sybil dipped a hollowed out reed into the font and placed a finger over the end so the reed captured some of the oil. She then touched the tip of the reed to the center of each of our palms, releasing a single drop of oil each time. "I anoint your hands that they may always rise to the defense of the weak."

She placed a drop of oil on her finger then touched it to Deacon's chest directly on the scar from when he'd given part of himself for my cuff. "I anoint your heart that it will be loyal and true."

Her finger took another drop and placed it at the base of my throat. "I anoint your voice that you may always use it to speak for those who are silenced."

Two drops of oil floated out of the font and above our heads. "And I anoint your head that your mind may always be clear." She lowered the oil onto the crown of each of our heads. "Now take each other's anointed palms and swear this oath."

Deacon and I clasped hands. My magic surged at the touch, but I held it back. We weren't bonding. Our magics weren't mingling. In an act of protest, my magic gathered in my stomach, fluttering wildly to make its displeasure known. With a deep breath, I calmed it, forcing it to still.

When I looked up into Deacon's eyes, they had softened from earlier. The weight wasn't gone, just pushed to the back. A gentle smile lifted his lips, so at odds with the giant hands that engulfed mine in their warmth. Even if he weren't sensitive to magic, he would have sensed the frenetic energy of mine at his touch. It wasn't fair that he should get such a clearer read on me than I could on him.

"Repeat after me," Sybil said. "I take upon me this day, freely and without reservation, the mantle of the Dragon Fae and Dragon Companion, to protect and defend the innocent until the end of days. May this oath bind us in service."

I had plenty of reservations, but Pint's words echoed in my head.

This was just another mission. Out of the corner of my eye, I saw the little dragon perched on the temple steps in front of the crowd, watching us. He rolled his eyes at my hesitation then gave an encouraging nod.

Deacon waited until I locked eyes with him, and we repeated the oath together. Where I was uncertain, he was sure. I wondered if he could see that to me, this was just one more lie in a lifetime of them. I'd pretend my reservations didn't exist. However, I took the oath to protect and defend seriously. My life had been devoted to service since the day Alistair took me into his care.

Sybil spoke when we finished the oath. "May this blessed oil that has anointed your palms act as a conduit, bestowing upon you and through you the gifts of the Dragon Fae."

At those words, some magic in the oil activated. Light beamed upward where our hands met. Energy surged through me, exciting my magic and gathering it up, pushing it toward my hands. It concentrated where the two drops of oil had touched my palms and crashed against Deacon's magic.

Some type of energy exchanged between us, a third magic birthed from both of ours. I'd never heard of anything like it. The energy travelled back and forth between us until it filled me, spreading my magic back through my body and leaving it as calm and tranquil as the sea after a storm.

Weight settled on my shoulders, and I saw that a mantle of shimmering green and orange dragon scales had appeared on Deacon. I wanted to look to see if an identical one covered me, but I couldn't tear my eyes away from Deacon. Something had shifted. Everything felt different now, and I wanted to explore these changes with him.

"I give you the Dragon Fae and her companion!" Sybil declared, and the crowd cheered.

Deacon pulled away first and faced the crowd, raising our still clasped hands in the air.

Had I misinterpreted? Did he not feel the same thing I did during the ceremony?

Pint flew to us. "You might want to tell your face to enjoy the adoration of your acolytes." His raspy voice brought me back to the mission, and I smoothed the confusion from my features.

"And now we feast!" Jaygar yelled above the crowd. People swarmed and led us to a clearing behind the temple. With every step we took, I searched for some sign in Deacon's face of the transformation that had taken place, but he appeared undisturbed.

In the middle of the clearing, a pyre stood ready for a bonfire. Wood benches dotted the area in little groups.

"Companion, might you do the honors of lighting the fire?" Jaygar said, gesturing to the pyre.

I didn't like Deacon being referred to that way. He had his own name, his own identity outside of being the Dragon Fae's companion. It didn't seem right to reduce him to a single role.

Deacon let go of my hand for the first time since the anointing, and I gasped. My magic stirred, bereft without Deacon's touch, but it was more than just the physical touch. It had to do with whatever happened between us. The entire thing was strange and unsettling.

If Deacon noticed, he gave no sign. He strode to the pyre and put on the show everyone wanted. With a deep breath, he blew a stream of fire several feet long through the pyre. If the crowd hadn't been so dense, he might have shifted. Poor people didn't know what they were missing.

The bonfire roared to life as Elustria's suns set behind the mountains that surrounded the valley. Light from the flames danced across the shimmering scales of Deacon's mantle. Music started playing.

"He does look quite magnificent, doesn't he?" Sybil said, appearing beside me. She wore a mischievous smirk on her face.

"Of course he does." Any other answer would be an obvious lie. I'd look ridiculous if I tried to deny it. "Now that this is done"—I faced Sybil and waited for her to turn away from the celebration to focus on me—"we need to get back to work."

"What you need to do is enjoy this moment. I doubt there are many more like it in our near future." Sybil eyed me knowingly.

"There's nothing that can be done right now. I know I don't talk about it a lot, but as the Oracle, I do know things. It's no secret that the future isn't going to be easy for you. You may find that you need the memory of tonight to get you through. The memory of all these people who are excited, who are here, who are hopeful because of you. It's just you, Deacon, me, Alistair, and Pint most of the time. You need to be reminded that there's a world outside of us."

Before I could respond, Jaygar and Deacon approached, Jaygar's hand affectionately around Deacon's shoulder. "And now it is time we eat and perhaps discuss a few things," Jaygar said. The way he looked between me and Deacon, I knew whatever he wanted to discuss was serious.

Sybil was right, but what she didn't get was that I had made peace with my lifestyle long ago. I knew the lonely road ahead of me. It was the same one I'd traveled all my life. My only detour was made in the name of love, and it had ended badly.

However, I wasn't such a fool as to think that we could do without Jaygar's support, and despite his affectionate manner, the look in his eyes said that I needed to appease whatever was on his mind if the affection were to continue.

There were too many precarious variables at the moment. I didn't need the followers of the Dragon Fae to withdraw their support. For now, there could be no doubt that I was the Dragon Fae. I feared Alistair's life depended on it.

9

I followed Jaygar to a table set with true Elustrian cuisine. My stomach growled, eager to partake of the foods I hadn't seen in years. While I enjoyed the food on Earth, especially the food in Arizona, there was nothing quite like the food from one's youth. The familiar smells, the comforting flavor palette, I could at least enjoy this for now. Besides, off to the side I saw Pint enjoying his own feast. I couldn't tell from here exactly what it was, but I bet he had been craving the wildlife of Elustria for some time.

We sat around the table, and the firelight danced across the firm expanse of Deacon's chest. I wanted him to put his shirt back on but couldn't exactly ask him to. It would be bad form in this company, but the sight of him was distracting. Not only was there the obvious distraction of his well-muscled chest but also of the scar that, even in this dim lighting, could still be seen.

The sight of it still felt intimate to me, knowing what it signified. While I had often thought of my dragonhide cuff as a shackle keeping me on Earth, the truth was, it was the only way I'd been able to survive this long. All because of him. The constant reminder made me uncomfortable. But to Deacon, and to the people here, it was an important sign. It was the mark of the Dragon Companion. Deacon

49

had spent years preparing for this role, and this was the only place and time where others could look upon that scar and know what it was. It meant something to these people.

I didn't even realize I was staring until Deacon caught my eye and smiled. I felt like a child being caught out, so I turned to Jaygar to change the subject. "What is it you want to discuss with me?"

"You get right to the point, don't you?" He took a bite of one of the meats on the table.

"Oh, I'm sorry, I didn't realize you were one for chitchat. Lovely weather we're having." I wouldn't eat until this conversation was over.

Jaygar looked across the table at Sybil. "I'm surprised you two get along." I couldn't blame him. It shocked the shit out of me too. He turned back to me. "What I need to know is why you two haven't been mate bonded. I thought Sybil would perform the bonding at the same time as the anointing."

Deacon spoke up for the first time since sitting down. "That's none of your business."

"Oh, but it is my business. What two people do between themselves is private, but you're not two people. You're the Dragon Fae and Dragon Companion. The prophecy says you're to be mate bonded."

"What you want to know," Sybil said, "is if they can still fulfill the prophecy as they are. I don't see any problems. If I say it's all right, it is."

"I wish that was enough, Sybileen, but it's not. There are certain powers that they share as a mated pair. How are they going to do what they have to without that advantage?"

"That's not all there is to it, Jaygar. During the anointing, they were given special powers. They didn't need to be mated for that."

"But it won't be everything they're supposed to have. You can't talk your way out of this one. The prophecy says they're to be mated. If they're not willing to do what's required, then why are we settling? Why aren't we continuing the search? A sorceress with barely a drop of fae blood in her declares herself the Dragon Fae, and now we're all supposed to fall in line? When she's not willing to do what's required?"

"If you don't accept her as the Dragon Fae, what then?" Sybil asked. "She's already declared, we've publicly anointed her, so what exactly would you say? We were wrong? We made a mistake, everyone, but trust us the next time we come to you with the Dragon Fae. Or better yet, don't see the Dragon Fae in our lifetime, train up another generation to search for her. Is that what you want, Jaygar?"

"What I want is for her to fulfill her duty."

"It's not happening," Deacon said, his voice low and filled with ice. "The Oracle has declared us, and we've been anointed. It's done. I suggest you make your peace with it. She's the Dragon Fae whether we're all friends or not, but I'd much rather we leave this table as friends."

I'd expected to be the one fighting for the independence to not bond, but here Sybil and Deacon were doing it for me. I understood Sybil's position. As she said, she was here for me. The decision was made, and she was defending it to Jaygar. She knew we needed his support and the support of the acolytes that came along with it. That's why she defended my choice even though she'd rather we were bonded.

Deacon, on the other hand, surprised me. Was he simply defending my decision? I remembered back when he had said he didn't want to be bonded. His answer had come so quickly. Was it my imagination, or had something changed? Had he never intended to mate bond with me? In the beginning, he'd been willing to do whatever was required. The sudden deviation alarmed me.

I'd been prepared to argue, and now I sat as a spectator to a staring contest, a battle of wills. I didn't have any doubt as to who would come out the victor.

"Fine," Jaygar said as he lowered his gaze and shook his head. "I'll continue to support you. I'd rather we be friends as well."

It was time for me to speak. "Thank you, Jaygar. Your support means a lot to us and particularly to me. I spoke honestly earlier when I told you I'm ready to try. Those who know me would tell you I'm often a disappointment, but I always get the job done in the end."

"See that you do. I'll go reassure the others. There have been questions. I'll quell any speculation and rumors, but you'd be wise to make yourselves visible, to display the camaraderie and power that people expect from the Dragon Fae and her companion. If you're not going to be mated, at least look like you are." Jaygar nodded to us and left the table, disappearing into the dancing crowd.

With the conversation over, I took the opportunity to eat some of the food laid out for us. I had too many things on my mind to have much of an appetite, but I didn't want to pass up the opportunity to eat Elustrian food. I didn't know when it would come again.

Nothing tasted as good as I remembered. My memories of eating these foods were sweeter than the foods themselves. What I really wanted was home, and that wasn't Elustria anymore. Once I was picking at my food more than eating it, Deacon stood and extended a hand to me.

"Come, let's join the revelry. You heard Jaygar."

More than anything, I wanted to feel Deacon's hand in mine again, so I accepted his invitation. When our skin touched, my magic leapt as it had before. I looked up into Deacon's eyes and could tell that he felt it too. So it wasn't just from not wearing my cuff. Something had changed.

Around the bonfire people danced and clapped along with the drums and flutes and stringed instruments. Even from where we stopped outside the dancing area I could feel all that happiness and magic mingling, forming a cloud of energy that sparked the air. I'd forgotten what an Elustrian celebration was like, or perhaps my absence had made me more sensitive to it.

"All this is for you. You should enjoy it," Deacon said beside me as he let go of my hand to clap along with the music.

I joined in the clapping for appearances. "This doesn't feel right, celebrating while Alistair is captured."

"No, it doesn't." Deacon faced me and we both stopped clapping. "But there's nothing else you can do right now to save him. I know you don't realize it, that you don't like to think of yourself as the Dragon Fae, but imagine for a moment what they're feeling." He looked over the crowd of merry dancers. "They've waited their whole lives for this. Most of them probably didn't believe this day would actually come, and now it has. This is bigger than us, bigger than Alistair. You give them this night, and they'll give you the rest of their lives."

The timbre of his voice spoke of like recognizing like. He recognized their commitment because it mirrored his own. I already had the rest of his life, mated or not. The warmth in his voice contrasted with the ice he'd used to shut down Jaygar earlier.

We stood in silence for a moment, taking in the music and the dancing, the laughing and cheering. Then he took my hand. "Forget for a moment who we are and let the world slip away. Come, dance, and celebrate the return of the Dragon Fae with me the way you would have if you weren't her."

I let him pull me into the dancing crowd. He was right. If I wasn't the Dragon Fae, I'd be celebrating. The Feast of the Dragon had been one of my favorites. After my parents died, I didn't really have family, so Alistair and I would attend together until I met Julien. Then I had joined his family for the celebrations.

Every year the scene was the same. We would feast and talk about the way the world would be when she returned. People would compare notes on when they thought she would come or if she would come at all. Then, with our bellies full, we would dance into the night around a bonfire just like this one. It was a time for us to celebrate the way we wished the world was, even if we didn't really believe in the Dragon Fae. I'd never been a true believer, but I'd always enjoyed the camaraderie of the holiday.

The Feast of the Dragon Fae was one of the only feasts celebrated by all the races of Elustria. The only other feast that united the entire continent was the Friendship Celebration commemorating the signing of the pact that had led to our current peace. That holiday was met with a tepid response. We knew we held the peace in name only. There were too many factions both along racial and geographic lines. It was those divisions that made the Feast of the Dragon Fae the biggest celebration of the year.

I let the steady beat of the drums infiltrate my hips. I raised my arms in the air and flung my hair behind me. I closed my eyes and shut off my mind, forcing myself to just feel: the rhythm of music, the heat of the fire, the cool night breeze. I breathed in the charged air, letting the happiness fill my lungs along with the scent of smoke from the fire mingled with cooking meat. All around me, magic acted as my dance partner, caressing and swaying with me.

I opened my eyes and saw Deacon looking back at me, the bonfire reflected in his eyes. The heat of his gaze affected me more than all of the magic and excitement in the air.

Underneath his gaze was a smile of pure joy. It lit me up from within. I laughed. "Why are you looking at me like that?"

"You're so damn beautiful when you're this carefree. I wish it could last forever."

"Me too. Like you said, let's forget that for now." I led him further into the crowd, and we joined the sweaty mass of jubilation. I wasn't pretending anymore. I surrendered myself completely to the moment.

Every time we touched, it was like an electric pulse through me. Deacon's chest was slick with sweat. My hair stuck to the back of my neck. I didn't care. I was having too much fun. We had no problem convincing the onlookers that while we may not be mate bonded, we were still one in purpose. We danced together with the familiarity of a mature couple and the passion of the newly bonded.

As the music slowed, I didn't want the night to end. I didn't want to return to the world where Malev held Alistair prisoner, where these people expected me to be some kind of savior. I wanted only this moment, this night, to last forever. I wanted Deacon to keep looking at me like that, and I wanted to surrender to him.

Overhead, an explosion sounded. The music stopped as people screamed. It wasn't the sound of a bomb, though, more like fire-works. Above us in the night sky, one word formed out of red sparkles.

LIAR.

10

Chaos broke out on the island. The word *LIAR* pierced through my heart. For a split second, I felt naked in front of all these people.

Sybil ran to me and Deacon. "It has to be Queen Malev."

Deacon nodded in agreement. "I'm going to get a better look."

"Don't," I said, reaching for him. Either not hearing me or pretending not to, he leapt into the air and shifted, taking flight.

"I don't know what he thinks he's going to find," I said to Sybil.

"He probably wants to examine the magic. With his abilities, there's no telling what he can discern." Sybil looked at me. Her eyes lacked the perky spark I'd come to associate with her. "I'm going to port to the fae court."

"That's foolish. We don't know what you're going into. It's too dangerous." Running into situations blind was reckless. Alistair would never approve of something like this.

"She can't do anything to me. I'm her direct line to you. Obviously, she wants to send a message. If I don't go, she'll take action, and who knows what she'll escalate to. In the fae court, this amounts to a summons."

Before I could say anything else, Sybil disappeared. At some point, being the Dragon Fae meant people would start listening to me, right? At least I didn't have to worry about Malev showing up now. Sybil was right about that.

All around me, the priestesses of the temple and the acolytes scrambled. Someone doused the bonfire, likely in an effort to hide our location. From the shouting around me, several different theories circulated.

"This is it. This is the end. We're under attack."

"It's from the Origin. We've got the wrong person."

The priestesses were back at the temple, examining the font and pillars for any signs. I caught Jaygar's eye and motioned for him to follow me. Deacon and Sybil may not listen to me, but I'd make these people listen.

I strode to the temple, and the priestesses made room for me, stepping aside so I could stand in front of the font to address the crowd. Pint followed and settled on the steps where he'd been for the anointing.

Jaygar raised his hands and shouted, "Be still! Listen to the Dragon Fae!"

Everyone stopped and faced me. Jaygar turned and nodded, giving me the floor. I returned the nod in thanks, not just for his help but for the way he addressed me. It would go a long way toward keeping the calm, and it went a long way in bolstering my confidence. I welcomed any endorsement that would help these people listen.

"There is nothing to fear. Why would you believe a word put in the sky by our enemies?" I gestured to the red *LIAR* that sparkled above us. Speaking in front of groups didn't come naturally to me, but I viewed it as a mission. I didn't need to be a commanding orator, I just needed to play the part of one.

I channeled my undercover skills and pretended to be the prophesied leader these acolytes needed. "We all know why I have come. It is a time of great turmoil for all the peoples of Elustria. You cannot expect the road forward to be easy. I don't. Some of us have been fighting this battle for a long time, and others are newer to the struggle. What makes us strong is that we're here together."

"And how do we know that this isn't a sign that you're not the Dragon Fae?" a voice shouted.

"Who said that?" Jaygar turned, examining the crowd.

"No, friend." I stepped forward and placed a hand on Jaygar's shoulder. "It takes bravery to speak up, especially if the words you say are in the minority. We will not dishonor that bravery by exposing the speaker." I resumed my place in front of the font so more of the crowd could see me.

"It's a good question, one we should all be asking. Don't take anything on the word of others. I have come here without the protection of my dragonhide cuff so that you could all feel the imprint of my magic and know who I am."

"You're the assassin!" someone shouted.

"That makes her a hero!"

"It also makes her a spy and a liar."

I raised my hand to silence the shouts. "You're both correct. I am the assassin. And that does make me both a spy and a liar. My entire life I've traded in deception, lies, mistruths. I don't know if I'm a hero. I wouldn't call myself that. I can promise that every life I've taken I've done so because I believed in my heart that it protected others. Whether that is right or wrong is not for me to judge."

I didn't intend to reveal so much of myself. This was meant to be an act to placate the crowd. My hint of vulnerability grabbed their attention, and they leaned forward. Like any good agent, I knew when to change course.

"I've spent years on Earth, hiding among the humans. Every day I've had to pretend like I'm not a sorceress, but I've never lost sight of who I am. When I came here today, I came here as myself because this is the one place where I don't have to hide." The more I revealed, the more they appeared to trust me.

"I don't blame you for being suspicious. I was too when I was first told that I was the Dragon Fae. I didn't believe it. Frankly, it's not a fate I want. But fate didn't ask me what I want. Fate was there the night I killed Bernhardt. It's the only time in my career that I've been seen during a kill. I didn't know at the time that I was fulfilling an ancient prophecy."

I turned to the priestess closest to me in the temple. "Priestess, if I weren't the Dragon Fae, what would've happened when I touched the dragon eye?"

"Only the Dragon Fae and her companion can touch the dragon eye. Any other will die."

An audible gasp rippled through the crowd.

"That's what the Oracle told me as well." I turned back to the people. "When I placed my hand on the dragon eye, I communed with the Origin herself. She confirmed to me my destiny, and I stand before you now to tell you that I have not taken on this mantle lightly. I used to serve the Circle of Sorcerers, and now I serve and protect all the people of Elustria."

Hundreds of eyes looked up at me. I held the crowd in the palm of my hand.

They reminded me of Nicholas's followers. How was I different from him? I felt the weight of their hope, their expectations. Something about my words drew them in. With their belief came an immense responsibility. This wasn't something I could walk away from. I couldn't rescue Alistair and go back to the way things were before. That life was closed to me forever.

A breeze threw back my hair. The sound of flapping wings grew louder in the silence that followed my words. I looked up as Deacon flew down to meet me. He shifted with perfect timing as he landed, appearing with the same pants and mantle he wore before. He looked at me and then at the silent crowd. He must've seen the trust in their eyes because he addressed them.

"All is well. Our location is not known." He faced me. "The writing is so high in the sky that it can be seen from all over the Spineback Mountains. An evil magic placed it there to scare us, but it cannot do us harm."

"We are not so easily scared." I had meant the comment for Deacon, but the crowd cheered.

Jaygar climbed the steps to join us. "That's right. We do not scare easily. We are the acolytes the great Dragon Fae, of the Origin, and of her successor. We are not mere followers in need of protection. We are disciples. Together, we swear fealty to the Dragon Fae and Dragon Companion." He knelt and bowed his head.

To my astonishment, the crowd behind him followed suit. With each bowed head, a wave of something—trust, loyalty, devotion, faith—rolled off of them and crashed into me. The last row of people knelt and revealed Sybil standing behind them.

Jaygar raised his hand and then dropped it. As one they all said, "I swear fealty to the Dragon Fae and Dragon Companion."

Jaygar rose, and the rest followed. He addressed the crowd. "It is time for us to return to our work. We look forward to the day when we can celebrate together again."

The crowd dispersed and went to start clearing up the food. No one bothered to relight the bonfire or resume the music. This wasn't the end to the evening they had hoped for, but maybe it wasn't such a bad thing for them to know people wanted to terrorize us.

Deacon and I headed straight for Sybil with Jaygar and Pint following.

"It looks like that went well," Sybil said.

"Aye, you did the right thing," Jaygar said to me. "I think you have their support, at least for now."

"Thank you for your help," I said. "You didn't have to do that."

"Yes, I did. Normally, each one of the acolytes would swear fealty one by one. Time constraints being what they are, I thought this would be a good substitute."

"Thank you, friend," Deacon said, slapping Jaygar on the shoulder. "We owe you a debt of gratitude."

"I'll go help with the cleanup. And I'll remind everyone of the importance of discretion before they leave here tonight."

"Before you go, Jaygar, you need to hear what I have to say," Sybil said. She looked at me. "The fae queen knows that you weren't anointed when you saw her earlier."

"But how could she know that?" If it was something she could sense from me, she would have made an issue of it earlier. That left only one option. In my experience, people were always the vulnerable point. "There has to be a spy."

"If there is, they didn't give away our location," Deacon said. "The lights are too high. If she knew our location, she would have used her magic closer to the ground. It would be more effective in scaring us."

My mind went over the events of the day, looking for the weak spot. The most obvious answer was that someone here reported to Malev, but that didn't make sense. "I thought that the enchanted boats took care of any spies?"

"They do," Jaygar said. "Whoever it is, they might have been under her influence. Or perhaps they take issue with you. They may not believe you are the true Dragon Fae. I don't know that the enchantment on the boats would account for that."

Magic was as fallible as the person wielding it. Would the Origin have put such complex thought into the boat enchantment? "Do you have any suspicions as to who it could be?" I asked Jaygar. "I don't recall seeing anyone leave here. What exactly was said before I arrived? Why did everyone gather here today?"

"The shade who you revealed yourself to spread word quickly. The news has been going around Elustria like wildfire. As soon as that happened, people started pouring in. Usually there's hardly anyone here, just a few priestesses attending the temple. We knew at some point you'd have to be anointed, so we all waited. We trusted Sybil would bring you here as soon as she could."

"So is it possible the spy was never even here?" I asked. "It could just be someone who let it slip that I hadn't been anointed before the announcement."

Jaygar rolled that thought around. "It's possible. I prefer that explanation over the idea that someone attended the ceremony and then reported to the fae queen. I'll see if I can find out if anyone left early. However, I don't know how easy it will be to find the mole or if it's even possible."

"Then we need to watch what we say and whom we say it in front of." With that, I looked around before asking Sybil, "What else did you find out?"

"Queen Malev was upset at being deceived. She said that if you have time to deceive her like this and attend parties, then you clearly don't take this seriously enough. If you don't get her the information she wants, she'll declare you an imposter."

That didn't sound so bad to me. She was the one who wanted me as the Dragon Fae. If she now wanted to leave me alone and pick someone else to do her bidding, fine by me.

Sybil hesitated slightly before she finished. "And she'll destroy all of your followers as heretics."

"Since when does the Dragon Fae work for the fae queen?" Jaygar asked.

"Since the fae queen kidnapped the Dragon Fae's handler," I said. I could see in his eyes that he knew what it meant to have one of my people taken even if he didn't understand the handler-agent bond. "And since she threatened the lives of all these innocents."

All the people on this island looked up to me. They thought I was some sort of savior, but in reality, their lives were in more danger now that I was here. I couldn't let them down. "We need to get back home. I need to get to work somewhere beyond Malev's reach. The longer I stay, the longer there's a target here."

"Safe journey," Jaygar said. "If I find out anything that can be useful, I'll pass it to you, Sybileen."

"Thank you," Sybil replied.

"And thank you for all of your help today," I said to Jaygar.

"Thank you for being honest with me, Dragon Fae." Jaygar nodded to me and then to Deacon and went to join the others.

"Come, we'll talk more at home." Sybil opened a portal, and Pint flew through first.

"Wait," Deacon said and grabbed my wrist. "Your cuff."

I dreaded putting it back on, but he was right. I couldn't afford to spend any time on Earth without it, especially now.

I pulled it from my pocket and fastened it onto my wrist. My magic chafed at the restraint and recoiled, curling into a ball of nausea in my stomach.

It was a familiar feeling, one that reminded me it was time to get back to work.

11

The sun sat low in the Arizona sky, casting a pink glow into Sybil's already colorful apartment. Deacon and I sat side-by-side on the sofa where we had been only this morning, relaxed, laughing, enjoying each other's company. The mantles we'd worn didn't come through the portal, and Deacon had put on a shirt—thank goodness. There were so many things I wanted to talk to him about, just the two of us. I loved Sybil and Pint, but I needed to know what the anointing ceremony had been like for him. Had he spoken to the Origin as well? What was his experience in the nether?

So many questions swirled in my head, some that Sybil could answer. "You mentioned that the anointing gave us additional powers even though we aren't bonded. What specifically did it do? We're going to need every advantage we can get in order to free Alistair."

Sybil rummaged around in the kitchen making tea. "There are a few, though not as many as you would get if you were bonded. They're useful, but Jaygar was right. The prophecy really intended for you to be bonded. I'll defend your choice publicly, but you do need to give serious thought to what you're doing."

"Thank you, Sybil," Deacon said. "We'll take that under advisement, but as it stands, what are we working with here?"

"For starters, the cuff now protects you both. So Deacon's imprint will be hidden from others the same as yours is, Nadiya."

That brought with it a lot of advantages. Deacon's magic emanated from him so strongly that it was difficult for us to have any kind of stealth. However, it did have its drawbacks. "Does that mean when he performs magic, when he shifts, it will hurt the same way it does me?"

"That's a good question. I would think so."

"Even if it does cause pain, it'll be worth it. That's a great advantage for us," Deacon said.

I knew firsthand that Deacon's capacity to handle pain was great, perhaps greater than my own, but it was hard to describe the kind of pain that came from having the very essence of your being suppressed. It was one thing to endure pain when inflicted by an enemy, when exerted by some external force, and it was quite another to experience it every time you did something as essential to your being as breathing. It was something I did not wish for him.

"The other ability that you have now is the fae ability to glamour," Sybil said.

That was even more interesting in combination with the cuff. We could hide both our imprints and our physical appearance.

"So how does glamouring work? Can we make ourselves look any way we want, or is there one set alternate glamour that we can take on?" I asked.

"I'm not sure since you're both only part fae. That's the advantage of having been anointed now. You can tap into those fae powers. Different fae have different levels of glamouring ability. And like most other magic, it's an ability that can be strengthened. You'll have to see for yourselves how far you can take it."

"And can we glamour each other? Or just ourselves?" Deacon asked.

"That's another thing you two are going to have to figure out."

"If I haven't mentioned it lately, there's quite a lot you don't know for an Oracle," I said.

Sybil shrugged and cocked her head to the side. "I don't know what to tell you. I only know what I know, and that's not much besides the fact that you're the Dragon Fae and Deacon's your companion. The rest of it is all up in the air except for the hard and fast parts of the prophecy. But even that's open to interpretation."

My life had been turned upside down by a prophecy that was open to interpretation? No one asked me what my interpretation was.

Speaking of glamouring, something Malev said stuck out at me. "When Malev showed us the image of the fae she suspected knew something, she said he was using his glamour. That implies that he has only one."

"Yes, it's common for fae that travel to Earth to have one standard glamour that they use. There's not much reason to learn to maintain multiple glamours. It's really just about hiding the fact that they're fae."

"Which means that we can look for this fae that Malev suspects based off of his glamour. Do you have any way to create a picture of the image we saw?" I asked. Sybil would be better equipped to magically create a portrait. I had no artistic abilities whatsoever.

"Yes, that's not a problem."

"Good. I want to take it to my tech guy. These humans have some advanced facial recognition systems that he may be able to use."

"Do we really have no other information to go off of?" Deacon asked. "All she did was show you an image of the fae glamoured?"

It was an extraordinarily small amount of intel. We didn't even know where on Earth he was, what country or continent.

"Sybil, when you make the portrait, do you think you could add in any details that were behind him? Do you have a way to capture that entire image, not just him?" I asked.

"Yeah, I can do that."

The smell of strawberry frosting filled my nose as Sybil performed the spell. I needed to compare notes with Deacon and see if it smelled the same to him. Her whole apartment smelled like cupcakes and made my mouth water.

When the spell finished, a picture of the fae floated in the air in front of her. The smell diminished to the point that I couldn't tell if what remained was my memory or a slight hint of the scent itself.

Deacon snatched the portrait from the air and laid it out on the coffee table. "Look there. That looks like a sign of some kind."

I squinted at the image. "It's too far away to make out. I'll take this to my tech guy and have him take a look. It's a long shot, but we might get lucky."

"Yes, we are quite lucky," Sybil said, not a hint of irony in her voice. I wondered what kind of childhood she must've had that led her to be this optimistic about the world. "And if that doesn't work, we can show this picture around the enclaves, see if anyone recognizes him."

"We'll have to be careful. We don't want to tip off this rival court. If it's a serious enough threat to have the queen worried, then we need to be wary as well," Deacon said. With every move he made, his magic moved against my skin. I wanted to know if he felt the same, but I didn't want to ask in front of Sybil.

"I can go drop this off to him now and get him working on it. The sooner we get Malev her name, the sooner Alistair's returned to us." I folded the picture and put it in my pocket as I rose.

Sybil stood in front of me. "That's a great idea. It's getting dark, so after you drop that off, I think you and Deacon should take advantage of the night and go somewhere secluded to practice with your new abilities."

"You don't want to come teach us how to glamour?" I asked Sybil. So much had happened today, and I needed to process it with Deacon, but we might need her help.

She shook her head. "No, I think you'll figure it out on your own. You need to see how the anointing changed things for you." I could see that she knew how important it was for us to have time alone together. I wondered how much Sybil knew about what happened during the anointing ceremony.

"Sybil's right. We can't really plan a mission if we don't know what we're working with." Deacon's warm hand rested on the small of my back, and I looked up into his eyes. I saw in them a desire to speak privately that matched my own.

Trevor's identity and location were a secret from even Alistair. While I trusted Deacon, it wasn't my secret to reveal. "I'll go drop it off to my guy and be back here in an hour. Then we can go practice."

12

"So how'd it go with that guy in St. Louis?" Trevor asked. It took me a moment to realize what he was talking about.

"Oh, it went well, thanks. We couldn't have pulled that off without you."

Trevor blushed the slightest bit and shrugged. "Just glad I can help. What do you have for me today? Or is this just a social visit?"

I missed the days when I would come play video games with Trevor and just, in his words, shoot the shit. In the beginning, I'd visited fairly often on social calls to learn as much as I could about Earth culture and get a crash course in technology. "Afraid I don't have time to hang out. There's a lot going on right now."

"How can I help?" Trevor asked.

I pulled the picture from my pocket and flattened it out on the table. The creases disappeared, and the image looked brand new.

"Is that some kind of magic?" Trevor asked.

I nodded. "Yeah. I need to find this person, and I have absolutely no idea where he is. I was hoping you could use some sort of facial recognition to see if he's shown up anywhere."

Trevor took the image and laid it in his scanner. "I can certainly try, but I doubt I'll find anything. If I do find something, there's virtually no chance I'll be able to get any info on him."

"That's fine. All I need is a location. It's not likely that he'll show up in any databases anyway."

"So what is he? A mage?"

"No, he's a fae. A mage would at least pretend to be human. This fae just wants to move about without attracting attention."

Trevor's face darkened, and his mouth twisted like he tasted something sour. "Fucking fae."

Generations ago, the fae had attacked Trevor's clan. A sorcerer had saved one of his family members, a great-great-great-uncle or something, and that's how they came to know about sorcerers and subsequently help us.

I'd forgotten how deep-seated Trevor's and his entire family's hatred of the fae was. If he ever found out that I was part fae, I shuddered to think how he would react. He'd view it as a betrayal. I didn't want to lie to him, but I couldn't afford to lose him either. All I could do was hope that he wouldn't find out some other way.

"They are slippery bastards. The sooner I can find this one, the sooner I can rescue someone who's very important to me."

Trevor removed the picture from his scanner and handed it back to me. Then he sat at his computer and started typing away. "Well, lucky for you, police departments are using facial recognition more widely. I don't agree with it myself, but it does work in our favor in this instance. It'll most likely take at least a few days running around the clock."

"Just text me as soon as you have anything, doesn't matter what time of day or night it is."

"Will do. You said this has something to do with saving a friend?"

I worked hard to keep Trevor separated as much as possible from my work. Alistair didn't even know his name, only that I had a tech guy. Someone at the Circle knew who he was, but I didn't know who. "Yeah, my handler. He was kidnapped."

Concern entered Trevor's eyes, and his face softened in sympathy.

He was a rarity in my world. For all the work he did—some of it in legal gray areas—to help me track down mage terrorists, he was much too innocent for this life. I hoped that never changed.

"I'm sorry," Trevor said. "Is he a sorcerer like you?"

A week ago, it would've been so simple and easy to answer in the affirmative. It felt like a loaded question, even though Trevor had no way to know or even guess that I wasn't one hundred percent sorcerer like he thought.

"Yeah, he's a sorcerer."

"It's so weird to think that sorcerers like you can get kidnapped." Underneath his voice flowed a current of fear. If sorcerers weren't safe, then what about humans? I didn't know how to comfort him.

"It's rare. Magic isn't everything. It's just a tool, like technology." And after the anointing I had more tools at my disposal. I needed to get back to Deacon and see how we could use our new powers. "Sorry I can't stay longer, but this one's personal. I can't spare any time."

Trevor waved off my concern. "No worries. We'll catch up after you've rescued your handler. Seriously though, I hope you have some other leads to track down. If the facial recognition works, and that's a big if, it could take quite a bit of time."

We didn't have any leads, but I didn't want to put more pressure on him. "Then I better get going."

13

I drove us to the far side of Red Mountain, deep into the desert. On the off chance someone came by, I didn't want to draw attention, so we would work by the light of the moon. It hung fat in the sky, nearly full. Deacon wouldn't have trouble seeing with his enhanced senses, and I could make do.

We walked about a hundred feet from the car, and I reached for my cuff. Deacon's hand covered mine, stopping me.

"What are you doing?" he asked, his forehead crinkling in confusion.

I glanced around the barren desert for effect. "I don't think there's much risk out here. What are the chances an Elustrian comes out to this desert and finds my imprint?"

"Even if it is safe, we might as well practice the way we intend to continue. Out in the field, you'll have your cuff on."

Deacon was right. Normally, I'd agree. "I don't think you understand how much it hurts to perform magic with it on. It'll be difficult enough for you to learn new skills without the addition of the pain." I hoped it wouldn't be as intense for him as it was for me, but I still wanted to ease him into it.

Deacon stepped closer to me, close enough that I could feel the heat radiating from his chest. "I'm no stranger to pain."

He was the first partner I'd had for whom that was true. All the others had been hopelessly naïve.

"I know you're not, but this is different. You don't know what it's like to have something that comes so naturally, that is so essential to your being, cause you pain. It's like a betrayal. Imagine if every time you took a breath, lightning shot through your heart. It's unnatural and unnerving on top of everything else. You're also used to healing quickly. If the cuff works for you as it does for me, then even using your ability to heal will hurt."

His intense gaze held mine. "And you've managed for the last three years. I can handle it. Maybe now that we're anointed, the pain will be shared between the two of us, and it won't be so bad for you."

I didn't like the thought of it hurting him every time I used magic. "That's not a very persuasive argument."

"We don't really have a choice. We're going to have to get used to this new situation."

I dropped my hand from my cuff, and his arm fell away. "All right then. We'll see how this goes."

I wanted to know if he could already feel the effects of the cuff, if he could feel my magic against his the way his magic squished against mine. It was as if the cuff acted as a vice, suppressing his magic, holding it to me.

But our most important job was figuring out how to use our new abilities in the field. Everything else could wait. "I don't know anything about glamouring. Do you?"

Deacon stepped back and took a deep breath. "I don't, but I wonder if it's like shifting. I'm able to make myself look like a dragon or like a man on command."

I'd never thought of shifting in those terms. The man before me was not a man. When he shifted into his dragon form, he wasn't really a dragon either. His identity was neither man nor beast. It was something separate entirely.

"So you're thinking you can try to shift into a different human form?"

"I think that's a good place to start. What about you?"

"I don't know much about fae magic, but I do know that the fae are able to do magic on the mind. I don't think glamouring is about changing our physical appearance as much as it's changing the way others perceive us." I closed my eyes and concentrated. "So, for instance, if I want you to perceive me as a blonde, I would use my magic not to change my hair color but to change the way it appears." I opened my eyes. "What do you see?"

I could tell before he opened his mouth that it had worked. His eyes were slightly wider than normal. Then he smiled. "I can't believe what a difference hair color makes."

I laughed. "Well it's a good start, but I think we're going to have to learn more than hair color."

"Does it hurt?" Deacon stepped closer and hovered his hand above my hair.

"No." I heard the surprise in my voice. "It's not comfortable, but it's not the normal pain that I experience. I wonder if, because it's fae magic, the cuff handles it better?" I looked up at Deacon to see what he thought of that, but his eyes were still transfixed by my hair. I sighed. "You can touch it. I don't think that will affect the magic."

His fingers slid through my hair. My mind flashed to last night in the shower. It seemed so long ago. He had taken my broken body and cleaned it and made me whole again.

I couldn't think about that now. We had too much work to do, and too many things had changed.

"It feels real. I can smell the magic around it, but if the cuff is really working, then no one else will be able to."

"What do you mean?" I asked. "Can you not tell if the cuff is working?"

He lowered his hand and stepped back. "Ever since the ceremony, something changed. I think it's because the cuff protects me as well now. I don't sense it the same way I used to. And it never completely fooled me like it does others, but I always wondered if that was partly because it came from me. How could something that comes from my own skin hide the truth from me? But now it's different. I feel your magic close to me at all times, like the cuff is somehow..." He searched for the right word.

"Like the cuff is hugging your magic and mine against your skin."

His eyes lit with recognition. "Exactly. It's different."

"It's different for me too. I can also smell magic in more detail than I could before."

Deacon raised his eyebrows. "Really? That could be helpful. How strong is it?"

"Not as strong as your ability. Is it just me, or does Sybil's smell like cupcakes with strawberry frosting?"

Deacon threw his head back and laughed. "I've never had a cupcake with strawberry frosting, but that sounds about right. You're lucky her magic is so pleasant. Can you smell mine?"

I didn't want to think about the smell of Deacon's magic. It was distracting enough as it was.

"Your magic is so strong I could smell it the first time I met you. Before the anointing, I only had a whiff of something sweet lingering around Sybil. Even now I could only smell it in detail when she was doing that spell. Some of the scent lingered afterward, but I couldn't tell if it was really there or if it was just my memory. Yours is much stronger." I turned my head to the side, closed my eyes, and took a deep breath.

"Yes?" Deacon prompted.

"You smell like the mountains after a good rain. Earthy. Smokey. Like a campfire that has just been doused." When I looked into Deacon's eyes, I could see desire there. I'd never wanted to kiss him more than in that moment. I could see he wanted it too.

Deacon shook his head and stepped back. "Good. Most dragon shifters have a similar scent. The more you're around magic, the more you learn that certain scents are attached to certain types of magic. Shifters in general tend to be very earthy. The fae can get quite rank, which is why we're lucky with Sybil. And then we have mages who smell almost like plastic. They're odd. I didn't have a word for their scent until I came to Earth."

"And what about sorcerers?"

"Their magic has a wide range of scents, but there's one around the edges of it that I can only describe as electric. I know that's not a scent, but it's the only thing that comes to mind."

"And what does mine smell like?"

Desire flashed in his eyes again, but it quickly disappeared. "Wouldn't you like to know?"

Yes, I would. A little spark of mischief in his eyes told me I wouldn't anytime soon.

"You've gotten us quite off-track." Deacon put some distance between us, all business. "We need to know how to do more than have you change your hair color. Let's see if I can do it."

Deacon took a few steps back and closed his eyes. He shimmered slightly as his appearance changed. His hair shortened and turned white. His skin darkened a shade and his nose lengthened the slightest bit and got thicker at the base. His lips thinned and a full beard grew. He opened his eyes. Instead of the green I'd become accustomed to, they were bright blue. "What do you think?"

My face twisted into something of a grimace. "I think it's weird. This is going to take some getting used to. Did it hurt?"

Deacon frowned and shook his head. "Not really. It tingles a bit. My skin is a little tender. You try again."

Intent on one-upping him, I closed my eyes and imagined myself looking like the star of the sitcom we'd watched this morning.

"Good choice." Deacon said, admiration ringing in his voice. I opened my eyes to see what he meant. "Being able to look like other people is a good skill. You've got it almost perfect."

This time, it did hurt a little more than just changing my hair color. It wasn't bad, though, like a severe sunburn. Something that was definitely bearable for however long I would need to be glamoured in the field. "I think it came easier basing it off of someone I've seen. There was less to think about. Your turn."

Deacon transformed flawlessly into the male lead from the show. It seemed the Origin had given us quite the aptitude for glamouring.

Back and forth we went, changing into different characters, learning how to do it while keeping our eyes open. Then we tried again to take on wholly original appearances, which ended up being combinations of people we'd seen.

We discovered that we could glamour each other, and the anointing gave the cuff more powers. We could now use it to glamour our imprints. That way we could choose to appear as voids or as some other magical creatures.

Pretty soon our practice devolved into each of us trying to make the other laugh by doing more ridiculous mash-ups of people. When Deacon appeared with a long white beard and wrinkly face with rock-hard arms and torso and big hairy feet, I lost it mid glamour. I didn't even try to contain my laughter.

"Okay, you win. I think it's safe to say that we are adequately prepared to glamour in the field." I let the bit of glamour I had fall away. "Besides, it's getting late, and we have some other things we need to try."

Deacon assumed his regular appearance. "Do you want me to shift?"

"Yes, and heal. We need to see if it hurts when you do it."

Deacon nodded and immediately shifted. I'd expected him to prepare himself. Even after all these years, when I used magic with the cuff, it took a little preparation on my end. Then again, he didn't know what he was in for.

As soon as his body changed into his magnificent dragon form, pain wracked my body, the same kind that came when I used magic, but it was less intense. I wondered what distance the connection would cover. Would the cuff protect him if he were miles away? Would I be able to feel it then? There were too many things we needed to test.

He shifted back, and the surge of pain returned. It was only during the moment that he shifted that the pain happened. It didn't sustain while he was in his dragon form, which made sense. Who was to say which form was his true form: the man or the dragon? Both or neither?

Deacon shook out his limbs and nodded. "Okay, that was worse than I expected. I can't believe you go through that each time you use magic. Did you feel it?"

"Yeah, not the same as when I use magic, but I can definitely feel it. I'd like to say you get used to it, but you really don't. Now, I need you to tell me if you feel pain when I do magic."

I levitated a rock into the air. The amount of pain I expected didn't come.

Deacon's cheek twitched, the only sign of the pain he must be feeling. Just as we shared the protection of the cuff equally, we apparently shared the pain in equal measure.

I lowered the rock, and he nodded. "I definitely felt that."

"It wasn't as strong as normal for me. It was about half the pain I expected."

Deacon's eyes widened a little, and his eyebrows rose "So we share the pain equally, which means it's normally twice that painful for you to perform magic?"

"I suppose."

Deacon shook his head. "Wow. I don't know how you've managed. I can't imagine it being like this every time."

"Guess that's just the curse of being the Dragon Fae. Now that you're my companion, you get to join in the fun too," I said with sardonic acid dripping from my voice.

"At least we know the cuff is going to protect us both, and it won't be so bad for you now."

No one had ever shown such concern over the effect the cuff had on me. Deacon appearing grateful at the opportunity to carry half my burden unsettled me. I needed a distraction, and we needed more data.

I picked up the same rock I'd levitated and with a swift motion sliced open my palm. I held it out to him. "Heal me."

Deacon took my hand in his and breathed on the cut. From his wince and the shock that went through me, I knew it hurt him. Then he stuck his tongue out and licked the blood, tracing the cut and closing it with his saliva. That also sent a steady thrum of pain through me, at odds with the tickle of his tongue on my palm.

When the cut was healed, he met my eyes, still cradling my hand in his. No trace of pain clouded his features. All that stared back at me was hot desire.

I wanted to reach out and touch his chest, feel the firm muscle beneath his shirt. I wanted to let him grab me, hold me to him the way he clearly wanted to. It didn't need to mean anything. We could just be two people attracted to each other beneath the desert's full moon.

But we were partners. He was my companion who didn't want to bond with me. Giving in to physical desire would only complicate matters, ruin the relationship we had as partners. Alistair's life depended on us working well together. He needed us to be sharp, not confused by feelings.

I snatched my hand away and broke eye contact. "We should get back. It's been a long day. Are you staying at Sybil's?"

Deacon stepped back, shaking his head once in a sharp motion like he was reprimanding himself for something. "She has kindly offered her couch. I'll be staying with her until I find something more permanent."

The entire drive back to the apartment we sat in silence. I didn't understand how we could have such a connection out in the desert and yet the thought of bonding with me seemed to disgust Deacon earlier.

We had so much to talk about. I still wanted to know if he had gone to the nether during the ceremony, but that discussion would have to wait. It was too involved to have now.

14

The next morning, I told Pint all about my new powers over a breakfast of cold cereal.

"Do you know what kind of powers you'd get if you bonded?" Pint asked.

"No, and Sybil hasn't given us any details, only that it's necessary for us to eventually bond. I'm not even sure she knows the details herself. I think she's just going off prophecy." The Origin had told me the same thing, that I needed to bond.

I hadn't told Pint that I traveled to the nether. I didn't want to sound crazy, and I still hadn't had an opportunity to talk to Deacon about it. Last night would've been perfect, but we were too busy with the practical side of figuring out our powers. The mission always had to come first. Discussing our feelings about the ceremony wouldn't help us get Alistair back.

It would take time to adjust to this new normal. When I woke up this morning, I could feel Deacon's magic against my skin due to the effects of the cuff. Having another person's magic so close to me first thing in the morning, in bed, was an intimacy I hadn't experienced since Julien.

"Show me one of your new glamour looks," Pint said.

My phone vibrated with a new voicemail. I had it set up so only a few favorite contacts rang through. "Sorry, I have to check this."

The message was only a few seconds long. Meilin's voice played in my ear. "Meet me at the safe house immediately."

It was strange for Meilin to contact me herself. When she told me I was the Dragon Fae, that was something that required someone of her standing to convey. But why was she getting involved again? Whatever the reason, it couldn't be good.

I turned to Pint. "Don't tell Sybil and Deacon about this."

"What are you going to do?" Pint asked.

"I'm going to go without them. I don't like bringing them into a situation where I don't know what to expect."

"And how do you plan to get there?"

I didn't know the directions to the safe house. I had no idea where it was actually located. Information like that was kept secret to prevent it from falling into the wrong hands. I'd only gone in and out of it one way. "I'm going to teleport."

I prepared myself for the familiar pain that would assault me.

"Then Deacon's going to know anyway," Pint said.

"Shit." He was right. I'd already forgotten. If I teleported, Deacon would feel it with our new powers. If I told him where I was going, he wouldn't be happy with me going alone. He'd insist on coming. If I still went without him, it would hurt him and our bond. But if I left now without telling him, once he felt my magic and the subsequent pain, he'd worry about me. That wasn't fair to him. "I'll go tell him what's going on."

Closing the door to my apartment, I realized for the first time that I was accountable to someone. Before, Alistair would go along with whatever I did and smooth it over with the Circle. The mission and survival had dictated my actions, nothing else. My partner's safety always concerned me, but I'd never made a decision based solely on the feelings of my partner.

"Nadiya, how are you doing? It's been a while since you've been over for a chat," Harry Harmon said from behind me.

I turned to see my retired neighbor sitting on his lawn chair in front of his door. Potted plants and a garden gnome covered the area around him. I wondered why he had chosen a second-floor apartment when one on the first floor would have been more conducive to gardening and his aging knees.

"I'm sorry, Mr. Harmon. I've been busy." Harry had befriended me the day I moved in despite my best efforts at avoiding connections. Maintaining my cover with him was essential. I didn't want him dragged into my world anymore than he already was.

"I have some news. My nephew Freddie is coming to visit."

"That's wonderful!" In the three years I'd lived here, Harry had never had family visit. It'd be good for him to have some company.

"I can't wait for you to meet him," Harry said. "He's a real good kid."

"I look forward to it." With any luck, his nephew would hold his attention off of me and keep him occupied. I didn't know when my life would resume some type of normality, and I already had too many balls to juggle. Knowing Mr. Harmon was taken care of would make my life that much easier.

I needed something to be easy, because I doubted this meeting with Meilin would be.

15

I delivered the news as soon as I entered Sybil's apartment. "Meilin has summoned me to the safe house."

Deacon's eyebrows lifted in that subtle way they did when he heard something unexpected. Sybil chewed her lip and look to the side.

"And you didn't go on your own?" Deacon asked.

"Yeah, don't give me too much credit. I'm only here because I knew you would feel me using my magic."

"What do you think she wants?" Deacon asked.

"I doubt it's anything good. The last time I saw her, she declared me the Dragon Fae, and look where that's gotten us."

Sybil nodded and looked at me. "I agree. I don't see this being anything good. We should all three go together."

Sybil hadn't been with us at the safe house last time, so she wouldn't know where to take us. I'd have to do it. I held out my hands to Deacon and Sybil and gritted my teeth as I teleported us.

◊

Nothing had changed in the safe house since the last time I'd been there. Meilin sat in the same chair as before at the same simple square table. Only this time, instead of Alistair sitting opposite her, a man I'd never seen before occupied that seat.

I quickly bowed my head in a respectful greeting to Meilin. Deacon and Sybil did the same.

"How nice to see you, Nadiya," Meilin said.

Interesting. She called me Nadiya and not Dragon Fae. Meilin never spoke carelessly. This was her way of letting me know that no matter what's happened, to her I was still just a loyal agent.

"Hello, Chancellor. I've seen you more in the last week and a half than I have the rest of my time working for the Circle put together. You must be pretty happy."

All I got in reply was an arched eyebrow.

"You got everything you wanted. I averted the attack at the Feast of the Dragon, and I took on the role of Dragon Fae. It's even more than you wanted."

"Oh, is that how you view things?"

The question was intended to put me off balance. Meilin was skilled. It's how she got to where she was, but I'd been a spy my entire life. I'd been trained by the best. It took a lot to rattle me.

"No, it's the reality of the situation. As is the fact that the queen of the fae has kidnapped my handler, and you don't seem to be doing much about it."

"That's why I summoned you here. I want to introduce you to your new handler. This is Gordon. He'll be handling you in Alistair's absence."

Absence, as if he were on leave and not held prisoner by the fae queen.

The man sitting opposite Meilin stood and held out his hands palms up in the Elustrian greeting. I did not return the gesture. Unlike Meilin who wore her usual Elustrian robes, Gordon was dressed as a human in jeans and a white T-shirt. His spiky red hair and round face made him look young, too young and inexperienced to possibly handle me.

"It's an honor to meet you, Nadiya. I've heard so much about you. Your case reports make for very entertaining reading."

I looked back at Meilin. "He is not my handler. Alistair is my handler."

"Gordon is a temporary replacement to help you get Alistair back."

"I don't need to train a new agent while I'm also searching for Alistair. He'll only get in the way."

In Gordon's defense, he did speak up for himself instead of letting Meilin fight his battles. "I'm a seasoned agent. I've been doing this as long as Alistair has. I can help you."

Nothing in Gordon's appearance or temperament led me to distrust him anymore than I distrusted anyone. Still, I couldn't develop the trust I would need with him in the timeframe necessary to save Alistair. He would only be one more hurdle, one more life for me to consider, one more distraction.

Deacon, who'd contented himself standing a few steps behind me, now joined me shoulder to shoulder. His physical closeness leant weight to his emotional support.

"Why is there any need for Nadiya to have a temporary handler? The Circle can communicate through Sybil," Deacon said.

I didn't know if Deacon objected to the idea of Gordon, but the fact that my objection was enough for him meant a lot to me. The only other person who had ever done things for no other reason than that I wanted them was Alistair.

Sybil came out from behind us and went to Meilin's side. "That would work well for me. I could act as an intermediary between Nadiya and the Circle. I could step in as her temporary handler. It would make things simpler, and I'm already going to be helping on this mission anyway. It might make things smoother for me to communicate directly with the Circle. My knowledge of the fae court can provide valuable context."

"See? There's no need for us to adapt to working with someone new. We don't have time," Deacon said. Meilin didn't have the same power over Deacon that she did me. Technically, Deacon didn't fall under her jurisdiction. He could talk to her however he liked.

"Having Sybil work as your handler is a waste. There's no need to take up her valuable time running back and forth communicating with us. Better to work through Gordon. While he's reporting to us, Sybil can help you get Alistair," Meilin said.

I didn't trust a word of it. Meilin had her own reasons for wanting Gordon, and they had nothing to do with me or Alistair.

I'd long suspected the Circle wasn't happy with how little control they had over me. It would be too easy once Alistair was free for them to keep Gordon as my handler. Now that I was the Dragon Fae, Meilin would want even more control.

All this would be moot if Alistair wasn't freed. Arguing with Meilin would only waste more time, and I didn't see what other choice we had. The resources of the Circle could help this mission. Once I had Alistair back, he'd be able to think of a way to get rid of Gordon. I realized now more than ever that it was Alistair and the cause that I was loyal to, not the Circle.

I looked at Gordon. "Fine. You want to be part of this, have fun." Before he could respond, I turned back to Meilin.

"Tell us what happened with Malev," she said.

Everything about this felt off. I had worked one way my entire life. I did the mission, reported to Alistair, and he handled the rest. In theory, he was supposed to tell the Circle everything. In reality, I knew that he exercised discretion. I didn't have the same knack for politicking as he did. I could handle a mark just fine, but the woman who held my job and my life in her hands was a different matter. I was acutely aware of how much Meilin outranked me.

"What exactly is it that you want to know? Alistair's an agent of the Circle, Queen Malev kidnapped him, and I haven't gotten any orders to go in and free him. I haven't been given an action plan. Nothing."

"We've been waiting to hear what happened between you two. We know she has Alistair, and we know she summoned you. Other than that, we don't have anything to work off of."

She could be lying. I didn't know how much information she had or what the Circle's involvement was. What was their relationship with the fae court? Before now, I thought they were working together, perhaps not closely, but at least toward the same end.

It seemed clear that the Circle wasn't going to do much if anything to rescue Alistair. They were scared of Malev like everyone else. Knowing that, I wanted to keep my knowledge close. Intelligence was power, and I didn't want to give mine way. Then again, it might be in Alistair's best interest for the Circle to know. They might be able to offer some help.

"Queen Malev suspects she has a traitor in her ranks, someone setting up a rival court here on Earth. She wants me to discover their identity and provide her with their name."

Meilin sat back in her chair with a satisfied smile. I'd never seen her that relaxed or happy. "Excellent. We had thought this for some time. Malev's grip is not as tight or as strong as it used to be. We suspected dissension in her ranks. We haven't been able to figure out how deep the rift goes or how willing some of the fae might be to act on it."

She nodded as she thought through the implications. "You have the full resources of the Circle to complete your mission. Discover the name of her rival and report to us. We will give you additional instructions after that."

"So you're saying instead of giving the name directly to Queen Malev, you want me to give it to you first?"

"You will give the name to Gordon." Meilin nodded to my interim handler, her gaze lingering on him meaningfully. "And then you will await further instructions."

The implication was clear. If I tried to sidestep Gordon, then Meilin would keep him as my handler even after Alistair was saved.

Of course, Meilin and the Circle wanted the name so they could choose who to side with.

I gave her the answer she expected, the one any good agent would. "Understood."

Meilin's grin widened. "Excellent." She stood. "I'll leave you to discuss the mission. Let us know where to direct our resources."

She nodded to Gordon, and he returned it. Then she made a portal and stepped back into the Starlight Palace. This time, seeing the portal shimmer just a few feet in front of me, I didn't have the desire to step through it. What I wanted wasn't on the other side of the portal.

Once Meilin was gone, Gordon gestured to the chair opposite him.

I shook my head. "No, there's not time. Do you have my contact protocol?"

"I have your cell phone number. I'll be using standard protocols. Tell me what information you have."

"We don't have anything to go on right now. We're heading out to the enclave in Queen Creek to ask around. Right now, all we have are rumors. We need to track them down and see where they lead."

"The fae queen didn't give you anything else to work with?" Gordon asked. I couldn't help but notice that he didn't use her name. Like most Elustrians, he was scared to use it.

"No, she didn't give us anything else. If she had more, she wouldn't need us."

Gordon took a deep breath and pursed his lips, trying to figure out how to handle me now that he had the job. "Look, I know you're not happy with this situation. Neither am I. Alistair is a great handler. The best. I'm not claiming to be as good as him, but I do know what I'm doing. I wouldn't have survived this long if I didn't. I know it doesn't feel like it, but I'm on your side. If this is going to work, you're going to have to trust me."

"If you've been with the Circle for as long as you say you have, if you really think I'm as good as my reputation, then you would know better than to ask me to trust you right away."

The corner of Gordon's mouth lifted and genuine mirth entered his eyes. "Fair enough. Don't trust me. But trust that the Circle trusts me and that right now your interests and the Circle's interests are aligned."

I wasn't going to give him anything more. "Like I said, we're going to the enclave to see what we can find out. When we have something, we'll let you know."

The air in the room tensed. He thought I was holding out on him, but he couldn't figure out if he should push the issue. In this battle of wills, I wasn't going to bend. I didn't want him knowing that I had a picture of the fae we were looking for. Yes, the Circle might be able to find him quicker, but I didn't know what they would do with the information they got or if they would pass it on to me. I had to stay in control of this mission to make sure Alistair made it out. Gordon would have to be content with the information I gave him.

Gordon's pale blue eyes were cold, but they didn't give anything away. He didn't make any movement to acknowledge what I said. He simply maintained eye contact. I couldn't get a read on him.

"Oh! Look at that!" Sybil exclaimed, pulling our attention to her. "It's getting quite late. We best be off. Too-da-loo!" She grabbed my hand and Deacon's and lifted them up to wave at Gordon as she teleported us back home.

16

_I_ could hug Sybil for getting us out of there. She had the advantage of not being under the Circle's jurisdiction as well as the prominence of being the Oracle.

Sybil went to the kitchen and started a pot of coffee while Deacon and I sat on the sofa.

"You're the Dragon Fae," Deacon said when we were settled. "You don't have to take her orders like that."

Deacon may not fully understand the workings of the Circle, but given his position in the dragon court, he understood better than most the chain of command and hierarchies. "No, in this situation I'm an agent rescuing her handler. Agents don't get their way. They obey their superiors until they see how to get away with not obeying."

It'd be easy enough to ignore Gordon for the short term. All I had to do was keep my phone off. Alistair had arranged my apartment, but he never reported the location. There'd be no way for Gordon to know where I lived. That only left one potential weakness.

"Sybil, does anyone in the Circle know that you live here?" I asked.

"No. As far as I know, only Alistair has your address. I went through him when I made my arrangements here. You don't need to worry about any unexpected visits." She levitated three mugs of coffee to the living room and sat in her armchair with her legs tucked underneath her.

Deacon and I grabbed the mugs floating in front of us. I took a sip without looking. A sickly sweet liquid flowed over my tongue, and I had to quickly hide my grimace. This bore no resemblance to the bitter black coffee I preferred. A glance at Deacon showed a pleasant face. Too pleasant. He didn't like it either.

"Sybil, you see if there's anything you can find out about who this fae is. While you're doing that, Deacon and I will head to the Queen Creek enclave. The people out there might've heard something. A fae setting up a rival court on Earth would certainly get tongues wagging." If there was one thing humans and magic folk had in common, it was gossip.

🔥

On the way out to the enclave, I went to a drive-through and grabbed us some burgers and fries. With one hand on the wheel, I ate my hamburger and then proceeded to the fries. The greasy little sticks of salty carb goodness were one of the best parts of Earth.

"You really shouldn't eat while you drive. It isn't safe," Deacon said as he ate his burger much slower than me.

"I'll remind you that I've been driving for the last three years with nary an accident, and that was back when I was just a sorceress. Now I'm a sorceress who's part fae and the Dragon Fae at that, driving along with my dragon shifter partner. I really don't think you have to worry," I said and grabbed another few fries from the bag.

"My reflexes are amazing," I added on a more serious note. While I didn't fear getting in an accident, I did take the safety of the other people on the road seriously. To Deacon, who hadn't been on Earth long, cars were a new and unpredictable thing and therefore dangerous.

When the fries were gone, Deacon handed me a napkin and my

bottled water. Soda was something I had never liked. "So, have you ever been to an enclave?" I asked.

"No. My time on Earth has mainly been spent with you or Sybil. What should I know?"

"Oh, there's really nothing you need to know. Better for it to be a surprise." I'd been to a few enclaves. While there might be some differences between them, they all had something in common: an odd population.

The people who were attracted to the enclaves were always a little strange. Some of them held almost religious beliefs about Earth and its connection to Elustria. Many were looking to escape Elustria for one reason or another. It was a fresh start. There had to be something a little off about someone who would abandon a world of magic to come to a place devoid of it where they'd have to constantly hide who and what they are.

Personally, I didn't care for the enclaves. They had both too much magic and not enough. Stepping into one, the rush of magic could be intoxicating, but it wasn't the ubiquitous presence that it was in Elustria. This half in half out set up only made the homesickness worse. It made it harder to stay content on Earth.

I liked it when I could ignore magic, when it could just be part of my job. It couldn't be who I was, not anymore, so I didn't like pretending in the enclaves.

"We both know that you're better at deception than I am, so I'll focus on maintaining our glamour," Deacon said.

From anyone else, it would've sounded like a criticism, but coming from him, all I heard in his voice was admiration for my skill. In my experience, people were often made uncomfortable by others who could easily lie and deceive.

While there were some enclaves that were segregated—only allowing one species—most of the enclaves were more diverse than even parts of Elustria. The segregated ones were usually either mages or elves, both liked to keep to themselves. The only hard and fast rule was that any magic folk on Earth had to be able to blend in, so that meant adapting either a human or animal appearance when outside the enclave.

"Do you want to come up with our cover story?" I asked Deacon.

I caught the lift of his eyebrows. He hadn't expected that. "Since you're the one who's going to have to sell it, wouldn't it be better for you to come up with it?"

"I can sell anything," I said without even thinking. I'd never had a choice. The Circle gave me my orders, and I became whomever they wanted me to be.

"Ooh, a challenge. Let's see." Deacon rubbed his hands together. "We're two lovers who have escaped Elustria after falling afoul of the Brotherhood. Our only way back is to find this fae and bring him to the Brotherhood."

That story might sound outlandish to him, but it wasn't for the enclaves. The Brotherhood was an organized crime group akin to the Mafia on Earth. If anything, that was a pretty mundane cover story.

The road out to Queen Creek was empty, so Deacon and I took the opportunity to glamour ourselves. When I parked outside Bubbles and Brews, a popular restaurant and bar in the enclave, we were Dylan and Carolina, two lovers on the lam.

Our car doors closing sounded loud in the unnatural silence. The main thoroughfare was deserted. The few times I'd been here in the past, this walkable downtown area had bustled with activity. Today, the shops stood empty.

"Is it usually like this?" Deacon asked as he squinted against the sun and peered into a shop window.

"No, this is a first for me." If everyone was gathered in one place, I had a pretty good idea where'd they'd be.

I led Deacon down an alley between Chad's Doodads, owned by Chadukarikus Lipstenpulerapi, and Fangtastic Flowers and Ferns that specialized in carnivorous plants from Earth and Elustria. Behind the shops hid the only park. It wasn't much, just a gazebo and some picnic tables, but it served as the main gathering spot. It was also the only place with grass in the enclave, maintained with magic.

Sure enough, it seemed the entire enclave was gathered at the park. Someone was speaking to the crowd from the gazebo, but they had a shield up so we couldn't hear.

We faced the speaker, and he spotted us. He must've said something to that effect because the crowd turned their heads to see the newcomers and then dispersed, quietly walking back to their businesses and errands for the day. More than a few cut sideways glances toward us and then whispered as they walked off.

"Should we leave?" Deacon asked.

Unease filled the air. They clearly didn't want us here. "No, just ignore it and act normal."

At this point, nothing would make us seem inconspicuous, so I decided to forgo any pretense. Besides, they wouldn't be able to describe us in any accurate detail should they be suspicious about something. That was the nice thing about glamouring. We could burn identities as quickly as we created them.

A woman chatted with a small group, clearly gossiping either about what the speaker had said or about me and Deacon. When her friends left, I approached her. She'd be eager to tell me what she knew. If not, she'd at least be willing to talk so she could tell others about me.

"Excuse me, I hate to bother you, but I was wondering if you've seen this man," I said as I showed her the picture. I deliberately withheld my name hoping she'd ask and that I could tell her our cover story, give her a little bit of gossip in trade for the information I wanted. She took a quick glance at the picture and then met my eyes.

"No, I'm sorry. I can't help you," she said as she walked away.

"Did you see that?" Deacon asked beside me.

"Yep." Her eyes had widened when she saw the picture.

"She recognized him," Deacon said.

My next target was a man who eyed me up and down. He might want to impress me. "Excuse me, sir. Do you recognize this man?"

He looked at the picture, clearly expecting to brush it off, but did a double take. He shook his head so vigorously I thought he might hurt himself. "Never seen him before."

As he walked away, he glanced around at the other people leaving the park, wondering if anyone had seen him talking to me. The people still present spoke in hushed tones. The serious atmosphere of the gathering hadn't yet lifted. It'd be better to come back in the evening, go to Bubbles and Brews and see what we could get from a drunk patron.

"I might have better luck," Deacon said and extended his hand for the picture. I shrugged and handed it to him. He approached a group of women, and I held back. If he could get them in a flirty mood, he might get some answers. My presence would only complicate matters.

I looked around. Everyone regarded us outsiders with suspicion. They all behaved the same, speaking in hushed tones, giving me and Deacon a wide berth. It all had a very cult-y feel to it. As someone with recent experience with cults, it seemed too familiar.

"I can't get any answers from these people," Deacon said from behind me. I turned, and he handed me back the picture. "It was the same with all of them. They clearly knew who he was but weren't willing to say."

I scratched my Bubbles and Brews idea. Getting to people in a relaxed environment wouldn't make a difference in this situation. If the cult vibe was correct, these people would all keep silent, especially to outsiders. It'd just be a waste of our time. "I agree. Let's get out of here."

I'd never felt so grateful to leave an enclave.

"So it's not normally like that?" Deacon asked on the drive home.

"No, that was weird even by enclave standards. Something's going on. Maybe Sybil will have news for us."

17

Sybil wasn't home when we arrived. Coming back to an empty apartment felt somewhat anticlimactic. We'd been going for so long, and now there was nothing left to do but wait for her. We either needed her insight or for Trevor to get a hit on our missing fae.

Waiting around never sat well with me. I wanted to be going, doing. Anything else seemed an awful waste of time.

However, spending this time with Deacon did provide a level of enjoyment I wasn't used to. I usually didn't have this kind of rapport with partners. In the past, it had been a strictly business relationship. My partnership with Deacon was something different. Since Alistair —who was the person I normally turned to for emotional support— was gone, it was nice to have Deacon here.

"Do you want me to make some tea or coffee or something?" Deacon asked.

I smiled as he looked around the kitchen perplexed. "Do you even know how to make either of those?"

"No, but it can't be too difficult. I mean, it's just adding hot water, right?"

"You'd be surprised how easy it is to mess that up."

Normally, I'd have a whiskey about now, but the bottle was in my apartment, and I didn't want to fetch it. Besides, this was a chance for me and Deacon to talk. Even with all the time we spent together since the anointing, we hadn't really discussed what had happened. I didn't need or want a drink for that.

I sat down on the sofa and invited Deacon to join me with a look.

"Do you want to pick up where we left off on that show?" Deacon asked.

That had only been yesterday morning. How I wished I could go back to that time, cuddled up against him, watching his face collapse into laughter. I could spend my whole life in that moment. It seemed I never fully appreciated those times until everything came crumbling down around me.

I could say yes. We could turn on the TV and pretend like none of this was happening. I could lay my head against his chest, and he'd wrap his arm around me. We could pretend even for a moment that we were normal.

But we weren't normal. We were a far cry from it.

"No, thanks. I was hoping we could talk about the anointing ceremony."

A shadow crossed Deacon's face, and I could see walls go up in his eyes. So there was something to talk about.

"I want to know what it was like for you. Did you go to the nether? When I came back, the look on your face, I could've sworn you had, but you didn't say anything."

He didn't meet my eyes. "Neither did you."

Fair, but even if I hadn't, I was talking about it now. "When I was there, the Origin spoke to me. I was wondering, did she speak to you? Or was it her companion who spoke to you?"

Deacon's guard didn't drop. "It was her companion."

"And? What did he say to you?" I leaned in, wanting to gather more information than he was giving.

Deacon shifted in his seat. He didn't often fidget, and the uncomfortable uncertainty didn't sit well on him. "He explained my role to me and what's to come."

A strange anguish filled his face.

"Can you tell me more?"

Deacon's mouth open and closed. He sniffed the air and took a deep breath, his brow furrowing in concentration. I caught a whiff of it a second after him: the smell of putrid garbage.

"I think it's just trash day," I said.

Deacon shook his head and stood. The smell got stronger, and a knock sounded at the door. Deacon opened it after peeking through the peephole.

"Hi, Deacon. I thought I saw you and Nadiya come in a little while ago," Harry said jovially.

I came to stand beside Deacon. Next to Harry stood a man who appeared to be in his thirties and taller than Harry. He stank of garbage. Like a flash of lightning, Deacon's words illuminated my mind. *The fae could get quite rank.*

"I wanted to introduce my nephew Freddie here to you." Harry slapped Freddie on the shoulder and beamed with pride.

Freddie stuck out his hand. "It's a pleasure to meet you, Nadiya. I've heard so much about you from Uncle Harry."

I didn't want to take his hand, but I didn't see any way around it. If I refused, it would be rude to Harry, and he wouldn't understand. I couldn't tell him the truth about his nephew. Right now, he was an innocent bystander. But if I made him aware of the fae standing next to him, he'd be more involved than he already was. There'd be little reason for the fae to keep him alive. So I took Freddie's hand and shook it, forcing back the instinct to recoil.

"It's a pleasure to meet you too. Mr. Harmon has been so excited for your visit." I stepped outside and Deacon followed, shutting the door behind us. We didn't need to let this strange fae into Sybil's apartment.

"Sybil isn't at home?" Harry asked.

"No, I'm afraid not. She popped out for a little while," I answered.

"Nuts. I wanted her to meet Freddie. Oh well, we'll catch her later." Harry waved away his disappointment.

"We'll be sure to let her know you came by," Deacon said.

Harry started to turn away but remembered something else, snapping his fingers in the air. "I want to invite you and Sybil over for dinner tonight. All my favorite people in one room together. You can come too, Deacon." Mr. Harmon nodded at Deacon with a broad smile.

I hated disappointing him. I hated that my life had brought this danger to his doorstep. I didn't know if the right thing was to accept or not, but I couldn't commit to a dinner appointment. Not now with so much in the air. When Sybil got back, she'd know what to do about the Freddie situation. "I'm afraid not, Mr. Harmon. I have a work thing."

Harry visibly deflated in front of me, his smile losing some of its width but not disappearing completely. "I understand. We need to get together sometime, though. I need to hear all about what you've been up to."

"And I'd love to get to know you while I'm here," Freddie said.

My magic tingled in my fingertips, wanting to unleash on him. Deacon stepped closer, his chest against my back. It was the most he could do with Harry standing right there. "We'll have to take a rain check," I said.

"All right. We won't keep you any longer. I know you're busy." Harry looked at Deacon suggestively and waggled his eyebrows.

I laughed and swatted at him the way I would if there weren't a fae standing next to him.

"Come on, Freddie." Mr. Harmon turned back to his apartment with Freddie falling behind. Just before he stepped over the threshold, Freddie turned and waved his fingers at us in a smug farewell.

In Sybil's apartment, I shut the door and slid the deadbolt into place, as if that would protect us from the fae across the way.

"How did he find us?" Deacon asked.

No one had ever found me. Other than Sybil and Deacon, only

one person knew where I lived. Alistair would never tell a soul, not for anything—not willingly at least. "Malev had to have gotten the knowledge from Alistair. It's the only explanation that makes sense."

"Is it possible Freddie's a changeling?" Deacon asked. "He could've been in Harry's family from the beginning."

Changelings were fae who were swapped with human babies. It happened, though it wasn't common, especially these days. I shook my head. "No, it's too much of a coincidence that my next-door neighbor would have a changeling for a nephew. That's putting aside that the nephew happened to visit in the middle of all this. I've lived next door to Harry for three years, and he's never had family visit."

I appreciated Deacon's effort to come up with another explanation. I shuddered to think what Malev must've done to Alistair to get this information. There wasn't much I was sure of in life, but I was sure that Alistair would rather die than give up my location. That meant Malev must have done some type of mind magic on him.

Nausea roiled in my stomach as I thought about the violation. I wanted to puke, but that wouldn't help anything.

Deacon's hands rested on my shoulders. "It's going to be all right. We'll figure this out together."

I looked up into his eyes. I wanted to believe him, but I wasn't equipped to handle this. I was an agent of the Circle. They gave my orders to Alistair, and I obeyed them. Simple as that. Who was there to give orders now? How was I supposed to figure out how to rescue Alistair when I couldn't even keep my neighbor out of the grasp of the fae?

My mind went back to what Malev promised when we made our deal. She wasn't supposed to hurt him. Or had she not agreed to that specifically? I thought back to her exact words.

You have my word that after you give me the name of my rival, I will give you your handler.

Dammit. What a rookie mistake. I'd spent so much time on Earth, where I almost never dealt with fae, that I'd forgotten to be meticulous in the wording of Malev's promise.

"Hey, what's going on over here?" Pint said as he flew in from the balcony. I must have looked a fright because he took one glance at me and flew over. "What happened?" He looked to Deacon for an answer.

"Your neighbor's nephew came to visit. Turns out he's a fae."

"Fucking fae," Pint spat. "I ought to go over there and roast his ass. This is our territory. When he comes here, he has to reckon with me."

I smiled at Pint's protectiveness. "There's no indication that Harry knows Freddie is a fae. While we're working on getting Alistair back, I need you to keep a discrete eye on Freddie. Let me know if he does anything unusual or becomes aggressive with Harry. I think that as long as we're peaceful and working on Malev's assignment, he won't do anything. She already has Alistair. She should know that hurting Harry won't get me to work any faster. This is just a threat, that's all."

I wished I was a certain as I sounded. Fae were tricky creatures. They were loyal to themselves above all.

"Don't you worry. Harry keeps his blinds open most of the time. I can keep an eye on him through the balcony. Are you any closer to figuring this all out?" Pint asked.

No, but I didn't want to tell him that. "I've got my tech guy working on some leads, and Sybil should be back soon with some information for us. Don't worry about the mission. You just keep watch here."

"You got it." Pint flew to the refrigerator and opened it with his talons. He grabbed a piece of steak that Sybil had for him and flew off with it.

"Come sit down," Deacon said. "There's no use fretting over this. We need to wait for Sybil to get back, and we'll plan our next move." He placed his hand on the small of my back and nudged me toward the sofa.

I stepped to the side, away from his touch. I couldn't go back to the way we were, sitting on the sofa, talking. As much as I wanted to know what happened to him in the nether, I couldn't simply sit and talk. Besides, it didn't seem that Deacon was going to share any more than he already had.

I didn't know how long Sybil would be. That only left one person who might give me some answers. "Stay here and wait for Sybil."

"Where are you going?" Deacon asked, the furrow of his brow showing his displeasure at this turn of events.

"I can't just sit here with you. I need to find some answers. I'm sorry." Sorry for leaving and sorry for the pain it was going to cause.

I opened a portal to Elustria and stepped through.

18

The temple was calm and serene compared to last night. Only a few priestesses attended the grounds. They looked in my direction. One started to approach, but I waved her away. She bowed her head and left me alone. This was, supposedly, my temple, and I was relieved not to see Jaygar. I didn't want to talk to anyone except the Origin.

I walked to the pillar and placed my palm on the dragon eye as I had before. I had no reason to doubt that it would work. All around me, the color faded until it was black-and-white and shadowy. This time, my mind swirled with a sense of vertigo.

"Origin," I called in my mind. As before, I couldn't see anyone, just the black-and-white world around me.

"What are you doing here?" It was the disembodied voice of the Origin.

"I need your help."

"No, you don't. You have all the help you need."

Grrr. I needed her to take me seriously. I wouldn't come here for nothing. "Malev has found me. She's threatening the people I love. I don't know how to stop her." Repeating my situation made me despair even more. Coming here was dumb. I didn't know what I expected.

"You expected me to give you some answers."

"Don't do that." I forgot that she could read my thoughts.

"You're thinking too small. You're the Dragon Fae. It may be a lonely position, but you are not alone."

I wanted to see her, to face the woman I spoke to. I wanted to know that she had really survived her own time as the Dragon Fae. I looked around, but there was no one.

"I don't care about being the Dragon Fae. This isn't about that. I need to get Alistair back. Malev is torturing him or at least violating his mind. There's no other way she could have the information that she does."

A chill filled the air, and a sense of foreboding overcame me. The Origin was mad.

"This isn't about you. It's bigger than that."

"Fine. If you won't help me with this, then what the hell am I supposed to do as the Dragon Fae?"

"You're supposed to lead."

"Lead whom to what? I didn't sign up to be a leader. All I did was save those people Nicholas wanted to kill. That's it. I figured if I could spread a little hope while I was at it, why not? But I'm not giving up Alistair for the stupid prophecy."

Wind roared in my ears and whipped my hair around my face. "You'd be wise not to disrespect the prophecy. It governs your life whether you want it to or not."

"So tell me what to do."

"You have an entire community around you. The fae, the dragons, all magic folk, and yet you come here asking me for help? You trespass into the nether? This is no place for you."

"I don't have a place. I don't have a home. Or didn't you read that part of the prophecy?"

"When you first came here, you called for Deacon. Why aren't you talking to him?"

"Because he doesn't have any answers either. And what exactly did your companion say to him?"

"He talked to him about the prophecy and his role in it."

"Whatever it was, he didn't seem happy about it. If you want me to live up to this destiny, then I'm going to need help. I can't do this without Alistair. Whatever it is, whatever grand plan is in store, I promise you, I cannot do it without him. I know you think Deacon should be enough as my companion, but Alistair, he's my rock. If I lose him…" I choked on the words. But I didn't need to say them; she could read them in my mind. The grief would kill me.

Warmth surrounded me, like the sun breaking through the clouds. "It wouldn't. That's not how you die. No matter what happens, know that."

I didn't care. How does Alistair die? Hot tears of frustration and sadness mourning the life I used to have flowed down my cheeks.

"No, I don't know what happens with him. I only know your destiny. If you say you need him, then he will survive. Everything you need will be provided for you."

"Provided for me to do what? I don't understand my purpose. Why can't you tell me more? Why is it that everyone knows more than I do about what's going to happen in my life?"

"We don't. It only feels that way. It wasn't easy for me either. There are things I could've done better."

I didn't know much about the original Dragon Fae. I just knew the legend, the same as everyone else. The legend didn't include her failures, her humanity, the complexities of her life.

"My failures are going to cost innocent people their lives. As if Alistair weren't bad enough, at least he signed up for this. He knew what he was getting into. It shouldn't have ever happened because he's a handler. He never went on active missions. Still, he knew the danger of our work. But my human neighbor? He has no part in this. Same as those followers of Nicholas."

"You're right. That is why you are here at this time. Earth and

Elustria are mixing in ways that could have permanent consequences."

"That's all you have for me? Isn't there anything you can say that'll help me?"

"All I can tell you is that every time you come here, you pay a toll. It's not natural for the living to enter the nether. Your ties to the humans are a strength. When I said you had a community, I meant them as well. Humans can help you find the answers you seek. One may even be trying to help you now."

I didn't understand what she meant. Harry was the only human in my life I could think about right now. Sitting in his living room was a fae who wouldn't think twice about killing him. He might do so just for fun even after my task was done.

"Lean into the community around you. And most importantly, lean into your companion. You haven't bonded. That will hinder you, but you have all the answers you need around you."

The vertigo I'd fought back earlier returned with a vengeance. My stomach twisted, and my mind clouded. Pain throbbed inside my skull. I felt myself being pulled. What was happening?

"You're paying the toll. Everyone pays a toll. It's how we get to places worth going."

I collapsed on the ground, and my hand slid off the pillar. When I opened my eyes, a priestess stood in front of me offering a cup of water. It was cool and sweet on my tongue. It had the flavor of the water I drank in my youth at Moonlark Academy. It came from the same snows. I drank it all and handed back the cup. "Thank you."

"You're welcome, Dragon Fae."

She stood so serene, as if she'd never had a care in the world. I wanted that. The simple life. Maybe the channels of destiny had gotten crossed. Maybe I was meant to be a Dragon Fae acolyte and not the Dragon Fae herself. "How did you know I needed that?"

"We are forbidden to touch the dragon eye, but we have long suspected that it would transport you to the nether. Traveling to the nether always takes a toll on people. I figured you might want a drink when you returned."

"You're right. Has anyone else been here since the anointing?"

"No, Your Highness."

I shook my head no. "I'm not a highness."

"It is the appropriate honorific for the Dragon Fae."

"All right, but it freaks me out. I just…" I suddenly became very aware that I was still sitting on the ground. I stood and brushed myself off. "Sorry, I didn't mean to be rude. I just, I need to get back."

"Of course. Do not worry. We will take care of the temple in your absence." She bobbed a little curtsy and went off to her work.

Coming here had been a mistake. All it did was weird me out and make me feel worse. I came with questions, and I left with nausea, a headache, and no answers.

19

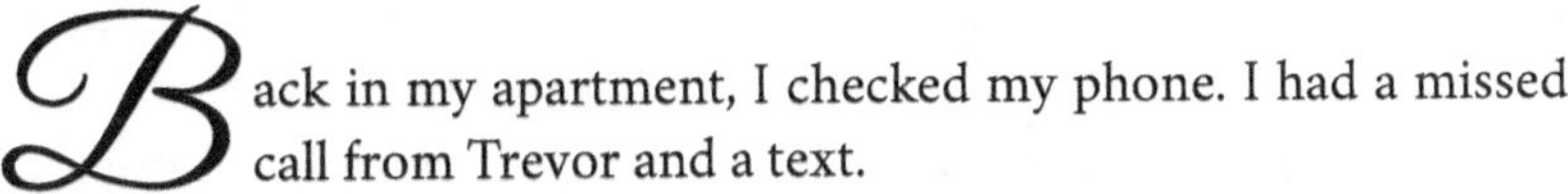

ack in my apartment, I checked my phone. I had a missed call from Trevor and a text.

I have something for you. Come see me ASAP.

The message had come in while I was in the nether. My stomach fluttered as I remembered the Origin's words about a human helping me. This text had come in right about the time she'd said that. Huh.

A knock sounded at my door. It wasn't Sybil's light rapping. Deacon's familiar scent reached me. I opened the door, and he looked relieved to see me even though he would've detected my magic.

I stepped outside, locked the door, and headed to my car, Deacon following. He broke the silence. "I felt it when you opened the portal to come back. Where did you go? What did you do?"

I stopped walking. "Oh? You could feel it even though I was in Elustria?"

"Yes."

"Huh. Interesting." I resumed walking. "I went back to the temple, to the nether. I was hoping to get some answers from the Origin."

Deacon reached out and grabbed my arm, stopping me. "And did you?"

"I'm not sure." It was the most honest answer I could come up with. "It all seemed like a bunch of nonsense. But she did tell me that a human would help and I came back to a message from my tech guy. I'm sorry, I would stop and talk more, but he said to come as soon as possible."

"No, no. Of course. Go. We'll talk when you get back."

⟡

I knocked on Trevor's door, and he yelled for me to come in. He lived in a converted garage apartment. It was just one big room with a TV and gaming system set up at the far end and a long table running against the garage door where he had computers and various electronics that he worked on. A futon, beanbag chairs, and two stools at his workbench were the only furniture.

Trevor looked up from his computer when I entered and smiled. No matter what was going on in his life, he was always quick to smile. From him, it was contagious.

"Come here. I can't wait to show you this," he said as he waved me over.

"What have you got for me?" I stood behind him and saw the fae's picture on the screen.

"I got a hit on him. Get this, it was in Oslo."

He looked over his shoulder when I didn't reply, and I raised my eyebrows.

"It's in Norway. The other side of the world." He pulled up a map and showed me. I had a sense that it was a European country and cold, but I didn't know much else. My work had never taken me there.

"This is good, Trevor."

Trevor laughed. "It's okay. What's good is what else I found. Turns out our fae has a whole human identity."

Trevor tapped on his keyboard and pulled up a dossier on the guy. I leaned in to read it as he continued speaking. "His name is Lars. He's registered as living in Bismo, Norway. It's crazy small. We're talking a few hundred people, less than a thousand."

What was he doing in Norway? There might be an enclave there. I'd have to ask Sybil. "But he wasn't in Bismo, right? You said the camera picked him up in Oslo."

"Yes, and that brings me to another interesting point. He was meeting with this man." Trevor brought up a picture of a man wearing a cowl.

Trevor skipped through the footage of their meeting. The cowled man's face never appeared. After Lars left, the mystery man pushed his cowl back and stared straight into the camera, smiling. He replaced the cowl and left.

"Go back to where we saw his face," I said.

Trevor chuckled and brought up a picture. He had already singled out a frame of the footage and enhanced it. The man's face was a map of deep creases. I'd never seen someone who looked so old.

"Now, the interesting thing about him is that he pings all over the world, even right here in Maricopa County." Trevor brought up another picture of him. "However, none of that is as interesting as the fact that there is no record of him. He's a ghost."

"If he can travel around the world like that and not leave any kind of paper trail, he's got to have magic." I took out my phone and snapped a picture of the mystery man. "How far back has he been showing up on cameras?" I wanted to know if this was someone who occasionally visited from Elustria or if they were a more permanent resident.

"Footage tends to get deleted pretty quickly, but faces are stored in a database. His face has been catalogued for as long as they've been using facial recognition."

The way the man smiled directly at the camera, it was as if it were a game to him. Like he knew the camera was there and also knew that it didn't matter. No one would be able to find him. The fact that he'd been seen in Maricopa County could be coincidence. "When was he seen in Arizona?"

"He's been here a lot and recently. Within the last week."

That didn't feel very coincidental to me. "Okay, thanks. You got a lot more than I thought you would. Can you jot down Lars's address for me?"

"Already done." Trevor handed me a piece of paper with all the relevant details.

"Are you any closer to getting your handler back?" Trevor asked, sincere interest in his eyes. He often worried about the innocent people who got caught up in the work I did.

"No, we had nothing to go on until you got this. For the first time since he was taken, I have hope that we'll get him back."

Trevor smiled. "Glad I could help. Let me know if there's anything else you need."

"Thanks for seeing me right now. I know you're normally sleeping about this time." Trevor was a confirmed night owl.

"This is better than sleep." He gave a little shrug.

"Get some rest. You've earned it." I put the piece of paper in my pocket, gave him a smile, and left.

I drove with the top down back to my place. It seemed I'd be going to Norway soon. Better enjoy the warmth while I could.

20

The stench of garbage assaulted me as I climbed the stairs to my apartment. Freddie was still here. As I got closer, a sweet, familiar scent appeared behind the garbage. Sybil was home. I changed course and knocked on her door instead of going to mine.

"Yay, you're back!" Sybil said as she waved me inside. Deacon stood when I entered, a cute, old-fashioned gesture.

I went to the sofa and sat next to him. "Freddie is still with us based on what I smelled on the way up here. Did you fill in Sybil?" I asked Deacon.

"We were just talking about that," Deacon said.

Sybil took her usual seat and grabbed a throw pillow to hold in her lap. "I don't think he's a changeling from birth. It's too much of a coincidence. The fae do play a longer game than humans do, but frankly, I don't think Malev would've cared enough to plant him that long ago even if she knew everything that was going to happen. It's much more likely that the real Freddie is being held somewhere."

Great, another person who needed saving. "Do you think they're going to hurt him? Kill him?"

"I don't think so," Sybil said. "I think it's much more likely that when this is all over they're just going to let him go with his memory altered. There's really not much benefit to hurting or killing him. Even if this other fae wanted to be mean, there's no fun in killing a human like that."

It was hard sometimes to remember that cheery Sybil came from the fae court where people did things like torture and kill for fun.

"Well, my tech guy came through in a big way for us. Our fae was caught on camera in Oslo, Norway. Not only that, he has an entire human identity under the name of Lars. He's registered as living in Bismo, Norway."

"What was he doing in Oslo?" Deacon asked.

"He was meeting with this man." I pulled up the picture on my phone and showed it to Deacon then passed it to Sybil. "This person has been seen literally all over the world, even right here in Maricopa County. The interesting thing is that there's no info about him in any database. As my guy put it, he's a ghost." Neither Deacon nor Sybil showed any recognition at the picture. I'd hoped Sybil would recognize him.

"He has to be magic folk," Deacon said. "You said he's been spotted in Maricopa County. Maybe the people in the enclave would recognize him."

"It would be nice to figure out who he is, but I'm more interested in getting the name of Malev's rival so we can get Alistair. We can worry about this other person later." I took my phone back from Sybil. "Isn't there an enclave in Norway?" I asked her.

"I'm not sure. I know that they're all over the place. I've never paid much attention."

"Can you find out?"

Sybil looked to the side and fidgeted with the corner of the pillow she held in her lap. "I didn't want to have to tell you this. I hoped we could finish this without any help, but the Circle's freezing me out. They want everything to go through Gordon." She looked up at me for my reaction.

The Circle had always been big on protocol and everything going through an agent's handler, but these were extraordinary circumstances. They had a relationship with Sybil. She was the Oracle. That position demanded a certain level of respect. There was only one reason not to help her: they felt that she was more loyal to me than the Circle.

They were right, but I'd hoped it wouldn't be this big of an issue for them. After all, we were getting Alistair back. This was a one-mission situation. But it did confirm my suspicions. They wanted me to go through Gordon because Gordon was loyal to them and not to me, which meant I couldn't trust him.

"Shit. Deacon, do you think Drake would know the location of more enclaves?"

Deacon shook his head. "No, the Syndicate has no business on Earth. Their presence here is strictly for you."

We could try at the enclave, but given the reception we received earlier, that didn't seem like a viable option, especially since time was an issue. I didn't want Alistair imprisoned any longer the necessary. That left me with only one option.

I pulled out my cell phone and dialed Gordon's number. He'd called and left me a voicemail earlier so I'd have it. I didn't bother with any protocols. They were designed to keep me and my handler safe. Right now, my handler was in a fae cell, and I didn't really care what happened to Gordon.

As for my safety, I had a dangerous fae holding my neighbor hostage, so screw that. Gordon picked up, and I got straight to it. "I have a chance for you to make yourself useful."

"Oh really, what's that?" Gordon's voice was warm and welcoming, conveying a desire to please and be helpful.

"I need a list of all the enclaves on Earth with their locations." If this were Alistair, he'd give me the information no questions asked. I didn't expect to be so lucky here.

"What are you looking for specifically?"

I wasn't about to tell him that. I didn't need the Circle sending more eyes to Norway. They didn't care if they got the information on the rival court from me or someone else.

"I'm not sure yet. I'm just looking for places where I can ask questions, see what answers show up."

There was silence on the other end of the line. Would he deny my request for information? It'd be difficult to justify that without outright admitting that he was there to get information for the Circle, not to help me. This information wasn't a huge secret. I just didn't have it conveniently available.

"All right. I'll send it to you. It would help matters if you looped me in a little more. I know you want Alistair back. We all do. The more open you are with me, the sooner that'll happen."

Gordon sounded so sincere that I wondered if he actually believed what he said. Did he really think the Circle had Alistair's best interests at heart? Or that they even cared about him at all? He was either too green and naïve to know better or he was putting on one hell of an act. I couldn't let either scenario be my problem. As long as I got the information I needed, it didn't really matter.

"I'm glad you think so. Thanks." I hung up the phone. A couple of minutes later, I got a text with a link to the document. Sure enough, there was an enclave in Norway. When I brought up a map, it was right outside Bismo.

"So where do we look first, Oslo or Bismo?" Deacon asked. He leaned over my phone to see the map.

Even though the fae had been seen in Oslo recently, I thought our chances were better in Bismo. He was likely only in Oslo to meet with the stranger. Besides, Oslo was a much bigger place. The chances of finding him without an address weren't great. If we went to Bismo and the enclave, even if we didn't find him, we were more likely to get some workable intel.

"Let's start at Bismo and the enclave."

Sybil jumped up from her chair. "Great, I can make us a portal."

"I appreciate that, but you need to stay here. We don't want someone recognizing the Oracle." Unlike me and Deacon, Sybil only had one glamour.

A hint of disappointment flashed across Sybil's face. "Good call. I'll just make the portal and wait here. I'll check in with Pint for you."

"Thanks. I'll just go grab a light jacket. We need to get something for Deacon."

"Don't worry about me. I don't get cold." He stood, calm and collected, ready to go as always.

Come to think of it, he hadn't appeared the least bit cold even when we were in the Spineback Mountains. I wondered if it was due to him being a shifter or from spending so much time in the mountains. Or was it just him?

He hadn't seemed cold in Washington as we watched the remains of Nicholas's house burn. I could still remember the feel of his chest against my back as he enveloped me in warmth, guarding me from the chill in the air.

If I kept up this line of thought, I wouldn't need a coat either.

21

*L*ars exited the bank and looked both directions down the street. If we were lucky, he'd head left, to the bar next door. If we weren't lucky, he'd go right, and we'd have to work out here on the street in broad daylight.

We had tracked Lars in the Bismo enclave. He'd headed into the bank a little while ago. Enclave banks didn't deal in money. They were more like safe-deposit boxes for holding on to magical items that were too important to be left unsecured.

While he was inside, Deacon and I had come up with a plan. Whatever Lars had hidden in that bank, it had to have some answers for us, a clue to point us in the right direction.

Deacon stood at the other end of the block, pointedly not looking in Lars's direction. He casually window shopped and kept an eye out for my signal.

Lars turned left, a bit of luck for us. I signaled to Deacon, and we followed him into the bar at a distance, not walking in together. Lars sat at the bar. This would be a quick pickpocket job, something any petty thief could pull off.

I positioned myself to the left of our mark with my back to him. Once Lars had his drink, Deacon sauntered up to the bar.

"Hey, I need a firewater!" Deacon shouted. He gestured his arm frantically to get the bartender's attention, bumping into Lars and nearly spilling his drink.

"Hey!" Lars exclaimed, rocking back out of Deacon's way. I took advantage of the distraction and slipped my hand into his inner coat pocket. My fingers swept up against only one item, and I pulled it out in a fluid motion.

With my back to Lars, I looked at the item in my palm: a flat, polished coin. There were no markings or engravings or anything at all on the surface. When I looked at it, a cloud of fog descended on my brain.

This coin, there was something about it, but the knowledge that I could've sworn was in my brain just a moment ago turned into wisps and floated away. Why couldn't I remember what it was?

I glanced over my shoulder to see Deacon apologizing to Lars. The fog dissipated. I looked back down at the item in my hand, and the fog returned. Our one lead, and it was completely useless.

I caught Deacon's eye and shook my head. We didn't have it. We had decided earlier that we wouldn't keep whatever we lifted from Lars. We simply wanted to see what it was and return it. No need to alarm him or tip him off that someone was following him.

I took the barstool next to Lars. When Deacon passed by, I handed off the coin. Hopefully he'd have more luck with it. All I needed to do was keep Lars distracted and inside the bar.

"Excuse me," I said to the bartender. "Can I get a pixie sparkle?" It was a disgustingly sweet cocktail that women got when they wanted to appear flirtatious. When it came to distracting and occupying men, I only had one tool in my toolbox. I didn't need any others because this one never failed me.

"Sure thing," the bartender said and gave me a wink while nodding at Lars.

I pursed my lips into a little smile and eyed Lars, giggling. "I know, right? It's such an embarrassing drink order, but it's my favorite. I don't care what anyone says."

Lars smiled and nodded. "I agree. Life's too short to drink what you don't like." He raised his glass to me.

"Exactly! That's what I keep saying. I mean, if we're going to learn anything from these humans, it's that time's short, right? We have to grab life by the collar and wrestle it to the ground. Get everything out of it. Otherwise, what's the point?"

Given the way Lars leaned toward me, I had guessed his type correctly. It wasn't such a stretch.

Lars chuckled. "I like that. What brings you all the way out here?"

I wondered how long it would take him to ask me that. This was a pretty isolated enclave, and he was in on a covert plan to start a rival fae court. I'd think he'd be a little more suspicious.

Then again, I looked around the bar. A lot of magic folk found the isolation attractive. No need to worry much about blending in with humans. This was a nice place to lie low and get away from Elustria.

"Oh, my girlfriends and I decided to do this whole tour of Earth thing. We've been hopping around the enclaves, seeing the sights, the whole deal."

The bartender dropped off my pixie sparkle. It was a swirl of bright pink and blue, and it did indeed sparkle. The magic in the drink looked like glitter continuously falling. Getting drunk on a pixie sparkle always resulted in a happy, giggly, generally annoying drunk. Great for flirting.

Lars made a show of looking around the bar. "And where are these friends of yours?"

"Would you believe it? They both ditched me. Jennamori got bored after the third enclave and went back to Elustria. She didn't care for Earth at all. Then Mika, the bitch, ditched me for a bear shifter at an enclave in Denmark. Can you believe that? I mean here we are setting out on a grand adventure together and she just falls for a guy she could've met back home? Lame."

"Well, that's a shame. What are you going to do now?"

I took a sip of my drink. Instead of cringing at the sweetness, I smiled. "Oh, I'm finishing this adventure. I didn't come all this way to bail."

Over Lars's shoulder, Deacon slipped out of the bar, still with the item. I'd have to stall for a while longer. Time to lean in.

"I mean the nice thing now is that I don't have to worry about inconveniencing anyone, you know? I can just do as I please."

I rocked back and threw up my hands in a little gesture of glee. "That bitch Mika isn't the only one who can have a little fun. Let her have that bear shifter. I could get a bear shifter if I wanted a bear shifter."

"Oh, I'm sure you could," Lars said, inching closer. His voice warmed, and his magic probed mine. It was cold and strange. My magic naturally tensed and resisted. I had to soften it, open it up to let him in. If our magics didn't mingle well, this wouldn't go any further.

Yes, I told my magic, *it's not Deacon, but we have a job to do, same as we've done hundreds of times before.* When my magic gave way, I smiled shyly up at him, as if the initial resistance was just nerves.

He took my hand and leaned in, sucking my bottom lip between his. Then his tongue entered my mouth, and I hated my job.

Deacon still hadn't returned. I had no idea how long it might take. I needed to draw this out. I pulled back. "Can't a girl get dinner first?"

"I don't think it's dinner you're after," he murmured.

"I mean, I like to get to know a guy first. I don't know anything about you. Like why are you on Earth?"

That was the wrong question to ask. The atmosphere cooled, and he shut down. "Same as you. I'm here for the adventure."

He finished the last of his drink then tossed some money on the bar and stood. I couldn't let him leave.

I placed my hand on his bicep, making a little murmur of appreciation. Then I stuck out my bottom lip in a pout. "Don't be like that. I thought we really had a connection here."

"I'm sorry, I have to get going."

Dammit. I had to take this further than I wanted to. If he left before Deacon got back, it could jeopardize our efforts to rescue Alistair. I would do anything to keep Lars with me.

"Aww, come on. You're not going to leave me like this, are you? Not after our magics mingled so well. I haven't had a connection like that with anyone since I came Earthside. You're not really gonna let that bitch Mika one up me, are you?"

I got as close to him as possible without touching, letting the arousal build between us. I reached out with my magic and held onto his. I knew I had him when he slid his hands around my waist to the small of my back.

"Well, we can't have Mika win, can we?"

I shook my head no with my bottom lip still insufferably jutted outward. He sucked my lip into his mouth again, and this time as his kiss deepened, he pulled me to him. Then he pushed me against the wall and latched onto my neck.

He put one hand on my breast, and I knocked it away. We were in the middle of a bar for crying out loud. He took my meaning, or at least the meaning of my cover persona, and led me to the bathroom.

Wow. Classy. Just as our rather unappetizing bathroom sex started, a surge of pain went through me. Deacon had used magic. I didn't know what for, but it seemed like a good sign that he'd be back soon.

A minute later, the pain returned. Was it him shifting back into human form? I couldn't think of any other magic he'd be doing.

If only we had some way to communicate. If we were mates, I'd be able to sense his feelings which would make this so much easier. But that's not a reason to bond with someone. In fact, thinking about bonding just to make spying easier while having sex with someone else was probably proof that I shouldn't.

I didn't want this encounter to last any longer than necessary. But if it ended too soon, I'd be right back in the same predicament I started in.

Despite my best efforts, it ended fairly quickly.

"Ooh, if I had known this was how the enclaves were, I would've come to Earth a long time ago," I said as I put myself back together. At least with my glamour he hadn't seen the real me. It made it easier.

"We do like to have fun here," Lars said, as he held the door open for me like he were some kind of gentleman.

I walked out of the bathroom and felt Deacon's presence. We locked eyes across the bar. I had never felt shame about what I did. It was work, and it was necessary work. It didn't mean anything.

But when I met Deacon's gaze, it wasn't his eyes I saw. All I saw was Julien staring back at me, and I looked away. At least Deacon was back, and this job was almost done.

"Buy me another drink?" I asked Lars.

He smirked. "Sure, why not? It's the least I can do after skipping out on a meal."

I followed him to the bar. Deacon passed us, handing off the coin.

Lars ordered me another pixie sparkle then faced me to say goodbye while the bartender fixed it. "I hope you enjoy the rest of your tour of Earth."

"Oh, I don't think I'll enjoy anywhere as much as here. I'll have to find you when I come back." I leaned my head up and gave him a deep parting kiss as I placed the coin back in his inner coat pocket.

"You do that," Lars said. Then he turned and walked out of the bar.

"Did you get it?" I asked Deacon. I wasn't going to give him a chance to shame me for what I did. I wasn't going to let us stand there and dwell on it. This was business, and we had a job to do.

Deacon nodded. "Yes, I got it."

"Good. Let's go home."

22

More than anything, I wanted to shower. I knew Deacon could smell the sex on me. But when we got to Sybil's, she jumped up asking what we had found.

We were close to getting Alistair back. Then I could shower this whole awful mission off of me. This time, I doubted Deacon would want to take part.

"It went well. Nadiya improvised long enough for me to get what we needed," Deacon said. His tone confused me. It sounded like pride, but maybe that was the way bitterness sounded in his voice.

"So did you get a name?" Sybil asked.

"No," I said. "I talked to Lars, but as soon as any questions got personal, he completely shut down. That was a nonstarter." It wasn't surprising. If he didn't break under Malev, he certainly wouldn't spill everything to a stranger in a bar. "But we did lift something off of him, a coin of some sort. I think it may be a toll coin."

A toll coin was used to gain passage to a magical area, like paying a toll to cross a bridge, except toll coins were usually reused. "I couldn't figure out anything else about it. Just looking at it muddled my brain, but Deacon did something with it." I didn't know exactly what he'd done, so I let him finish the story.

He toed off his shoes and held one up. "The coin was made out of obscuron with a forgetfulness enchantment on it. I've spent a lot of time with this material, so I was able to break through the enchantment. Once I remembered that obscuron reveals its secrets under heat, I partially shifted and blew fire onto it. That's when the etchings appeared. Because of the enchantment, I knew there was no chance I'd remember the pattern to replicate it, so I heated the coin up and pressed it into the sole of my shoe until the pattern burned in." Deacon handed the shoe to Sybil.

"That was clever," I said. His shoe was the perfect material to preserve the coin.

"Thanks." Deacon focused all his attention on Sybil.

"I know this symbol!" Sybil exclaimed, her eyes lit with excitement. "I know who's setting up the rival court. This is the crest of the Calendyn clan. Specifically, it's used by the heir, Goffrey. This is big. It's been thousands of years since a man tried to rule the fae. His family has served generations of fae queens. The ramifications of this..." Sybil shook her head. "I can't even imagine."

"Well," I said, "the ramifications are someone else's problem. We have a name. We've done our part. It's time to get Alistair back."

"Are you going to tell the Circle?" Sybil asked.

I appreciated that she asked instead of telling me to. "No. If what you say is true, then they're likely to consider backing him. If this usurper is as close to the throne as you make it sound, there's a real chance he'll topple Malev. Meilin would love that. Whether she acts on it or not, it's quite a bit of power she'd get just from the knowledge. I don't have the time or inclination to deal with the politics of this. I made a deal with Malev, and I'm delivering my end of it."

"I think that's the right call. I can take us to the fae court now," Sybil said and handed Deacon back his shoe.

Before Deacon could say anything, I preempted him. "As before, you don't need to come. Stay here and take a break. You can check in with Pint or be here in case he needs anything. I still don't like the idea of Freddie being here without one of us nearby."

I didn't look at him. I didn't want to see whatever emotion was on his face. This was almost done. We could talk later. There'd be time for feelings and everything when we debriefed.

Sybil took my hand, and we went back to Malev's realm.

23

We appeared, once again, in the throne room. This time there was laughter, music, and fae of all kinds dancing around. The music was a mixture of stringed instruments and light tingling bells. Laughter filled the air, and it seemed almost every hand held a glass of some alcoholic beverage.

"What are they celebrating?" I asked Sybil. Was there some fae holiday I was unaware of? The entire room was a study in pastels. Clearly there was a dress code.

"No, this is just a regular evening," Sybil said, her glamour having fallen away. Even though this was her truest form, I didn't think I'd ever get used to it. She seemed happier, more perky, in her human glamour. It probably had to do with circumstance more than anything. I only saw her fae appearance in Malev's presence.

Malev spotted us and waved like a drunk girl on spring break. She ran our way. "Ooh, the Dragon Fae and the Oracle have returned!"

A cheer erupted from the crowd and they promptly went back to partying. When Malev reached us, she handed her drink to a woman who'd followed her then touched both me and Sybil. We were transported outside the throne room, standing at the base of the tree under which her throne room was built.

"Now, what do you have for me?" Malev's voice changed into a cold, sober tone. The sudden extreme change was breathtaking.

"I found out the name of your rival, just like you asked. It's Goffrey Calendyn." I prepared myself for Malev's fury.

The fae queen's face gave away nothing. Beside me, Sybil fidgeted. She seemed anxious to fill the silence. She was smart enough to know that wasn't a good idea.

"Well done." Malev met my eyes. "You'll have to kill him."

I'd assassinated quite a few people in my life. I didn't care about adding one more to my tally. I only cared about getting Alistair back. "As soon as you return Alistair to me, we can discuss an assassination plan."

Malev tapped her chin as if she were thinking and flew a few feet into the air. "No, no, that won't do." She landed back on the ground and looked me in the eye. "I think I'll keep Alistair here as my guest a while longer."

White hot rage surged through me, but I held my temper. "That's not the deal we made."

"And since you like making grand gestures and letting people know it's the Dragon Fae killing the enemy, I want you to kill him in such a way that the world knows it was you."

"Of course," Sybil said. "If he were assassinated on your order, it would show that you feared him. But if the Dragon Fae kills him, then it's proof that he was evil and needed to die. You can't use the Dragon Fae's reputation like that."

I didn't think telling the fae queen what she could and couldn't do was such a good idea.

Malev's face hardened. "I want this coup to die, and it will only die with his head."

If there was any chance that I could kill her and get Alistair out of there, I'd do it. In a fight in Malev's realm, I didn't stand a chance against her. What's more, even if I succeeded, it didn't mean I'd get Alistair. "You're a liar. I don't make deals with liars."

"Tsk, tsk, tsk." Malev's expression relaxed and she shook her head like an adult teaching a child a lesson. "It's not very nice to call people liars. Besides, fae are bound by their word. I said I'd give you your handler after you gave me a name. I didn't say how soon after. It's not my fault that you don't take better care with your contracts." She shrugged and turned away from us. "Now, I think it's time you go back home and work on how you're going to deliver Goffrey's head to me."

Malev waved her fingers, and Sybil and I appeared back in her apartment. We already knew that Malev had my address because of Freddie's presence, but to have her deposit us back into Sybil's living room felt like an intrusion.

Deacon stood and looked at us with a hopeful expression tinged with a little confusion at Alistair's absence. I couldn't talk. If I opened my mouth, I'd scream, and I didn't know if I'd ever stop.

I ran out the door and down the stairs to my car, Deacon following. He knew the drill. We'd been through this before.

At least, he thought he knew what to expect, but I'd never felt this level of violent rage in my life. I didn't know what I'd do.

24

I couldn't contain my anger, and I didn't want to try. I drove out to the desert. The cuff was coming off. Once I got away from traffic, I floored it, pushing my Corvette as fast as it would go.

Deacon had the good sense to keep quiet. I saw his knuckles go white where he gripped the door.

I wanted to rip the cuff from my wrist, but I was acutely aware of Deacon's presence. The cuff came from him. So when I parked the car and got out, I carefully removed it from my wrist and put it in my pocket.

My magic surged to life. I splayed my fingers in front of me and lightning shot out, striking the ground with a force that represented only a fraction of my fury.

Malev had never intended to release Alistair. She'd sent me on a ridiculous quest, used me like a pawn. I knew she'd already tortured Alistair or invaded his mind. It was the only way she could have the location of my apartment. She'd made him suffer. She played me while all along she intended for him to suffer.

I swirled the wind with my magic, kicking up sand and creating little dust devils. It wasn't enough. I needed to vent my anger, and nothing felt like it would even make a dent.

I forced the wind to blow harder and harder until it gathered clouds above us. I wanted it to rain. I wanted lightning, thunder, and destruction. I opened the heavens and let all the fury of a monsoon storm rain down around us. My hair whipped around my face. My car rocked side to side with the gusts of wind. I wanted to destroy it all.

I had destroyed so many things in my life, so many people, and I'd always done it for others. I had killed more times than I could count. I had destroyed lives without a second thought. But now, for the first time, I wanted to wreak destruction for myself.

The pressure inside me built: the anger, the fury, the rage. I wanted my body to open up and consume the earth. I wanted to unleash the darkness that swirled inside me and let it infect every-thing around me. I wanted it gone, and I wanted Alistair back.

I called down more lightning, dozens and dozens of bolts. The crack of thunder served as my voice, and I would be heard. Unable to hold it in any longer, I opened my mouth and let out a scream that tore at my throat but was drowned in the thunder. I kept screaming until I didn't have any air left in me, and I fell to my knees.

Strong arms wrapped around me from behind. Deacon's cheek rested against mine, and he pulled me against him. He had watched the scene without comment. I realized that he didn't even know what had happened. He hadn't asked. He just let me be.

"She's not releasing him. She changed the deal, and I was a fool. Now she says she won't release him until I kill Goffrey."

I let out a humorless chuckle. Killing her rival. A difficult task, but one I was well suited for. It should be easy. It should've come to me like second nature. But who was to say after I killed him that she'd release Alistair? She had already changed the deal once. I wouldn't be played for a fool again.

"As a fae, she's bound by her word," Deacon said. I didn't know why he said it, if he was advocating for doing as she said or not.

"They are, but fae like her are tricky."

"Exactly. We need to examine precisely what she promised you. We don't want any more surprises. We can't plan our next move until we scrutinize exactly what she said."

I closed my eyes and thought back to the moment. "She said she only promised that she would give Alistair back after I gave her the name." I opened my eyes. "She didn't say how long afterward."

Deacon looked away, rolling the implications of Malev's statement around in his mind. When he looked back at me, he saw that he didn't need to explain his thoughts. This was a game Malev could draw out for as long as she wanted.

"What do you want to do?" he asked.

The question brought me up short. I didn't think I'd ever been asked that. What did I want to do?

"I want to kill her." I said it with such a cold, deep evenness that it scared even me.

"Can you?" It was an honest question from one fighter to another.

Could I? My skill couldn't be denied. So far, I had a perfect kill rate. None of my targets had ever escaped me. I held a certain power knowing that I could take the life of almost anyone I met. But I never felt powerful. I'd never had the heady rush that I did now, because all of those kills had been done at someone else's behest. For the first time, I wanted to kill for me. But wanting and doing were two different things.

"In her realm? No, I don't think so. I wouldn't even attempt it. If she ever left? That I could do. I know I could. Which is why she'll never leave her realm while I'm alive."

It sounded dramatic, but it really wasn't. She could live hundreds of years. For her, staying in the fae realm was nothing. She probably didn't even have an interest in leaving.

"It sounds like that's a mission for another day then," Deacon said, pragmatic as ever.

I appreciated that he didn't try to talk me out of it. He didn't try to talk reason to me. He simply accepted me. He also didn't flatter me, bolster me up with fake words. He was my partner.

"I hate feeling powerless. I'm so tired of it all. I've known from the beginning that this would be my job until the day I died. I find myself wishing for that day to come sooner and sooner. I'm sick of destroying everything and everyone around me."

At least now as the Dragon Fae I knew it would come sooner rather than later. She died young and alone. It's what scared me most about the myth. Not the dying so much, the dying alone.

I'd always thought I'd die on a mission. Quick, no sentiment. I'd fooled myself into thinking I had made peace with it. But it wasn't until I was told of my identity as the Dragon Fae that I realized how much it scared me.

When I put myself there mentally, I didn't want to be alone. I wanted there to be something to show for my life, something that said I was here.

Deacon stood up behind me. I didn't move, just watched as he walked away. He went a few dozen feet then knelt on the ground. I felt a rush of magic. Without the cuff, there wasn't any pain. I felt his magic uninhibited for the first time since we'd been anointed.

Deacon must've partially shifted. His hand looked like a talon that he used to dig at the ground. I wondered what he had felt of my magic as I'd thrown my little tantrum.

Deacon stood with something in his hand and walked back to me. He held it in front of me: a small glass sculpture.

"Sometimes when lightning hits sand, it makes glass. I used to find it back in Elustria. I always liked how something so beautiful came to be without any magic."

He handed it to me. I understood what he meant. In Elustria, magic was part of everything. Almost all acts of creation involved magic. When I first came to Earth, I worried that it would be a dull and dreary place, devoid of beauty the same way it was empty of magic. How wrong I'd been. It seemed at every turn these humans confounded me.

I didn't know why he'd handed it to me. I looked up at him from the ground, searching for an answer.

"Watching you, I noticed something. You like to think you're destructive, that your darkness unleashed on the world is a negative force. You know what's rather remarkable? Amidst all your fury, all that wind and rain and lightning, you didn't strike a single cactus. You didn't throw a single animal. You unleashed all that, and you didn't destroy a thing. In fact, you created something, this glass, probably several more like it."

I looked around. None of the precious saguaros, the guardians of the desert, had fallen. "It's just coincidence. I didn't mean to do it that way."

"That's too much of a coincidence. Something inside you resists destroying the innocent. It always has. It's why you fought so hard for the humans who were under Nicholas's spell. You may be an assassin, but you're not a killer. You're not a destroyer. It's not who you are."

I stood and faced him. "But it is. I want to kill her."

"You want to kill her to preserve Alistair's life, to preserve justice."

The desire for vengeance burned inside me, but if this was the version of me he saw, then what harm was there in letting him believe it? Whatever delusions he had to feed himself to keep working with me, I wouldn't disabuse him of them.

He probably told himself a similar story about what I'd done with Lars back in Norway. Let him think what he wanted. Life was cruel enough without me pointing out its cruelties.

"It's good you came out here," Deacon continued. "You got it out. Let's go back home and figure out what we're going to do. Malev's made her move. It's time for us to make ours."

"I already know what my next move is." I tossed the glass sculpture to him. "I'm going to get him out. I'm done killing for other people. I'll rescue him myself."

Deacon smiled. "Then we have a prison break to plan."

25

I walked up the stairs to my apartment with a plan already forming in my head. I was done being a pawn.

"Perfect timing!" Harry said in front of his apartment door. Freddie followed him outside carrying a pink bakery box and closed the door behind him. "Freddie and I were just getting ready to go to a movie, and he wanted to drop this off for you before we left."

As much as I didn't want Harry going anywhere with Freddie, I had to swallow my feelings. It was best not to bring him into this anymore than he already was. Making him aware of the danger next to him wouldn't lessen that danger at all. If anything, it would make it worse. Hopefully we could all get through this with Harry none the wiser. I would deal with Freddie in good time.

"Here you go," Freddie said as he handed me the box. There was an envelope sitting on top of it. "I wanted to get you a little something to thank you for taking such good care of my uncle."

"Thank you," I said, putting on a cheery front as if this were a role for a mission. It felt strange to pretend this way at my home.

"Yes, that's very nice of you," Deacon said next to me.

"It's good to see you two getting out so much," Harry said. "I haven't seen Mr. A in a bit. Is everything all right? I hate to think that you two had a falling out." His eyebrows raised in question.

"No, it's nothing like that. He experienced a loss recently. His niece died, so he's been spending more time with his family." At least I could tell a partial truth.

Harry's face fell. "Oh, I'm sorry to hear that. Please, pass along my condolences when you can."

My heart ached at the sight of the sincere concern on Harry's face. He was too pure for the lot of us. "I will, Mr. Harmon."

"Well, Freddie and I have to get going. You two enjoy your evening." Harry nodded to us.

"Yes, and enjoy your treat," Freddie said with a wink. How I wished I could punch that smug face.

Deacon and I went into Sybil's apartment. I had a headache, probably from my little outburst in the desert, but Freddie's games certainly didn't help. Whatever was in the pink box, I doubted I'd like it. I sure as hell wasn't stupid enough to eat it.

"Are you all right?" Sybil asked when we entered, looking from me to Deacon. I'd been quite a sight storming out of here earlier.

"Yeah, we're all right," Deacon said.

I sat on the sofa and opened the envelope on top of the box while Deacon went to the kitchen.

"Ooh, what's this?" Sybil asked. She sat next to me and looked over my shoulder as I read the note.

After our little chat, I felt bad about how we left things. It was so sad seeing how disappointed you were that it didn't work out the way you thought it would. So, I decided to send you this little gift. You wanted Alistair back, so enjoy your "hand"-ler.

I lifted the lid to the box, and Sybil screamed. Deacon rushed in from the kitchen at the sound. Sitting inside the box on a cushion was a hand.

Alistair's hand.

26

Bright red blood stained the cushion where the hand sat. Based on the forensic shows I watched with Harry, I knew this meant the hand had been removed while Alistair was alive.

"Deacon, can you keep it alive?" I asked, trying to keep desperation from my voice. I knew he'd do what he could.

Deacon lifted the hand out of the box and blew on the severed wrist. "I can keep it alive. The trick is going to be not healing the wound completely."

Deacon's healing ability could normally close up a cut, seal it, and heal it perfectly without a scar. If he closed up this wound, though, it wouldn't be possible to reattach it.

"What are you planning to do?" Sybil asked.

The current situation wasn't a long-term plan, and not just because of the pain from Deacon using his healing powers while I wore my cuff. We would gladly endure that for Alistair's sake, but I needed Deacon to help me if I was going to get Alistair released.

At the same time, the hand had been delivered to me alive. I couldn't stand to let it die on my watch. Perhaps it couldn't be reattached no matter what I did, but I had to give it my best effort.

"Is there any magic you can do to sustain the hand until we get Alistair back?" I asked Sybil.

She shook her head. "That's something that is far outside my ability."

I knew one person who could help, but it would require swallowing my pride. I pulled out my phone and dialed his number.

"Well, well, well. The Dragon Fae has deigned to grace me with a phone call," Drake said when he answered. The oiliness of his voice seeped through the phone.

However, he had cause for the attitude. "I'm sorry, Drake," I said with as much sincerity as I could. "I can't tell you how sorry I am for your loss. How are your dragons doing?"

"Our people are resilient. We've had to be." He took a beat, likely judging whether to be an ass or not. "But there's no need to apologize anymore for that. You already have, and I accepted it. I withdrew my support from you not because I blamed you but because I needed to protect my people. What offends me now is that after what I did for you, you and that bastard went off and got anointed without even inviting me."

I bit my tongue over the insult to Deacon. He was a bastard, and I understood why it was important for Drake to always consider him that way, but I didn't like it. Deacon had served the dragons his entire life. He deserved some respect. Not to mention that he was now the anointed Dragon Companion. But rising to Drake's bait wouldn't help anything.

"I'm sorry for the oversight. It was a spur of the moment thing. I didn't know it was going to happen until it did. There were extenuating circumstances involved."

"Still, I am the Dragon Prince. The lack of an invitation was bad enough, but I wasn't even notified. It's quite offensive to be overlooked in such a way, especially when you so often need my help."

Yes, I needed his help, but we weren't children. I wouldn't indulge these games. "Then you'll have to be offended on your own time,

Drake. I'm calling about the extenuating circumstances I mentioned. Alistair's been taken, and I'm a little busy trying to get him back."

"Oh, I am sorry to hear that." The attitude was gone from his voice. Genuine regret took its place. He understood what it meant to lose people. "Do you know who's taken him?"

"Malev."

Drake sputtered. "The fae queen? That Malev?"

"Yes."

Drake whistled. "You really are no respecter of persons."

"Maybe you can take comfort in the fact that you're not the only person I annoy." Normally, the people I annoyed ended up dead. For the first time, it seemed a little club was forming.

"I do, actually." I could hear a smile in Drake's voice. "So why is it you're calling me?"

"I need your help again." My breath caught for a second waiting for his reply, but he didn't make me wait long.

"I can't put my people in danger."

"I'm not asking you to. You've given too much to this fight already. This is about protecting my friend. I figured you, more than anyone, would understand that."

"Getting entangled with Malev endangers my people." It was a fair point, but I didn't think this would expose his dragons.

"I promise you, she won't even know you're involved. She sent me Alistair's hand in a box. Deacon's working on keeping it alive, but that's obviously not an ideal solution. We need someone to keep it alive for us while we work on getting Alistair back. He's done so much for me. I can't give up on this part of him."

A few seconds of silence passed. Then Drake said, "Bring it over, and I'll see what we can do."

He hung up, and I slid the phone in my pocket.

"What did he say?" Sybil asked.

"He's going to try. He wants us to bring the hand to him."

While I was on the phone, Sybil had removed the cushion from the baker's box and replaced it with a towel. Deacon placed the hand in the box and came over to join me.

"It would be great if we could get his help," Deacon said. "There are people in the Syndicate who are much more adept at this kind of thing. I've never had much need to heal others, just myself. I don't have the fine-tuned control that someone else would." He lifted up the box and blew slightly on the hand. It pinked up a little.

"I'll port us into the courtyard," Sybil said. She placed one hand on me and one on Deacon, and we appeared in the compound.

The courtyard stood vacant, a relief after the last time we were there and dragons had mourned everywhere. This time, it was the stillness that was eerie.

27

The stately door to the mansion opened before I had a chance to knock. The man who opened it gave us a little nod and gestured with his hand for us to enter.

The house was as silent as the courtyard. The shifter led us to the same great room where I'd first met Drake, but the scene differed from last time. Everyone stood to two sides, creating an aisle leading up to an ornate high-back chair on which Drake sat.

No, it wasn't a chair. It was a throne. The formal atmosphere and the way everyone looked at us when we entered made me uncomfortable.

Upon our entrance, Drake rose from his throne and walked toward us, a few of his shifters following. Deacon, as before, knelt in respect, but Drake gestured for him to rise before Deacon's knee even hit the ground. I wondered how many people in this room knew that Deacon was Drake's bastard brother.

"Is this it?" Drake asked, pointing at the box.

Deacon nodded. "I've kept it alive, but I'm not as talented as others at healing."

Drake took the box and handed it behind him to the three shifters who followed him. Without looking at them, he commanded, "Keep this alive so it can be reattached." One of the shifters took the box, and they left the room. "Those are my best healers. If it can't be reattached, the fault won't be on this end."

"Thank you." I made eye contact with Drake to convey my sincerity. After the harm I had inadvertently brought to his dragons, I didn't know why he showed me this kindness. His dark red eyes seemed mournful, like he had seen so much loss in his life that each addition weighed on him.

Drake gave a little nod in acknowledgement of my thanks. His eyes darted to the side, his confidence dimming. He took a deep breath then met my gaze again. "I'd hoped to do this at the temple."

To my astonishment, he grabbed my right hand and Deacon's left. While maintaining eye contact, he lowered himself to one knee. Behind him, the entire room followed suit.

The same feeling I had at the temple assaulted me again. I'd gone from an anonymous spy to having crowds kneel to me. It shook something inside my core.

When Drake got down to one knee, he bowed his head. "I, Drake Fafnir, the Dragon Prince, Defender of the Dragonkin, and Commander of the Dragon Syndicate, swear fealty to the Dragon Fae and the Dragon Companion. May all dragonkin do the same."

Behind him, those assembled repeated, "I swear fealty to the Dragon Fae and the Dragon Companion."

A spark of surprise lit Deacon's eyes that only I would notice. He still held himself with the same regal posture as always. I couldn't imagine his emotions at seeing this man who had been the source of so much sorrow in his life kneel to him.

I wished I could see Sybil, but she stood behind us. The anointing ceremony had been rushed, but she could have notified Drake. She chose not to, and I didn't blame her. I wouldn't have expected this behavior from Drake. Did her face show the same surprise I felt?

Drake rose to his feet, as did the rest of the dragon shifters. Despite what just happened, the room still felt distinctly Drake's. It didn't feel right for me to make any kind of speech like I had at the temple. The magnitude of what he'd done wasn't lost on me.

"Come, let's speak in private." Drake gestured to the doorway and led us to his office. When we were all seated, it was Deacon who broke the silence.

"Thank you for that, Your Royal Highness."

Everything Deacon did was deliberate. I couldn't believe that I'd ever thought he was anything less than competent. Drake had just given Deacon some of his pride, and now Deacon gave it back to him. After a show of humility from Drake, he made sure to accord him the proper respect due his position even though Deacon now outranked him.

"Thank you for not asking for it, or worse, demanding it. I understand why you didn't want me at the anointing. But I want you to know that, had I been there, I would've done the same."

"I was wrong to doubt you," Sybil said.

After our history with Drake, I thought that was stretching it. Based on Drake's face, he appreciated the gesture.

"Well, it's done. You're both anointed with the sacred oil. You are the Dragon Fae and the Dragon Companion," Drake said. "Ritual and tradition are all we have. It's what keeps the high fae and us ancient races going. That wasn't performative out there. I am the Dragon Prince, and I did just swear fealty. So tell me what's going on. What can I do to help?"

I relayed our current situation to him, leaving nothing out. As much of an asshole as Drake had been, he'd proven to be a man of his word, and he put the welfare of his people first. I wondered how much of the asshole persona was an act meant to create distance between himself and the people he was duty-bound to care for.

"Did you ever find out who Lars met with in Oslo?" Drake asked.

"No." I pulled up his picture on my phone and handed it to Drake. Before I could say anything, he laughed. "What's so funny?"

"That's Dorran. I'm surprised you haven't run into him." He handed my phone back.

"Dorran?"

"Yep. He has no other name. He's a druid who's probably older than Father Time himself. To hear him tell it, Earth is his, and we're all just guests on it."

"Is he violent?"

Drake pursed his lips and shook his head. "Not that I've ever seen. He's all talk. At the same time, I wouldn't cross him. He puts on the airs of a pacifist, but I don't trust anyone who's lived that long. Nothing happens concerning magic folk on Earth without him knowing about it."

"Do you know how I can get a hold of him?" I asked. If what Drake said was true, this Dorran would be a great source of intelligence.

"No. I have a feeling he decides who to grace with his presence and then does so."

"What are you thinking?" Sybil asked me. "Do you think he can help us get to Goffrey?"

I hadn't told her of my new plan yet. "Knowledge is power. He knows something about this rival court, and I want to know what it is. We need as full a picture of the situation as possible. But I'm not going to kill Goffrey for her. And I'm not going to do the Circle's bidding either."

"Then what about Alistair?" Sybil asked. She seemed confused, as if I was admitting that I was giving up on him.

"We're going to rescue Alistair. Then we'll decide what to do about the rival court."

Drake leaned forward over his desk, his eyebrows raised above wide eyes. "You're going to break Alistair out of Malev's realm? Are you insane?"

"The sanity of my plan is subjective, but I am going to rescue Alistair. It's my only option. I can't keep playing Malev's game."

Drake sat back, a bit of admiration in his eyes. "And what is your plan?"

"I don't have it all figured out yet." The throbbing in my head from earlier surged to the forefront of my consciousness. I had to work to keep a wince from my face. It appeared stress took its toll in the form of a headache.

"We haven't had time to work on it," Deacon said in my defense. "Now that Alistair's hand is being tended to, we can focus on our mission."

He spoke as if this were a regular assignment given to us from the Circle. His confidence was such that he didn't think our undertaking was suicidal.

"I wish you luck, but I hope you understand that the only assistance I can provide is with the hand," Drake said, his tone all business. He may have sworn fealty, but that didn't mean he'd let us endanger his dragons.

"I do understand, and I'm grateful. The only other assistance I would ask for is knowledge that might aid us. If you know anything about fighting the fae, it would help."

Drake smiled. "Dragon shifters are in the business of making love, not war, with the high fae. If you like, I can ask some of the families we regularly mate with."

From what I understood, the high fae who mated with the dragon shifters didn't have much of a familial relationship with them. I couldn't trust their loyalties. The risk that something would get back to Malev was too high, especially since I didn't think there'd be much of a payoff. People weren't usually keen on telling you how to beat them.

"No, thank you. I think it's best we leave them out of this."

"I agree." Drake nodded. "I wish you luck. You're going to need it."

I could tell in his tone and his eyes that he didn't think we stood a chance against Malev.

"Thank you," Deacon said, taking my hand in a show of support. "But it's Malev who needs luck if she thinks she's going to stay alive after this."

Drake laughed. "You were always the craziest of our father's sons."

His eyes drifted to the memory of their brothers, all of whom he'd killed to secure the throne. "I hope you're right."

The two men held eye contact, and it seemed a lifetime passed between them. I supposed now that each were in their rightful place there was no more need for the little dance they'd done around their shared paternity.

"Thank you, Brother," Deacon said, his voice thicker than I'd ever heard it. "We will make the dragonkin proud."

28

I lay awake in bed, staring into the darkness of my bedroom. My headache had intensified to a thundering agony accompanied by swirling nausea. The two shots of whiskey I'd taken hadn't been enough to calm it or numb me to the feeling. So I'd poured a glass and taken it with me to bed. It sat empty on my bedside table next to a clock that read two-eighteen in the morning.

Despite my best efforts, I couldn't sleep. Pint was out hunting and occasionally checking in on Freddie and Mr. Harmon. Deacon was asleep in Sybil's apartment. I knew I could wake him up to talk if I needed to, but I wanted him well rested. Besides, he'd already dealt with enough of my meltdowns.

It didn't matter. It was all an excuse. I didn't want to talk to Pint or Deacon or Sybil. I wanted to go to the nether. Just the thought of it temporarily soothed my headache and the nausea that refused to go away. In the nether, things would be better. I could get some answers.

Drake said that Dorran was an ancient. If that was true, it was possible the Origin knew him. She could give me valuable intelligence. She may even know how to break into the fae realm to get Alistair back.

I might be able to keep my actions a secret from Sybil and Pint, but Deacon would know. He would feel it as soon as I made the portal and again when I returned. Maybe it wouldn't be enough to rouse him.

I got dressed and made the portal. I needed the Origin's guidance.

My palm touched the smooth dragon eye and calm came over me, soothing an itch I hadn't been fully aware of. I felt more at rest here than I did in bed at home.

A cool wind blew, and the Origin spoke. "You. I didn't expect to see you here again."

Who else did she expect? "I'm trying to save my friend, and I think you may know something that'll help me."

"Oh? I thought the fae queen gave you a task. Did you not complete it?"

I pushed down my frustration. It wouldn't get me answers or be helpful here. "Yes, but she changed the terms of our agreement. I would've thought you knew that."

"The fae are bound by their word. If the terms changed, it means they weren't clear to begin with."

Yes, I knew the failure was mine. "I'm not used to dealing with the fae. Humans, mages, and sorcerers I understand, but not the fae."

"You are part fae."

I wondered again if I too was bound by my word. I lied plenty in my job, but I didn't often make promises. "I'm still not entirely sure on that point."

"You are. Otherwise you could not be the Dragon Fae."

I still wasn't convinced on that point either, but there was no point arguing the matter.

"You're right, there's no point arguing it now," the Origin said.

"Malev wants me to kill her rival."

"So? You've killed plenty before. At least this time the killing will give you a personal benefit."

Perhaps that was why I had such a problem with it. Killing for a cause or to protect others I could understand. This was different. Alistair wasn't a civilian. "I'm tired of killing for other people."

"Does the Circle want you to kill her rival as well?"

"I'm not sure. I haven't asked them. I haven't even told told them I have the name yet. But I'm fairly sure they'd want to back this rival. They'd be more than willing to let Alistair die. I don't want to do their bidding any more than I want to do Malev's."

The Origin chuckled.

"What's so funny? Does my predicament amuse you?" I don't know why I thought coming here would get me answers. She had never been helpful before.

"Nadiya, you're the Dragon Fae. You're beholden to no one."

A part of me still thought this wasn't real, that after this mission everyone would realize they'd made a mistake, and I'd go back to being a simple Circle operative. I didn't know how to lead. I knew how to follow orders.

"Apparently not," the Origin said, replying to my thoughts. "Otherwise you'd kill this rival, get it over with, and get Alistair back."

But even if I did that, I didn't know if Malev would actually release him. She had already eluded our deal from before.

And what did this have to do with being the Dragon Fae? I had seen the crowd at the temple kneel to me. The dragon shifters had done the same. All of these people swearing fealty to me. And what was I doing? I wasn't helping them. I wasn't making the world better. All I wanted was to rescue my friend. I didn't deserve their loyalty.

"I know it seems small, but this is just the beginning. The type of person who would risk everything, who would face any danger, who would take on an adversary they knew they couldn't beat all to save a friend is exactly the type of person these people want to swear loyalty to. They've already done it. There's no coming back from that. You're committed now. But you already knew that. You didn't need me to confirm it."

She was right, I didn't need it. But I did need someone to tell me that I wasn't crazy. That I wasn't making the wrong choice. That I wasn't letting my pride get in the way of saving Alistair.

"Nonsense. It's not prideful to refuse to take the life of another just because someone tells you to. Making this decision to go your own way may feel strange because it's the first time you've stepped out to lead. This is what it feels like."

It felt like being alone, exposed, vulnerable. The responsibility was crushing. Before, I'd always felt the weight of what I did for the Circle, but I also knew that if I died, there was another agent waiting to replace me. Cogs in the machine I had once told Alistair.

Now instead of a cog, I was the one working the machine. I got to decide what the machine did and how it was used.

I didn't have the first idea how to rescue Alistair from the fae realm. Sybil had spent most of her life at the temple. Her role as the Oracle meant that she didn't spend a lot of time in the fae realm herself. While she was proficient with her own fae magic, she wasn't an expert.

"Since you are the original Dragon Fae, you must know something about the fae realm."

"By that logic, so should you. You're the current Dragon Fae."

"But I didn't even know I had fae blood until this whole prophecy happened. I wasn't raised with it. I don't know how to use it or even how much of it I have. It doesn't seem like I have any fae powers."

The only thing remotely fae-like was my magic's affinity for growing plants. But that didn't mean anything. It had never seemed odd to me back when I thought I was only a sorceress.

"Fae magic is trickier than sorcerer magic. It's better at deceiving. If you want to know how to navigate your way around the fae realm, just think of what a fae would do."

That was almost worthless. I could gather that from my experience as a spy. "Can you at least tell me if I'm right in my assumption that I can't fight Malev in her own realm? There's not some secret Dragon Fae power that I have that would give me an advantage?"

"No, you're not wrong. If you want to rescue Alistair from the fae realm, the best way is to avoid a fight with Malev."

"Otherwise it could satisfy that whole dying young and alone part of the prophecy." The silence that answered my joke sent a chill down my spine. A whisper of wind tousling dried leaves on the ground was the only sound I heard. "Is that it? Is that how I die?"

"I can't divulge anything more. I can't see the future."

"Then why did you go quiet?"

"Your visits here aren't a good idea. You were never meant to return to the nether after your anointing, except for…"

"Except for when I die." A cold flash hit my body. The tenuous strings between life and death seemed so fragile in this moment. I felt my death. It was close, a breath away.

"It's time for you to go back."

The headache and nausea that had accompanied me since my last visit chased away the cold. The temporal realm was pulling me back. But I hadn't asked her the question I'd come for. "Wait. Do you know Dorran?"

The pulling stopped, and my headache and nausea receded slightly. "Dorran?" The Origin laughed. "Oh yes, I know Dorran. Has he sought you out yet?"

"No. I wouldn't even know of his existence except that I saw some surveillance of him when investigating who Malev's rival is." It seemed strange that everyone assumed he would find me.

"If you've seen him, it's because he wanted you to."

I opened my mouth to contradict her, but then I remembered the footage on Trevor's computer. The old man had looked up at the camera and smiled. "Is he a friend or foe?"

"He is loyal only to the earth. If he thinks you are too, then he is your friend. If you pose a threat to the earth, then he is your foe."

That didn't really help me. He could think whatever he wanted. I needed to know if he meant me harm.

"I can tell you this: Dorran is someone you can trust. If he offers you help, you can trust his word on it. If he tells you he's going to kill you, you can trust his word on that too."

"Do you know how to find him? I think he knows something about this rival court. If he does, it might help me."

"No one ever finds Dorran. Dorran finds you. He does spend a lot of time at the enclaves. Never just one. He likes to wander. The whole Earth is his. He won't be constrained to just one location. If you ask around the enclaves for him, word will get back to him. He'll make contact if he wants to."

The nausea swirled, and my head pounded. This was the price I paid for coming to the nether, more intense than last time. As the strands of life pulled me back to the temporal realm, they tore at my mind. It almost felt like I left some of it there in the nether.

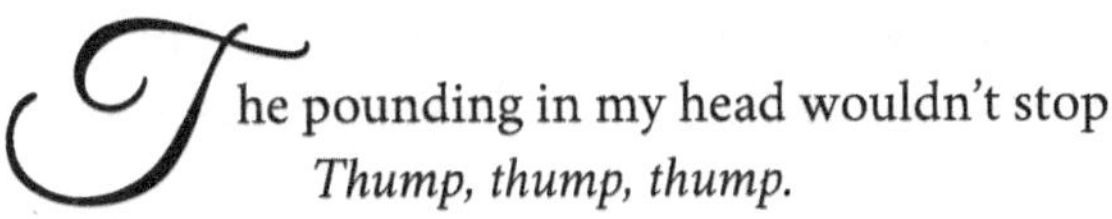The pounding in my head wouldn't stop.

Thump, thump, thump.

Wait.

That wasn't my headache. Rather, my headache was reacting to the knocking on my door. After I'd come home from the nether, I'd fixed myself a drink and gone to bed. Whatever time it was, I hadn't had enough sleep.

Thump, thump, thump.

Deacon, it appeared, would not be deterred. The smell and feel of his magic found me in my room. The only other person who'd knock on my door would be Harry or Sybil.

Deacon would've felt me going to the nether last night and my return. While I was grateful he waited until morning to come talk about it, I didn't look forward to this conversation. Still, he had been nice enough to wait, so I should return the courtesy.

Even after such a long night, and fatigued as I was, the feel of Deacon's magic as I got closer soothed me. I opened the door before he could knock again and squinted at the bright sunlight that poured into my dark apartment.

"Hey," I croaked. My voice was raspy, filled with sleep.

Deacon didn't say anything. He stood staring at me, his face etched with concern and some other emotion. Anger, perhaps? I didn't blame him. Not after all the shit I'd pulled.

"Is Sybil home?" I asked.

"Yes. She's doing some research into the fae magic we can expect to encounter on our mission to get Alistair."

Deacon and I definitely needed to have a conversation, and it would be awkward with Sybil there. Plus, she was the only one of us getting actual work done, so best to leave her to it.

Deacon had been in my apartment before, but this was the first time I'd invited him inside. I opened the door wider and gestured for him to come in.

While he walked into the living room, I went to the kitchen to get some coffee started. I still had a sour stomach from my trip to the nether, and I didn't think I could keep food down. I needed something to get me going.

What I really wanted was a whiskey to dull the pounding in my head, but I had too much work to do today. Even if alcohol didn't affect me the same as other people because of my magic, I needed to be sharp. The caffeine in coffee didn't do much for me other than get my magic buzzing, but I liked the smell of it, the ritual.

As I scooped the grounds into the coffee maker, I took a deep breath and let that delicious scent consume me. It sharpened my senses, made me more prepared to face the day. I needed all the help I could get with the conversation that was to come, especially when I realized the clock on the coffee maker showed twelve minutes past eleven. How had I slept so long? No wonder Deacon looked angry.

"Is Pint here?" Deacon asked from the living room.

"No, he's keeping an eye on Freddie."

"Is there any news on that front?"

"He appears to be on his best behavior from what Pint says." I willed the coffee to brew faster. I couldn't help but feel that Deacon was judging me. Judging me for going to the nether, for what I did with Lars, and now he was in my apartment, judging. It didn't help that with my open floor plan I could see him looking at me.

I drummed my fingers on the counter, waiting for the coffee to finish. As much as I dreaded this conversation with Deacon, I was itching to have it over with. We needed to get going. There was too much to do.

The coffee maker beeped. I poured my mug so fast that coffee sloshed over the sides. "Do you want a cup?" I asked Deacon.

"Sure, I'd love one." It was the first time I'd seen him smile since he arrived. It lit up something inside me, and I resented that it was for coffee and not for me. What a childish thought.

I pulled out a second mug and poured him a cup. He didn't sit until I came into the living room and handed him his coffee. Then we sat together on the sofa.

"I guess you're here because of my little trip last night," I snapped. I don't know why. Deacon hadn't done or said anything overtly irritating, but having him look at me, I felt inadequate.

"Yes. I want to know what happened. And I'm worried about you. I think you're addicted to the nether." Deacon's face appeared to show concern, but it felt patronizing, like I was incapable of making my own decisions.

"I'm not." Was I? It did soothe something inside me to go there even though it caused headaches and nausea. But that was normal. The Origin said we paid a toll to go there. That was simply my payment. "I'm not addicted."

"Really? Then why are you acting this way?"

I was acting strange. I knew it. I could feel it. Everything irritated me. There was no real reason for me to be upset with Deacon except that I was upset at the world. My handler, the man who'd been my rock for my entire adult life, was in danger. Captured by the fae queen. Tortured. And here I was, completely useless.

The hot coffee felt good going down. It soothed my body, but it excited my magic, which only increased my restlessness. I didn't know why I was acting this way. I could only hope that everything would calm down once I had Alistair back.

"You don't need to worry about me. I've lived this long without you."

Hurt flashed in Deacon's eyes, and I regretted the words. I didn't mean them, not like that.

"I'm sorry. That came out wrong." I think he could tell I was being genuine. I'd only meant that there was no reason for him to worry. I'd survived more perilous circumstances.

"I know you're capable, Nadiya. You'll never have to convince me of that."

"Then focus on the mission, not me." The way I felt right now, I didn't want him paying me any attention.

"That doesn't work for me. I'm always going to worry about you."

The way his green eyes bore into me with genuine concern made me want to crawl into a hole after how I'd treated him. I could tell he wanted to reach out to me, take my hand or rest his on my leg, but he didn't. He could tell it wouldn't be welcome given the mood I was in, so he used his eyes to their full effect instead.

In those green depths I saw vulnerability. I was his vulnerability.

"Then you're just going to end up getting hurt like everyone else." I hadn't meant to say that. Or rather, I hadn't meant to expose that part of me. People who worried about me got hurt.

The last time I cared about a man the way I cared about Deacon, I'd ended up devastating him. That was why we couldn't bond. That was why we needed to stay professional. Just partners. I couldn't live with myself if I devastated Deacon the same way I had Julien. In a way, I thought I loved Deacon more than I had Julien precisely because he was a partner.

"Why are you acting like this? Why are you trying to push me away?" Deacon asked. He reached for my hand, but I snatched it back.

Before I could think it through, I let out the anxiety I'd been holding. "I know you could smell it on me."

"Smell what?" Deacon asked. He sounded genuinely perplexed.

"Sex. Lars. You know what I did with him to buy time, what we were doing in the bathroom."

Understanding dawned on Deacon's face. "Yes, I know what you did. Why does that matter?"

"It's a part of my work most people find distasteful." I looked away, not wanting him to read my face. "It was enough for my fiancé to leave me."

Deacon grabbed my shoulders and forced me to look at him. His eyebrows knit in consternation. "I am not Julien. I am not some weak man so insecure in my place that I'm threatened by a job you did with a mark. It's the job. You did what you had to do. You completed your mission without hurting anyone. It was a success in my book."

"It really doesn't bother you?" That didn't seem possible.

He let his hands drop from my shoulders. "It really doesn't. I don't know, maybe that makes me strange. But we have a job to do, a mission to complete. We both put everything we have on the line. You do what you have to with no regrets. It's one of the things I lo—" he caught himself, "admire about you."

"I thought you'd be disgusted to know what I did."

"I will never judge you for doing your job. What kind of asshole would that make me?" A little smile teased at his lips. "Though it does make me a little happy to know you worry about my opinion."

I turned away from his gaze and took another drink of my coffee so he wouldn't see my awkwardness at his admission. Still, there was some reason that he refused to bond with me. If it wasn't that my job involved seducing other men, what was it?

Whatever it was, it didn't matter. We were in the middle of a mission, and there were more important things to attend to. Whatever reason he had, at least we were both on the same page not wanting to bond.

"I am concerned about you going to the nether. That is where you went last night, isn't it?" Deacon asked.

"Yes, I went to speak with the Origin."

"You have to be careful with that. This is the third time you've gone."

I didn't even know if it was worth it given what little I received in return. For some reason, I felt like I needed it. The Origin was the only person who'd ever been in my position. Something about talking with her made me feel more in control, like I was doing the right thing. It made me feel more sure of myself.

"Did you at least find out anything useful?" Deacon asked.

"The Origin knows Dorran. She seems to think that he spoke with Lars in front of the cameras to get our attention. To play with us."

"It's strange for a druid to know that much about human technology."

It was strange for anyone from Elustria to know that much. "He's been here for ages. Apparently he makes it his business to keep up with the happenings on Earth. He may have information to help us, but there's no way to contact him. The most we can do is ask around and hope word gets back to him."

"So what do you want to do?" Deacon asked.

I downed the rest of my coffee, and it did nothing to dissipate my headache. "It's time I introduce you to Bubbles and Brews at the enclave."

"You think we can get information about Dorran there?"

"If not, at least we can get a decent drink."

30

We got to Bubbles and Brews during the lunch rush. It was the most popular establishment in the enclave. Not only did they make great brews of the alcoholic and magical variety, they served the kind of comfort food people dreamed about.

Their menu philosophy was basically take Elustrian and Earth favorites and deep fry them. A good brew, a deep-fried dish, and a dipping sauce that could be enchanted with any number of enhancements. It was a winning combination.

At this hour, the bar had turned into a lunch counter. It was a great time to fish for information. We dodged the bubbles floating about and grabbed a booth in the back.

"What's with all the bubbles?" Deacon asked.

It was weird sitting across from him but not seeing him. We had glamoured ourselves before entering the enclave. We donned different appearances than we had in Norway and the last time we were here. No one would recognize us, but it also meant I didn't recognize us either.

We were both blondes with blue eyes. Our facial features hadn't changed much, just enough that we weren't ourselves. It was strange and felt like wearing a thick layer of makeup that I couldn't wait to wash off.

The bubbles were what made this place unique. They were a little gimmicky but helpful to us. A jar full of clear liquid sat on our table next to the wall with a couple of wands sticking out of it.

I took one of the wands and showed Deacon the circle at the end of it. A pretty standard bubble-blowing wand. I held it to my lips and cupped my other hand over my mouth so that Deacon couldn't see my lips moving or hear what I said. I whispered into the circle at the end of the wand. When I was done, a bubble appeared and floated across the table to Deacon.

"Pop it," I told him. He narrowed his eyes in question and cocked his mouth with a little glee. When he popped the bubble with a finger, his smile grew. I couldn't hear anything, but he could hear what I had whispered:

You can say whatever you like into one of the bubbles, and whoever pops it is the only one who can hear it. You can also put items inside the bubbles and they won't appear until someone pops them.

"I've never seen anything like this," Deacon said. He looked around at all the bubbles floating about and reached out to one. He popped it, and then a second later, he laughed. "Ah, I see."

"What?" I asked.

"Someone complaining about their boss."

"Yeah, you get a lot of that. Anonymous confessions and gossip are the most common whispers." Keeping in mind our primary reason for coming here, I picked up the wand again and blew a few bubbles asking about the druid.

"I don't expect we'll actually get any good info about Dorran. I just want to get word out that we're asking about him." We'd have to remember these glamours in case we needed to follow up with anyone.

With the bubbles sent off, I took a menu and placed my order for some deep-fried bat wings and mozzarella sticks that were supposed to be made from mammoth milk. The bat wings were from Elustrian bats that were raised here in the enclave. The mammoth milk would have to be imported from Elustria since a loose mammoth would be hard to explain to humans. They were about twice the size of elephants. My guess was they used regular Earth milk for the mozzarella sticks.

"Is there anything on this menu that isn't deep-fried?" Deacon asked as he flipped the menu over in his vain search.

"Nope, that's the beauty of it."

He placed his ordering stone on the menu over fried green beans, waited until it glowed to indicate the order had been received, then placed it on fried green tomatoes. "I've always wanted to try those."

"Excellent choice," I said as I placed an order for some dipping sauces with a mental clarity enchantment.

Deacon proceeded to order some Elustrian fried melon and squash.

"It's cute how you think choosing only fruits and vegetables somehow makes it healthy. Eat some of the meat too." I added an order of fried Elustrian cave fungus and konin, an Elustrian animal resembling a rabbit.

Deacon was huge, and as a dragon shifter, he burned calories at a rate that left me jealous. He could eat anything he wanted and not have to worry about adding any fat. I'd have to put in some extra workouts after this was over to keep myself fit.

"What do you want to drink?" I asked Deacon.

"Just a water, thanks," he replied, as if the question were ridiculous.

I blew a bubble in the direction of the bartender with my order for their house ale. I paid extra for an enchantment that would make my headache disappear.

The bartender, a tall dark blue elf, levitated my ale and Deacon's water to us. I sent out a few more bubbles asking about Dorran. A few minutes later, our table glowed red for a second, and then our food appeared.

As we ate, the chatter around us gradually quieted to whispers. Curious glances were tossed our way.

"I think they're on to us," Deacon said as he popped some fried melon in his mouth.

"It was bound to happen." The enclave was small, and we were likely the only strangers present. It didn't take a mental clarity enchantment to figure out that I was the one sending out the bubbles about Dorran. "At least we know that word will travel."

I took my time eating. For the best chance of getting information from my next source, we would have to wait until the place had cleared out a bit.

"You waiting to approach the bartender?" Deacon asked as he licked his fingers.

"Yeah." I finished my drink. The enchantment had barely made a dent in my headache. "If anyone here is willing to share information on how to break through fae magic, it's going to be him."

The bartender was a shade, a fallen elf. He came to the enclave to get a fresh start, live on the straight and narrow and all that. But once a mercenary, always a mercenary.

Once the bar had cleared and all that remained were a few tables of patrons, I sent a bubble to the bartender. A minute later, he appeared at our table.

"So it's not enough that you ask for Dorran's whereabouts, you also want to dabble in the black market?" He spoke directly to me, ignoring Deacon. It communicated both his respect for me and a false bravado that Deacon didn't intimidate him.

"I wouldn't tempt an upstanding shade such as yourself like that. I'm asking a question, that's all. Do you know how to break through fae magic?"

"Huh," the shade snorted in derision. "Yeah, I know how to break through fae magic, and I'm working at this place."

"There's no need to be rude. We'll just be going then." I started to scoot out of the booth, and Deacon followed my lead. "Do you happen to know someone with more connections than you who might be willing to make some money?"

The shade looked from me to Deacon and back again, weighing his options. He held up his hand. "Just wait. What is it exactly you're wanting?"

"Let's say I had something being guarded by a fae. Any information or objects you can provide that would help me retrieve the item would be greatly rewarded." I wanted it to sound generic enough that anyone who might get wind of this conversation wouldn't be able to connect it to me or Malev. No one would help me if they knew who I fought against. It would amount to suicide.

"I don't have anything like that just sitting around, but if you give me some time, I might be able to come up with something," he said.

"Time is of the essence. The item I aim to retrieve will be gone in a few days."

"Leave your phone number, and I'll call if I come up with anything."

He slid a small pad of paper and pen across the table, the kind for taking orders. I pushed it back to him. I wasn't stupid enough to fall for that. There was no telling what kind of magic the paper and pen held.

I pulled a business card from my pocket that had my phone number on it and nothing else. The shade took it and went back to the bar, smart enough to not ask for a name.

Driving home, I could only hope that more parts of Alistair wouldn't be waiting for me.

ack at Sybil's, we found Pint eating a steak on Sybil's lap as she petted him. She appeared absorbed in reading a large tome floating in front of her.

"You know, you don't have to keep getting him steaks. He does hunt quite well on his own," I said as I plopped down on the sofa with Deacon.

"Hush," Pint said. "Just because you don't know how to take care of me doesn't mean you should discourage Sybil." He let out a fiery burp.

"Do you at least have some news for us?" I asked Pint. We hadn't seen each other much since he had started spying on Freddie and Harry. I generally took no news to be good news.

"There's not much, but I do smell magic. Harry's sleeping a lot lately. It seems to me that Freddie's bored, and I think he's using a sleeping spell on Harry just to keep him out of the way. I don't get the feeling that it's anything dangerous." Pint took another bite of steak.

I trusted his judgment. I didn't like the idea of Freddie using magic on Mr. Harmon at all, but at least this way Harry wouldn't get curious and start asking questions. Sleep might be the best thing for him.

Sybil shut her book and looked at me. "And what about you? Did you find out anything at Bubbles and Brews?"

"No, but I put some feelers out. From what I've learned of Dorran, I think he's likely to reach out. I made contact with a shade who's going to try to get us something to help against Malev." At least it had been a nice lunch with Deacon.

"You should go there sometime, Sybil. I think you'd like it," Deacon said.

I did not doubt that Sybil would love it. After this was all over, we could celebrate there.

Sybil didn't react with the enthusiasm she usually did. The only time I'd seen her this somber was when she delivered the news that Alistair had been kidnapped. Seeing the usual perky, happy-go-lucky Sybil acting any other way was unsettling.

"At this point, I'm just reading books hoping I stumble upon something that'll help. I don't really expect to find anything."

"So what are you saying, Sybil?" I asked.

"Malev's going to start wondering where Goffrey's head is. You're the Circle's most successful assassin. She has the person closest to you as her hostage. It's not going to take her long to figure out something is up. You might get another day, two at most, and that's only because she perceives time differently," Sybil said. She leaned forward, urgency in her eyes, as if she could will me to come up with a solution.

"I'm open to any ideas either of you have. I'd storm in there right now if I thought there was any chance I could rescue him. At this point, it would be a suicide mission," I said, looking between Sybil and Deacon, imploring them for ideas.

If we attempted a rescue and failed, I had no hope that Alistair would survive. We had one shot to get it right.

"I don't know anything about the fae," Deacon said. "I've barely had any contact with them. In my time protecting the dragons, I staved off a few fae attacks but none from high fae. My battles were always fought on the defensive, a completely different situation to the one we face now. You tell me where to go and what to do, and I'll do it. When it comes to physical fighting, I can take on anyone. But as for forming a plan to invade the fae realm? When it comes to subtlety and subterfuge, I'm not one for coming up with ideas."

"So you're saying you're all muscle and no brain?" I asked with a smile. It wasn't true, especially after his quick thinking with the toll coin, but it was fun to tease him.

"In this instance, yes," Deacon said.

"There's only one option we haven't tried," Sybil said. She stared at me meaningfully, and I got her point.

"If I call Gordon, he's going to want to know what we know."

"I don't see how we can go further without assistance from the Circle."

"And how's that going to work? I can't let them know what our plan is. If I ask them about ways to defeat the fae, they're going to assume that I'm out to kill the rival. They're not going to help."

"Maybe not, but Gordon may help you," Sybil said.

"I can't trust him. He was appointed by Meilin."

"So was Alistair."

That may be true, but Alistair and I had developed trust over years of working together. I didn't have that with Gordon. I'd never had another handler. Alistair made it sound like all handlers were as devoted as he was, but I had a hard time believing it. His allegiance had always been to me above the Circle. While I would like to think that other handlers felt the same, there was no way to know, and it seemed too naïve a thought for me to entertain.

"What's the worst that could happen if you ask Gordon for help?" Deacon asked sincerely.

My mind ran through all the different scenarios that could play out. "Worst case, the Circle actively works against me. Really worst case, Meilin determines that I've gone rogue, which I have, and orders my death."

Deacon considered this with pursed lips and finally nodded. "Okay, so that's pretty bad. But aren't we also working under the assumption that's going to happen eventually anyway? How much longer do you think the Circle can hold on to this fantasy that they control you?"

I hadn't considered it. I'd never planned a life separate from the Circle. This wasn't a job anyone retired from, at least not someone on the front lines like me.

I didn't think the Circle would tolerate me much longer. At least this way I had a chance of getting some helpful information. I pulled out my phone and called Gordon.

"I was wondering when I'd hear from you. Do you have any news for me?" Gordon asked. His voice was inscrutable. I hated that I couldn't tell what he was thinking. It put me at a disadvantage that I wasn't used to.

"No, I'm calling for some help."

Without missing a beat he asked, "What do you need?"

He took that same urgent I'm-here-to-help-you tone that Alistair did. The tone that said nothing else mattered other than getting me the help I needed. The question was whether I could trust it. We would soon find out.

"I need any information you can give me about breaking into a fae area. If I were to try to steal something from a fae, what information could you give me that would help?"

I tried to word it in a way that it could apply to me retrieving the name of the rival. I doubted they had heard about what Malev did to Alistair. At least, I hoped they hadn't. If they had, that would mean they knew about it and weren't doing anything.

"I'll see what I can find out for you, but nothing immediately comes to mind."

"Thank you."

"It's what I'm here for." He paused for a long moment, and when he spoke again, his voice was lower. "I know you went to Norway. Or rather, the Circle knows."

How could they know that? I stared at the phone in my hand. Of course. I hung up without replying.

At Sybil and Deacon's questioning looks, I said, "They know we went to Norway. The only way I can think they would know that would be from our phones. Specifically mine, but who knows if they're tracking yours as well."

The only other way they could know would be if Trevor told them somehow. Normally, I would've never even considered the possibility. Trevor was loyal to me. He was more than just a colleague. He was my friend. Except, if he had found out I was part fae, that could push him to answer questions from the Circle. I kept his identity secret for his protection, but someone at the Circle had to know.

I dreaded the thought that Trevor might know I was part fae. Curse my fae blood. I didn't feel fae. I felt more human than fae. The thought that this would drive a wedge between us made me sick.

I felt shaky, but looking down at my hands, they were as steady as ever. My headache throbbed to the front of my consciousness. I was being paranoid. I couldn't entertain the thought that Trevor might've turned on me. It was ludicrous. But it wasn't paranoid to take care of our phone problem.

"We all need to get burner phones. I'll go pick some up. From here on out, don't use your phones for anything. I'll keep this one either here or at my apartment strictly to receive calls from Gordon or the shade if he comes through for us. Don't use it for anything else, no searching the Internet, no looking something up, nothing. And it doesn't leave these two apartments. Understood?"

Sybil and Deacon both nodded. Deacon asked, "What else did he say?"

"Gordon doesn't have any information for us off the top of his head. He said he'll get back to me. That leaves us with nothing. It's possible one of our intelligence sources will come through, but we can't bet on it. Like Sybil said, Malev's not going to be patient. When she realizes I have no intention of bringing her Goffrey's head, this mission is going to go from insane to suicidal real quick."

I locked eyes with Deacon, and somehow I could tell that we were both thinking the same thing. We only had one option.

"Well it seems like if we want information on how to penetrate Malev's court, we should go to the source," Deacon said.

I nodded. "It's time I meet Goffrey."

"And worst-case scenario, you leave with his head to get Alistair back."

32

$\mathscr{B}$efore we left for Norway, I bought some burner phones and left my old cell phone in Sybil's care. She wouldn't be coming with us. She only had one glamour, and there was a chance that she could be recognized. This plan was already likely to fail. We couldn't take any additional risks. She would call if anyone left a message on my phone.

Deacon and I stood together atop a mountain outside the Bismo enclave. I had on a light coat and a beanie pulled down over my ears to protect against the cold. Deacon, predictably, wore his usual T-shirt and jeans, enchanted to stay intact when he shifted. I liked the look of his biceps in the tight material, but the absence of goose-bumps in this cold seemed unnatural.

"So how are we going to do this?" I asked.

We knew the rival court had to be close, but its exact location was still a mystery. Even if we could find Lars again, I didn't want to expose ourselves to him. Following him was out of the question since fae could teleport. There was a whole lot of nothing in every direction.

"The only option I can see is to fly. I can shift into my dragon form and go above the clouds. Even from that distance, I should be able to find it."

No matter how well the fae had concealed their rival court, Deacon would be able to smell the magic. Dragon shifters were the best magic sniffers in Elustria. There was no hiding from them.

Sorcerers had strict rules against dragons flying on Earth, but I didn't think it made much difference here. The sky was blanketed in clouds. Once Deacon got above them, no one would be able to see him. And that was on the off chance that there was anyone to see. The only humans around were the five hundred or so inhabitants of Bismo, and they were well away.

"I agree. I'll go down to the enclave and see if I can find out anything useful. You can meet me there once you're done." If I hung out at the bar long enough, I might overhear something useful.

"No, I'm not leaving you. You're coming with me." Deacon's tone made it clear that he considered any other idea ludicrous.

"But we're not bonded," I said as if it were the most obvious thing in the world.

Dragon shifters only ever let one person ride them: their bonded mate. Since many dragon shifters bonded with each other, that meant dragon riders were rare. Even if a dragon shifter mated with a sorcerer or high fae, they typically didn't bond. The mating was for reproductive purposes only.

Dragon shifters weren't domesticated beasts to be ridden at will. This offer from him said more about his devotion to me than the scar on his chest did.

"I'm well aware," Deacon said. "But I'm not going to have another rider. No matter what happens, Nadiya, it's always going to be you."

The way he looked at me, affection, desire, passion burning in his eyes, I knew he spoke the truth. For the first time in a while, a different physical sensation drowned out my headache and nausea. Giddy warmth flooded me. My magic jumped in my veins and fluttered in my gut. It very much liked this proposal.

But this wasn't a romantic overture. It was a pragmatic solution to a problem we found ourselves in.

"I'd be honored." They were the only words I could come up with. I needed to acknowledge what he offered, but there wasn't time to lose ourselves in sentiment.

"I had hoped our first time flying together would be more relaxing. I certainly wouldn't have chosen a place so cold, but you should get some warmth from my body." The fire inside dragons kept them warm.

"Don't worry. I'll be fine. Do you have any instructions for me?"

Deacon smirked. "Yes, hold on and grip with your thighs." He walked to the far side of the mountain, away from the enclave, and shifted.

For a moment, I got so caught up in drinking in the sight of him that I forgot what I was supposed to be doing. He turned and looked at me, cocking his head in question.

I climbed on and found that I fit nicely right above his wings, giving them full clearance. Once I was comfortably situated, I gripped with my thighs to let him know I was ready. His massive head turned, and he licked my cheek. Then he looked ahead and crouched down.

Without warning, he launched into the air, straight up like a rocket until we cleared the cloud cover.

We broke through from a world of gray into a sea of bright sunlight. I threw my head back and soaked in the sun. Up there, the only sounds were Deacon's breathing, the flap of his wings, and the air rushing past. My legs could feel Deacon's body expanding and contracting with each breath, a steady rhythm, slow and consistent.

My magic reached out to his, and the two intertwined, securing me to him in a way that had never happened before. This must be the dragon rider bond the myths talked about. The strands of our magic interlocked, holding me securely to Deacon's back. I felt like I could stand up and walk down the length of his body and our magics would keep me from falling.

I exhilarated in the freedom and speed of our flight. My magic settled in a way it never had before, and I knew then that all the times I'd raced down the road in my car, pushing it to its maximum speed, this was the feeling I'd sought. Something inside me had yearned for this without even knowing it.

Frost formed on the tips of my eyelashes, but Deacon had been right. His body produced enough warmth that I didn't feel much colder than I had on the ground.

Up here, out of the flight path of planes, Deacon could keep flying. We could explore, keep this feeling forever. But all too soon, Deacon lowered his altitude. He stopped and hovered, poking his head through the clouds.

I couldn't see what he saw, but after surveying the scene, he brought his head back up and kept flying until he got to a spot he had picked out. Without warning, he dove toward the earth.

I had to bite my tongue to keep from screaming with glee, but I released a little laughter. When Deacon landed, I slid off his back and couldn't control my smile.

Deacon shifted and grinned at me. "So you liked it?"

I stretched my arms out wide and lifted my face to the sky. "It was amazing." I dropped my arms and looked at him. "I can't wait until we do it again."

Deacon laughed. "It may happen sooner than you think."

"What brought you down here?" I asked, looking around the clearing he'd landed in.

He pointed to the base of a nearby mountain. "That's it. That's where the rival fae court is or at least part of it. There's a lot of magic coming from there, but not all of it's fae. There's something strange, something I've never come across before."

I could smell the magic, but I wasn't familiar enough with all the scents to discern between them. I had no doubt that Deacon could smell it better than me. I could only smell it because of our anointing.

Whatever that strange other magic was, it was probably the reason for the fae court's location. If Deacon couldn't even hazard a guess as to what it was, it had to be rare. Something like that would normally interest me, but right now all I cared about was getting Alistair. Whatever rare magic was here, the fae could fight over it themselves.

"Do you think this mystery magic will present a problem for us?"

Deacon pursed his lips to the side. "It's hard to say. How do you want to approach this? Going in covertly could be difficult with an unknown magic source."

"I'm here for one reason: to see if they will give me any knowledge that will help rescue Alistair. I won't be able to get that covertly or even with torture given the way they've held up to Malev. My only hope is to use the prestige of the Dragon Fae to get their help. Having the Dragon Fae turn on Malev and defeat her security can work in their favor when trying to depose her."

"So there's no need for glamour or the cuff then," Deacon said, nodding to my wrist.

"That's right, but I'll leave the cuff on until we get closer." Paranoia came with the job, and it had only increased recently. From my vantage point, everyone was a threat.

We walked in silence through the trees. I tried to anticipate Goffrey's reaction. This was a gamble, but I didn't see any other option. I needed someone to get me into the fae court, and Goffrey was our last hope.

As we neared what we assumed was the entrance, Deacon broke away from my side and took the lead. In our short time together, he'd grown accustomed to scouting out magical objects ahead of me. This was no different.

We came upon a rock face and Deacon held out his arm, blocking my way. "This is it. I'll see if I can find a way to activate it."

The magic centered on this rock. It smelled earthy and sour, like moldy leaves. I wondered if other magic folk could smell it or if it would simply blend into the surrounding scents.

Deacon stepped closer to the rock face, placing his hand as close to it as he could without actually touching it. He took a deep breath, getting more from the scent than I was.

"I think it's a fae portal, but there's also a hint of that strange magic mixed with sorcerer magic. I don't detect any traps."

"If you don't think it's going to harm us, then let's go through, see what we find."

I could tell by the look on Deacon's face that he didn't like going into the unknown. He was used to defending a position. At the Spineback Mountains, he knew every inch of the place he defended. He didn't go into the unknown. For me, every step I took was into the unknown.

Deacon reached his hand out to me, and I took it. We'd go through together. No need to risk being separated.

I stood shoulder to shoulder with him and hovered my hand over the rock face as he did.

"Three, two—" Deacon stopped as the smell of fresh magic came from behind us. I could feel the portal a split second before a bolt of electric magic crashed into us.

33

Electric pain sizzled over my skin. I whirled, drawing my void blade from its sheath at the small of my back. A lone sorcerer faced us. A Circle assassin. No other sorcerers would be outside the entrance to the rival fae court.

He'd underestimated how much magic it would take to kill us and squandered the advantage of his surprise attack. The spell he used could kill another sorcerer in less than sixty seconds, but split between me and Deacon, it was too weak.

The Circle must've placed surveillance on the entrance. It would be hard to detect it among all the magic of the portal.

Even if it wasn't enough to kill us, the pain weakened our abilities. The Circle already knew I was here, so there didn't seem to be much harm in removing my cuff. The second I unfastened the dragonhide, Deacon shifted. I knew he would hesitate to use his magic and cause me more pain as long as the cuff remained on my wrist.

The sorcerer blanched at the sight of Deacon. Despite the situation, I couldn't help a little grin. Deacon did cut an impressive figure. He blew a torrent of fire at the sorcerer. The pain from the sorcerer's spell stopped as he leapt out of the way.

My magic responded with a vengeance. I hadn't fought with magic in quite a while, but my power instinctually knew what to do. I levitated the assassin and threw him into the rock face further down from our position. Behind me, I smelled and felt more magic appear, but Deacon turned to take care of whatever threat there might be.

As the assassin flew through the air, I ran to meet him. He cracked his head on the rock and fell to the ground, blood gushing down his face. He tried to hurl a ball of fire at me, but I easily dodged it and swiped my blade down his arm, drawing blood in a superficial wound. It wasn't enough to kill him, but it didn't need to. He no longer had magic.

I looked down into his brown eyes, and I wanted to spare his life. He was like me, following orders. I was simply another target. But I couldn't spare someone who tried to kill me. Too much training worked against me. Besides, killing him at this point was a mercy. He wouldn't know how to live without magic. He wouldn't want to.

I cradled his head in my hands and with a quick snap broke his neck. If humans happened upon his body, they would assume he'd fallen off the mountain. I cleaned my void blade in the grass and sheathed it.

When I turned, I faced three fae. They must've emerged from the court to see what was happening.

I cut right to the point. "I'm the Dragon Fae, and I'm here to see Goffrey."

Two of the fae were indistinguishable from each other, like twins, except one glared at us, seemingly unimpressed with my title. He had the look of a man who had never been impressed by anything. They wore lightweight enchanted armor and each carried a sword that vibrated with magic. They stood a head taller than Deacon in his human form and seemed prepared for battle. I didn't sense any type of threat from them, but I knew that could change if Deacon or I moved.

The third fae was shorter and with lighter coloring than the twins.

He stepped forward and eyed me for a moment as if judging my words. He nodded. "Very well. Come, and we'll see if he'll admit you."

The three fae turned their backs to us and walked to the entrance. Only then did Deacon shift back into human form.

"Good kill," he said once I got next to him.

"He was an amateur. Such a waste," I whispered in reply.

The three fae stepped through the entrance. Deacon and I followed, holding hands in front of the rock face as before.

"I think I'll skip counting this time," Deacon said with a smile. We placed our free hands on the rock and were pulled into darkness.

I could feel Deacon's hand in mine, but I couldn't see it. The silence pounded in my ears. Until that moment, I didn't know such darkness existed. Reflexively, my free hand went to my void blade. I curled my hand around the hilt, prepared to draw it if necessary.

I couldn't tell if the darkness was due to lack of light or if we had been enchanted somehow. I could feel eyes on us, eyes that could see through the black. Working off of our theory about the toll coins, perhaps this was where the coin was supposed to be shown. In this instance, we were awaiting Goffrey's approval instead of providing a coin.

The silence dragged on, and I lost all sense of time. Rationally, I supposed it was only a few seconds. I was about to ask Deacon to light the area with his dragon breath when a voice spoke.

"He'll see you." It was the disembodied voice of the fae from outside.

Light flooded the space. I kept my eyes wide open despite the pain from the sudden illumination. We stood in a small cavern, a type of antechamber. The rock walls surrounding us shone with a blue light from within. Standing shoulder to shoulder, if Deacon and I extended our arms out to the side, we could almost touch the walls. About twelve feet in front of us stood the fae twins, prepared to kill anyone who they deemed an intruder.

They each took a step to the side, creating a path between them.

They touched the stone wall behind them, and it melted away, allowing us entrance.

"Hurry up. He's a busy man. Don't keep him waiting," said the one who had appeared unimpressed by my title.

I took the lead and stepped through into the new fae court.

34

We were teleported into a round cavern with half a dozen hallways branching out like spokes on a wheel. The cavern wasn't particularly large, a few thousand square feet, and it was completely bare. A few benches and chairs were placed against the walls in between the hallways. Fae cut across the hub, but none of them paid us any attention.

A man approached from one of the hallways, the only person to make eye contact with us. He smiled and walked with determination. I half expected him to stick out his hand like an American business-man. The plastered on smile gave me flashbacks to Bob with the Be Your Best Self movement. I got the same strange vibes from this guy despite the fact that he clearly wasn't human.

He was at least a head shorter than me, lean with pale skin that had a light greenish tint to it. His dark green hair had brown high-lights and was clean-cut except for the top that had that ruffled can't-be-bothered-to-care look that men took forever perfecting. He wore well-tailored pants and a crisp white button down with the top buttons undone. I could see green tattoos snaking up his chest. The smell of seawater hung like a cloud around him, irritating my headache. He must be some type of sea fae.

All in all, I didn't like him.

I snuck a glance at Deacon, and the slight twitch between his mouth and his nose told me that he didn't care for this fae either.

"So, you must be the Dragon Fae and her companion," the fae said, stopping a few feet in front of us and extending his hands palms up in greeting.

Deacon and I returned the gesture. "Yes, I'm Nadiya, and this is Deacon."

If I ever got some actual power as the Dragon Fae, I'd decree that my companion go by his name. All this companion shit was driving me nuts. The man was a dragon shifter, a guardian and warrior in his own right. He could be called by his name. "And you must be Goffrey."

Truth be told, he didn't strike me as the type of man who would try to establish a rival court. He seemed more like the PR department.

"Yes, I am. It appears our reputations precede us. I heard you ran into some trouble outside. Do you need attention from healers? Refreshments of any kind?"

Neither Deacon nor I were stupid enough to ingest anything given to us by a fae. "No, thank you. We're fine."

"Well then, let's have a seat, and we can discuss what it is you came here for." Goffrey went over to a group of seats against the wall and pulled a chair out to face a bench. He sat in the chair with his back toward the cavern, a courtesy I noted. Deacon and I sat side-by-side on the bench facing him.

I noticed Deacon's eyes cataloguing everything he saw. He wouldn't talk much during this meeting. I could trust him to take note of everything that happened behind Goffrey and to observe any physical signals I may miss. Years spent alone on a mountaintop made him an excellent observer.

Once we were settled, Goffrey asked, "Do you know who just tried to kill you?"

"Yes. Do you?" If he didn't, I wasn't about to enlighten him. The look in his eyes gave it away, though. He knew.

"I take it they've been protecting me from you," Goffrey said, raising his eyebrows to me.

Before I could answer, a fae came up behind Goffrey and bent down to whisper in his ear. Goffrey nodded his understanding of whatever the fae said. It gave me time to consider how much I wanted to reveal. This was one of the hardest parts of my job. Knowledge was power. Each little bit was currency, and the choice of how to spend that currency differentiated the amateurs from the professionals.

"If you think they're protecting you from me, why did you let me in?" I asked when the fae left.

Goffrey seemed surprised at the question. "You're the Dragon Fae. I wanted to hear what you have to say."

Deacon moved in his seat, the only tell that what Goffrey said didn't sit right with him either.

"It is true that Malev sent me to kill you. Once I found out who you were, I didn't tell anyone other than Malev. I have no clue how the Circle has your name or location." That wasn't entirely true. I assumed it had something to do with me, but it was unintentional.

"So if Malev sent you to kill me, why aren't I dead?" Goffrey asked. "Clearly you had no problem taking out whoever the Circle sent."

Another fae came up to whisper in his ear, and Goffrey held up a finger asking us to wait a moment. They whispered for a few seconds, and then he focused his attention back on us while the fae scurried away.

There was quite a lot of activity going on, fae running here and there. I wondered what else was hidden in this cavernous fortress. I suspected there were multiple levels, and we were seeing only a little part of it. For some reason, we weren't in a throne room or audience chamber. Maybe he didn't trust us to see more than the very basics.

"Like you said, I'm the Dragon Fae. I'm not Malev's puppet. Do you know why I gave her your name to begin with?"

"Yes, I have heard that she's taken someone close to you as a hostage, someone you work with for the Circle."

I wanted to see how much information I could get from him. "And what do you know about him and his situation?"

Goffrey leaned back in his chair, seeing that I was fishing for information as much as he was. "I know he's alive, but that's the extent of it. You still haven't answered my question. Killing me would get you your friend back. So why aren't I dead?"

Goffrey showed remarkable nonchalance while discussing his possible death. It was almost like he expected to be dead already and that he truly didn't understand why he was alive.

People reacted differently to the prospect of death. I had delivered enough killing blows in my time to see a wide range of reactions, but this one took me by surprise. It unsettled me in a way that I couldn't quite describe. I filed it away for later.

"You're right to assume that I would do anything to rescue my friend. However, I don't relish giving Malev what she wants. I came here in the hope that maybe we could come to our own arrangement. I've been trying to find a way into Malev's court to rescue him. Quite frankly, I have no interest in fae politics. It doesn't matter to me whether you or Malev is the victor in whatever quarrel you have. All I care about is my friend. However, I've come up empty-handed. I'm running against a bit of a clock here. Too much longer and I fear what Malev will do to him. So if you can help me free him, it would get us both what we want."

Goffrey raised his eyebrows in surprise. "Oh really? How does it get me what I want?"

Deacon spoke for the first time in our meeting. As always, he chose his words and his moment carefully for maximum impact. "You get to stay alive."

That deep voice coming from so much bulk and with such menace was enough to send chills down anyone's spine. Goffrey knew what Deacon was. He'd be a fool not to take his words seriously. Again, though, it seemed as if staying alive wasn't Goffrey's main concern.

"I take your meaning." Goffrey sighed and slapped his hands on his thighs as he stood up. "You've given me quite a lot to think about. Come back here tomorrow, and I'll give you my answer after I've had time to consider my options."

I didn't give him the pleasure of seeing how much his response confused me. Deacon and I both stood, and Goffrey gestured for a fae who'd been standing against the opposite wall to join our group.

"Luellen here will see you out. It was lovely meeting you." Goffrey gave us a little nod and walked down one of the adjacent hallways.

"All right, I can make a portal to anywhere you want to go, or I can put you right back out where you entered. Which would you prefer?" Luellen asked. The small fae was all business, polite but clearly with more things to get done today.

I wasn't foolish enough to give the fae any more information on me than they already had, and that included a location to send me to. "Just outside where we came in is fine."

Luellen nodded. She formed a portal and stepped back. "This goes right out where you entered."

Deacon stepped forward and peered through the portal. Satisfied, he walked through, and I followed. When the portal closed behind us, he turned to me. "That was strange."

"I'm glad you think so too."

"The only problem is I can't put my finger on why," Deacon said and started walking back the way we'd come, past the assassin's dead body.

"I can't figure it out either. It'll come to us. Just give it time." I didn't need to be reminded that time was something we didn't have. I knew from experience that we couldn't rush these things. We both had sharp minds. Even as we spoke they were processing everything we took in at that meeting. Once there was a clear answer, we would know.

"I'll make a portal to take us home," I said. "My magic's already around this place. A little more won't hurt. I want to get back to Sybil as soon as possible."

The faintest shadow of disappointment passed through Deacon's eyes, but he nodded. "Of course."

He'd wanted to shift and fly again. I didn't blame him. I wanted that to. I wished he could shift and fly us both far away from here. Instead, I made the portal then pulled my dragonhide cuff out of my pocket. My burner phone tumbled out with it.

I held the phone in one hand while I used the other to fasten the cuff around my wrist. Deacon gasped at the sensation. He shared more than just the pain the cuff caused when I performed magic. He also shared the discomfort simply wearing it caused.

Together, we stepped through the portal, and when we did, my phone went crazy.

35

Sybil and Pint jumped up from the sofa when we entered, and my phone started chiming. I looked at the screen.

"Sybil, I have thirteen missed calls from you. I must not have had reception there. What happened?"

"Nothing happened. Gordon called you. I called you once for every time he did." She didn't seem too terribly concerned about whatever had Gordon desperate to reach me. "Tell us how it went." Hope lit her expression.

Before I could say anything else, Pint narrowed his eyes at me and flew over, landing on my shoulder. He sniffed my hair. "You got into a fight."

Pint could always smell a fight on me, probably a mixture of adrenaline and blood.

"The blood you smell is from a Circle assassin."

"Are you sure?" Sybil asked. She didn't doubt me; she just didn't want it to be true. The Circle taking such a bold step changed things.

"I'm positive."

"You killed him, right?" Pint asked.

I reached up and scratched behind his horn. "Yes, I killed him."

"Good." Pint didn't mess around. He took revenge seriously. It was more than just a desire for me to defend myself. Pint regretted not being able to avenge his mother's death. During the attack that killed her, a curse had ricocheted and hit him, shrinking him down to his small size. I never thought he minded being small nearly as much as he minded not avenging his mother. He'd gladly go down fighting for someone he loved.

"Deacon, why don't you tell them what else happened while I'm on the phone?" With the attempt on my life and Gordon apparently desperate to get a hold of me, I wanted to know how he was going to play this.

Deacon nodded. "Join us when you're done."

Pint flew off my shoulder. I grabbed my regular phone from the coffee table on my way to Sybil's bedroom to make the call.

Gordon picked up on the first ring and sighed with relief. "You're alive."

"Yes, no thanks to the efforts of our employer," I said in a contemptuous tone.

"I tried to warn you. I've been looking into fae magic like you asked, and I think they found out. Between that and tracking your cell phone, they've put together a little picture for themselves. I don't know how much more they're going to involve me."

"I'm the Dragon Fae. Isn't it in their interest to keep me alive?"

"Not if you won't do as you're told. They want to back this rival. Meilin is sick of Malev."

"If that's the case, why did they send such an incompetent assassin?"

"Well, that's the one thing we have going for us. Meilin underestimated how difficult it would be to get other agents to turn against you. It goes against their code. You're one of them. Not just that, Meilin declared that you're the Dragon Fae and word's gotten out about Alistair. People aren't thrilled with the idea of leaving one of our own in Malev's clutches. I don't think Meilin realized how much this move against you was going to damage her reputation. She's retreating into her inner circle. I don't know how much information I'm going to get from here on out."

I had wondered something, and now seemed like the moment to ask, even though I didn't know if I'd get an honest answer. "She obviously trusts you enough to assign you to me. Aren't you part of her inner circle?"

"I have been a faithful and loyal agent of the Circle my entire life. I moved up the ranks swiftly because I'm good at my job and I know how to play the game. That's where Alistair and I differ. We knew each other from school, grew up together, and we joined around the same time." His voice got that faraway sound of someone reminiscing on better days.

"I'm good at my job because I've worked really hard at it. Alistair? He has natural talent, the smartest person I've ever met. If he'd played the game, he'd be challenging Meilin for power right now. But you came along. He spent every bit of political capital he had to get assigned as your handler. He devoted everything to you."

Gordon took a breath, and I could imagine him shaking his head. "He tried to explain it to me once, why he had no desire to climb higher in the organization. He really believed in you. He didn't tell me that he thought you were the Dragon Fae, only that you were special."

My eyes stung, and my sight got hazy. Alistair had been my rock, but I didn't realize that he'd given up advancing his career for me or that he'd fought to become my handler. I'd always assumed I was an assignment.

Our relationship was a strange one because it was just the two of us. We didn't have contact with outsiders. I didn't see how he acted with other people. I knew him better than I knew anyone, but parts of him were still a mystery.

"If you and Alistair grew up together, why did Meilin assign you to me? Wouldn't she surmise that you're loyal to him?"

"Honestly, I don't think she knows. In her eyes, I'm the perfect little soldier, doing what I'm told and delivering results. The way she has handled this entire affair shows that she drastically underesti-mated her agents. I think in her twisted mind, she really thought we were doing all of this, putting our lives on the line, for her. She doesn't really understand the code."

The code. We never spoke of it, but we all knew it existed. Despite what people thought, we weren't a bunch of killers for hire. We didn't do this for the money. For one thing, we could make more practicing our craft for pretty much anyone else. We did this work because we believed in it. Jaded as we were, we still believed. It was our downfall.

"What does this mean for my safety? Is she going to send someone here?"

"I don't know. Meilin's become unpredictable. I would guess that she'd want to keep you alive because of who you are, so she may stay out of your way as long as you don't try to kill the rival. Or she may have decided that she's had enough of this Dragon Fae business and try to eliminate you. I haven't been able to get close enough to her to gauge her mood. You need to go underground deeper than you ever have before. Be prepared for anything."

"All right. I'll consider it."

"Do more than that. I'm sorry I didn't get word to you in time. I tried. I know it may not seem like it, but I'm doing what I can to help. I'll pass along anything useful I get. I can tell you that you have some time. Meilin doesn't know that you're alive. You have until the assas-sin's next check-in time which is probably a few hours from now. Once he misses that call, you'll need to be underground."

"Thank you, Gordon. I misjudged you."

"No, you didn't. You were doing your job." The line went dead.

A sharp spear of pain pierced my forehead. These headaches were getting worse. I wanted to go to the nether, not to speak to the Origin, just to soothe the pain so I could think through everything.

Between the assassination attempt, meeting Goffrey, and the conversation with Gordon, there was a lot of information to parse. Even Deacon knew that we'd missed something with Goffrey. Deacon wasn't trained to figure out what it was, but I should already know, and I didn't because of my blasted headache. All I needed was some peace to work through my thoughts.

According to Gordon, I had some time. Deacon and Sybil were talking in the living room. It wouldn't take long. I formed a portal and stepped through. As it closed, I could hear Deacon enter the room behind me, too late to follow.

36

In the nether, my mind cleared. Instead of thinking over everything that had happened, I relished the feeling.

Peace.

Fake, stolen peace, but peace just the same. Here was my escape. I could stay here forever. No more pain, no more disappointment, no more responsibilities, no more people counting on me whom I'd inevitably disappoint. Why would anyone leave this glorious place?

"Because this place is not for mortals. You are trying my patience," the Origin said.

"Shut up! I didn't come here for you. I came here to let my mind rest." All I needed was a place to clear my head, to silence the pounding, to calm the nausea, and let my mind put together all the pieces that were laid out before it. I knew there was an answer somewhere. I just had to find it.

"This isn't the answer," the Origin said, and wind whipped my hair around my face. "This place isn't for you. You need to leave."

"Oh really? Then where is my place? Please, tell me. I'll listen. Because it's not on Earth. I'm not a human. No amount of pretending or wearing a dragonhide cuff will turn me into one. Apparently, I'm not a sorceress either. I'm part fae, but I'm not completely fae, otherwise I'd know something about fae magic, perhaps something that could help me save Alistair. Not fae, not sorceress, not human. I don't belong in Elustria, and I don't belong on Earth. This is the one place where I get a modicum of peace, but you're telling me I don't belong here either. So please, enlighten me. Tell me where I belong," I screamed, imploring the heavens with my arms.

I felt myself unraveling, but I didn't care. What was the use? I'd given my entire life to the Circle only to have them turn around and try to kill me. I'd done sane. I'd done calm, cool, and collected. Maybe it was time to give insanity a try, because it was about the only thing left.

"You belong with your people," the Origin said in her sage voice as if that were the obvious answer to all my problems.

"Oh." I spread my arms wide and exaggerated my voice. "Is that all? My people? And who, pray tell, are my people? I was just almost assassinated by my people."

"No, an incompetent assassin made an attempt on your life. You didn't almost die. Don't give him more credit than he deserves. And why do you think the attempt was unsuccessful?"

I saw where she was going with this, and I wouldn't let her lead me there. "It doesn't matter. All that matters is that two fae are fighting and somehow my friend got stuck in the middle of it. The only way I can see to get Alistair back involves teaming up with this rival fae, but that just puts me right back where I started. I don't want to be allied with any of these people."

"You don't have to be allied with them to use them," the Origin said.

"Oh, that's quite the noble motive coming from the Dragon Fae."

"You still don't get it. The Dragon Fae leads. You use what you need, and you lead."

"Maybe I could if you would leave me alone and let me think. All I need is silence."

Wind whispered in the uppermost branches of the trees. It was always just the wind here, never animals or insects, just that swishing breeze and the rustling of leaves.

My brain had felt so frazzled before I came here, but now it sat calm, giving me the space I needed to work through all the information I'd taken in. I knew the answer I sought was there. I just had to find it.

"This is not where you find answers."

Maybe if I ignored her, she would go away.

"Hard to ignore someone who can read your thoughts."

I refused to engage. Malev, Meilin, the Circle, an assassination attempt, a rival, his court, the wilderness outside of Bismo. Then there was Dorran. His meeting with Lars. It all fit together, and somewhere was the key to freeing Alistair.

"You won't find it here. You can only find it among your people."

When I returned from the nether, I needed to get Deacon, Sybil, and Pint out of there. We still had a few hours before the would-be assassin missed his check-in time. Once Meilin realized that her plan failed, she'd come looking for us. I had to get us away, to safety. We couldn't bring anything that might be traced back to us.

I had some money stashed away under another identity, money that even Alistair didn't know about. He'd prepared me for the possibility of the endgame. I wondered if other handlers taught their agents the same way he did me. It wasn't something we spoke about often, but he had trained me for the day when I'd have to run even from the Circle. I'd never fully expected that day would come.

"So that's your plan? Run?"

"My plan is to keep my people safe while we figure out how to get Alistair."

"And yet you still haven't done the one thing that will keep you the safest: bond with Deacon."

"He doesn't want to bond with me!" I shouted. "I can't force him. So chalk that up with every other disappointment you have in me. Can you blame him? I'm a mess. So if you want to be helpful, try suggesting something that is actually within the realm of possibility. Better yet, leave me alone."

Wind whipped around me. The breeze that had whispered in the branches now roared. I didn't care. At least her voice was silent. At least the ache in my head was gone. I breathed deep and choked.

"That's right, because this isn't air. This is the nether. Don't come back if you're not going to take my advice."

The wind whirled around me, faster and faster. All the while, I couldn't breathe. I clawed at my throat, willing my lungs to take in air. It was no use. As before, the strands of life pulled me back to the temporal realm and ripped at my mind, shredding it, leaving bits of it scattered across the nether.

Then it stopped. I lay gasping on the ground in the temple. I scrambled to sit up, leaning my back against the pillar that held the dragon eye.

Each gulp of breath I took didn't seem to be enough. The same priestess who'd attended me the last few times I'd come stood by with a cup of water. Once I had my breathing under some semblance of control, I took the cup and downed it.

"Thank you."

"It's what I'm here for."

I looked up into the young woman's face. Her long ears, tall and slender frame, and white skin marked her as a moon elf. The moon elves spent their days deep in caves underneath the ground until they came out at night. This one must've broken from her people to study at the temple. Because of that, her skin didn't have the blue hue that most moon elves' did. The lack of sun caused their skin to become almost translucent.

I bet she didn't know when she left her people to come here that she would end up serving water to a nether addicted woman. Just like when Alistair pulled me out of school he didn't think I'd become this mess.

My plan to figure things out in the nether had backfired spectacularly. I felt certain it would've worked had the Origin just left me alone long enough.

Already my headache and nausea were making it nearly impossible to think. If the Origin hadn't talked to me, I probably would've just lost myself in the peace and stayed there forever. What a waste that would be.

No, absence of pain wasn't the purpose. Rather, the pain gave way to purpose. Instead of trying to rid myself of it, I needed to let the pain sharpen my senses. Peace wasn't an option for me.

37

*D*eacon waited for me on Sybil's bed. He stood when I entered. I'd expected him. He likely hadn't left since he saw me leave through the portal.

I felt a mess and probably looked it.

"Are you all right?" Deacon asked.

"No, I'm not." I didn't know what I was, but I knew I wasn't all right.

"What did the Origin say?"

I waved my hand. "Nothing. All she does is nag me to bond with you. I'd hoped for some quiet to think things through, but she wouldn't leave me alone."

I could tell that Deacon wanted to talk more, but we didn't have time. I walked to the living room where Sybil and Pint sat.

"Good, you're both here. We all need to leave." I announced it in the same weary way I might announce that I was going to bed.

"What are you talking about?" Sybil asked.

Didn't they realize the Circle had sent an assassin to kill me? It was only a matter of time before another one came. "We're not safe. I spoke with Gordon—"

"Since when do we trust Gordon?" Pint asked.

I thought back to what he'd shared about his time with Alistair. I believed him.

"Since this last phone call. I don't know if he's on my side, but I do know he's on Alistair's, and that means helping me. Besides, what reason would he have to lie? He said that I need to go underground once Meilin realizes that I'm still alive and her assassin is dead. He doesn't know what she's going to do, but it's entirely possible that she'll come after me. I can't see what benefit there could be to feeding me this information if it's false. It's not like going underground is going to keep me from completing my mission. Gordon knows that. Anyone who's worked for the Circle any amount of time knows that. Scrapping identities, taking on aliases, this is what we do. If anything, I've been lucky to stay here as long as I have."

"Wait a minute," Pint said. "Are you talking about making a permanent move? What about Harry?"

"Right now, I'm not thinking far ahead. I hope it's only temporary, but I don't know." Pint did have a point about Harry. I didn't have a good answer for that.

"If Meilin were to send someone, she'd only send them after you. I don't think she would make a move against me," Sybil said. "Why don't you let me stay here and keep an eye on Harry?"

The look on her face wasn't one of concern for Harry. She had the look of a person approaching a spooked animal. Did she think I was being paranoid? I probably looked like I was.

"If Meilin is willing to make a move against the Dragon Fae, she is willing to make one against the Oracle. We should all go to a hotel somewhere."

"And Harry?" Pint asked again.

He was right. I couldn't leave Harry behind. Normally it wouldn't be a problem, but with Freddie here, it was a dangerous situation. Not only was Freddie a threat, but his presence might alert others who came looking for me that Harry was a weak spot.

"There's no reason for me to go," Pint said. "I'm not on anyone's radar. Besides, they'd have a hard time finding me. I can hide, and I don't even have to stay in the apartment. If I stay, I can keep an eye on Harry and let you know if anything happens."

"And I can stay here and watch over Pint," Sybil said. "We want to know if Meilin sends someone. I promise, at the first sign of trouble, I'll teleport away with Pint. He can stay here when he's not watching Harry."

I couldn't find any fault with her plan. If someone came looking for me, they wouldn't immediately think to attack Sybil or Pint even if they knew of their existence. They'd try for me first, and only after failing would they turn their sights on Sybil. She'd have plenty of time to get away. Plus her security charms were good.

"All right, stay, but you have to be vigilant. Increase your security, and get out of here at the first sign of trouble. I don't think the Circle will hurt Harry. If we want to save him, we have to first be safe ourselves."

"I promise, we'll be vigilant," Sybil said. "Where are you going to go?"

"I have some money and another identity stashed away. We're going to go to a hotel."

Before Deacon could say anything, I turned and pointed at him. "You are nonnegotiable. You're coming with me. Targeting you is as good as targeting me, and whoever comes will know that, especially given all the Dragon Fae mythology."

The thought of something happening to Deacon hurt so bad that I couldn't even let myself consider letting him stay. I wasn't one for pulling rank, but if he argued with me, I would in an instant. The experiences we had shared, the anointing, made the thought of him dying as unbearable as the thought of my magic being ripped from my body. I couldn't go there.

Deacon came to me and rubbed a soothing hand on my back. "It's all right. Of course I'll come with you. Where else would I be? I'm your companion. Where you go, I go."

I felt a strong sense of relief. Just knowing that he would do this for me lifted some of my worry.

"Okay, good. Thank you. I need to run a quick errand. Pack some things, and if you get a chance, get some stuff from my apartment for me too. When I get back, we'll go check into a hotel."

Deacon's brow furrowed. "Where do you have to go?"

"I need to get my new identity." Without another word, I left.

◊

I didn't take anything with me that could be tracked, just my burner phone that, as far as I knew, was still clean. It wasn't until I was halfway to Trevor's that I considered the possibility that my car was being tracked. It would make sense. There was no reason to think the Circle didn't know about it. All it would take was a simple GPS device. It could be hidden anywhere in the vehicle. I had no way to know, and I didn't have the time to search for it.

I couldn't risk bringing an assassin to Trevor's door, so I parked one neighborhood over from Trevor's and walked the rest of the way. I kept my go-bag at his house. After I grabbed it, I would swap my car for a rental and head back to get Deacon.

Trevor greeted me with the same warmth as always. "How's it going? Did you ever identify the mystery man?"

I really wished that someday we would get back to hanging out, talking about something other than work. I wondered what this friendship looked like from Trevor's point of view. He liked the work we did. Maybe it didn't seem so messy and frantic to him. "Yeah, I got an ID on him. I'm hoping to make contact soon."

"That's great. Any news on your handler?"

My mind flashed to the picture of the baker's box with the hand inside. I couldn't tell Trevor that. For someone who regularly assisted an assassin, he was remarkably sheltered. Something like that would turn his stomach. He liked our work to be only slightly more real than the video games he played.

"I haven't found a way to rescue him yet, but I'm getting close. I won't stop until he's free."

"I wouldn't expect anything less. You can do it. You've never failed yet." Trevor's encouraging smile lifted my spirits more than I thought it would. "So what brings you here?"

"I need my go-bag."

The happiness in Trevor's eyes dimmed. "So things can't be going that good."

I went to one of his cabinets and opened it. I moved all the knick-knacks aside and took out the false back. Inside sat my go-bag. I grabbed it and put everything back the way I'd found it. "This is just an extra precaution. Don't worry about me."

"So is this goodbye?" Trevor asked. The naked vulnerability in his voice hurt my heart.

I remembered the day I'd hidden this bag here. It had been pretty early on. At the time, I'd expected my relationship with Trevor to be strictly professional, the same as I'd had in Elustria with Circle analysts. But in Trevor I'd found not only a capable colleague but something of a kid brother. When I'd hidden this bag here, it had been with the understanding that it was for a permanent escape.

"I really think this is going to be temporary. I might not even end up using it."

I put the bag on Trevor's workbench and unzipped it. Inside was a passport, driver's license, and a few debit and credit cards tied to accounts that had a long history. There was also twenty thousand dollars in cash and some clothes. Everything I needed to start a new life somewhere.

But this wasn't for an escape. It was to hide for a little while. Once I got Alistair back, we'd come up with a better plan together. I zipped it back up and slung it over my shoulder.

"Is there anything else I can do? How do I know if I'm going to see you again?" Trevor asked.

I put my hands on his shoulders and stared into his eyes. "I promise, you're going to see me again. You're not getting rid of me this easily. If I go, who's going to kick your ass at first-person shooters?"

Trevor nodded, but he didn't say anything. I pulled him into a hug.

"I'll see you soon," I whispered into his ear. Then I left without looking back.

When I got to my car, a little bird hopped from foot to foot on the roof. I opened the door, and it hopped faster. Looking closer, I saw that the bird had something in its beak.

Once I gave it my attention, it stopped moving, looked me right in the eye, and dropped a piece of paper at its feet. I picked it up, and the bird flew off. I unwrapped the note.

Meet me at Bubbles and Brews for breakfast at eight o'clock. No glamour.
    Dorran

38

When I pulled back into the apartment complex, it was in a crappy rental, a nice modest compact car that wouldn't draw attention. My Corvette was parked at a strip mall.

Passing by Harry's apartment on the way to Sybil's, I smelled Freddie's stench. I hated how it had permeated our lives. It was always there in the background, like the rotting trash you had to walk by to get to your car. I couldn't wait until he was gone. I didn't know how long that might be.

If it came down to it, I might have to kill him. At some point among all of this I needed to find out where Harry's nephew was, the real Freddie. If he was already dead, there was nothing stopping me from taking care of this problem. If he was alive, I owed it to Harry to do everything I could to keep him that way.

One problem at a time though.

Deacon opened the door before I could knock. I couldn't wait to share Dorran's note. It was the first bit of good news we'd had, but I didn't want Sybil and Pint knowing. They needed to focus on the here and now.

"Are you ready to go?" I asked as I walked inside. I didn't want to drag this out. Time wasn't on our side, and I didn't want a scene.

Sybil and Pint were quite emotional under the best of circumstances. After what I'd just done with Trevor, I didn't relish goodbyes.

Deacon grabbed a bag from the dining room table. "Yep."

Sybil bounded over and gave me one of her big, exuberant hugs.

"Remember, only use the burner phones," I told her. "Don't let my cell phone leave the apartment. If Gordon calls, let me know. If anyone you don't know comes by, call me. If anyone with the slightest bit of magic comes, I don't care if it's a latent mage, you call me. You got it?"

Sybil stepped back from the hug and nodded. "Don't worry about us."

"At the first hint of danger, you port yourself and Pint out of here." I looked behind her through the apartment and noticed Pint was missing. It didn't surprise me. He never said goodbye before any of my missions. This would be no different. "Okay, we're off."

I lead Deacon down to the rental. He laughed as he got inside.

"What's so funny?" I asked as I started the car and pulled out of the parking space.

"This car. It's got to be killing you."

I let out a little chuckle. "It is. I just can't risk that they're tracking my Corvette. There's no way I'll enjoy driving this, but it'll get us where we need to go."

"And you're sure about this?" Deacon asked.

I looked over at him and then back to the road. I could tell he was worried about me, but he had the decency not to show the extent of his concern on his face.

I was a mess from the nether, and I knew it. My entire body felt shaky. I gripped the steering wheel harder just to assure myself that my hands were steady.

Every bit of light and sound hurt my head. If I had anything in my stomach, I'd throw it up just to try to feel better. I didn't think I'd eaten since breakfast. Everything was such a blur. We'd have to grab something at the hotel.

"I know how this looks, but I trust Gordon. I didn't expect to, but everything he said made sense."

Deacon spoke cautiously. "Are you sure you can trust your instincts with him? It's no secret that you're not your sharpest right now."

I didn't take offense. This was part of the job. I relied on him to call me out, find any weaknesses in my thinking.

"It's not just my gut I'm going off of, though my gut feels pretty sure. Like I said, there's really not much upside to lying, to driving me down this path. If he'd tried to convince me that the danger was in my head and I should hunker down and stay safe at home, then I'd mistrust him. He told me to go underground. He knows what that means. He knows as soon as I do, no one will be able to find me unless I want them to. It's not like he's trying to get me out of the way for something. No one at the Circle is stupid enough to think that anything can make me give up my mission to get Alistair back."

"All right then," Deacon said as he relaxed back into his seat.

"Oh, and I forgot the best part. I didn't want to say anything in front of Sybil because I just wanted to get out of there, but Dorran made contact."

Deacon sat up and looked at me. "Really? That's good. What did he say?"

"He had a bird deliver a message. He wants to meet at Bubbles and Brews tomorrow morning for breakfast."

When Deacon sat back in his seat, a genuine smile filled his face. "Okay, this is good. We'll go to the hotel, get a good night's sleep, then tomorrow things will finally start coming together."

I loved this part of having a partner, the part where we shared the tiny victories, the little steps that we took down the path to completing our mission. Dorran's note had given me hope, and that hope was amplified through Deacon.

Even if we didn't get anything useful from the meeting, it was progress. It was forward momentum. At this point, that's all we could hope for.

39

At the hotel, Deacon insisted that we share a room. I insisted that it had two queen beds. If side-by-side rooms wasn't enough for him, then side-by-side beds would have to be. In his words, there was no point in going into hiding if we weren't going together.

We ordered one of everything from room service and had a picnic on his bed. I sat with my back against the headboard, and he took the foot of the mattress. Eating actually helped the nausea a little, and the rise in my blood sugar cleared my mind a bit.

Once I'd eaten my fill, the true purpose of the meal revealed itself.

"So what is all this with the nether?" Deacon asked with too much nonchalance. He really did make a crappy spy. I could imagine Sybil told him the best way to avoid an argument when talking about something difficult was to prime the pump with food. I wanted to resent being played like this, but the meal was too good.

"Like I told you, it's nothing. I had hoped to get some clarity there, but the Origin wouldn't leave me alone. She told me not to come back if I'm not going to do what she tells me to."

"What did she tell you to do?"

"Bond with you." I kept my eyes trained on him to make sure I didn't miss the discomfort that washed over his face. "Don't worry, I told her it's not happening."

That only intensified Deacon's discomfort. I decided to face it head-on. "I'm with you on this. Though, there's something I don't understand."

"What's that?" Deacon asked.

"It seemed when I first met you that you were all in with this Dragon Fae business."

"I am." Deacon nodded. "I've always been all in." The warm sincerity in his eyes made my heart flutter. I looked away. I couldn't say what I needed to when he looked at me that way.

"What I mean is, you seemed sure that we were supposed to bond like the prophecy says. Then, after spending time with me, something changed. You didn't just waver at the idea of bonding. You're adamant that we not. Then you look at me the way you just were, and I don't understand it. What about me makes the idea of bonding so abhorrent?" I faced him again. I needed to see in his eyes what his words wouldn't tell me.

"That's not it at all." His face was stricken, as if I'd just taken something precious from him.

"Then what is it? I don't understand."

"It's just that I didn't expect things to go this way."

"And you think I did? I'm the one who was blindsided. You came here knowing that you were to be the Dragon Companion. You've been preparing for this for years. I had no idea until what? Not even two weeks ago? What is it that's changed? The only thing I can think of is that back when you agreed to this, you didn't know me."

"That's it exactly," Deacon said.

I used every shred of self-control I had to keep the hurt from my face. "Oh."

Deacon stood from the bed and pulled me up as well. He took me by the hand and sat against the headboard of the other bed. He pulled me down to sit next to him, wrapping his arm around my shoulders and tucking me in close to his chest.

"It's not that the idea of bonding with you is abhorrent. It's nothing of the kind. It's just that, before, I was prepared to bond with the Dragon Fae. It was my role, my duty, and I was prepared to fulfill it. It would be one more dutiful step in a long line of them. My life has been defined by the acts of duty I've undertaken. I was prepared to bond with you the day I met you."

"And then you got to know me."

Deacon placed a finger over my lips, shushing me. I looked up into his face, and the most pure expression of love looked down on me. My heart swelled, like golden sunlight filled it.

"I got to know you, and I realized I didn't want to bond with you out of duty anymore."

How could he look at me like that while rejecting me?

"I realized I wanted to bond with you for me. For us, not for the prophecy. When I realized that, the idea of bonding with you out of duty did become abhorrent. When we bond, and I hope we do some-day, I want it to be because you want to. The way I feel now, knowing that it's different for me than it is for you, it seems like it would be dishonorable to bond with you under false pretenses. You'd be doing it for duty, and I'd be doing it because I want you. It didn't seem fair to you."

My heart melted. I wanted what he offered. I wanted to let him love me. I already knew that, despite my best efforts, I loved him. But my heart was already getting too crowded. There was Alistair, Pint, Harry, and now Sybil and Deacon. They'd all found their way in past my defenses. They'd all laid claim to parts of my heart.

The part Deacon had claimed was the most tender, the part that would hurt the most if something should happen to its claimant. My heart already sat bruised where Alistair should be. He rotted all alone in a fae prison, without a hand, not knowing if he'd ever get out. And that was because of me. Because he'd gotten close.

I didn't fully believe in the Dragon Fae prophecy. I'd made no secret of that. But I had known that I would die young and alone, whether it was as the Dragon Fae or as a Circle assassin. That fate was sealed. As much love and affection looked down at me from Deacon's face right now, my death would cause an equal measure of devastation to him. Why bond to him, why get closer, when I was destined to hurt him so completely?

I was a coward, of that I was sure. I'd asked him his reasons, and he'd given me an honest answer. Yet, he didn't ask me my own reasoning. I thanked him silently for that. I knew it was another token of his love. But how did I explain to someone who was so important to me that I wouldn't get closer to him because I was scared? Because everyone who'd ever gotten close to me had ended up hurt?

My mind flashed to the picture of Julien's face when he'd found out about my betrayal. I knew Deacon didn't have the same issues Julien did. My work wouldn't interfere with our relationship the same way. I knew that. I didn't need to be convinced. But that didn't mean he would come out of this relationship unscathed.

The absolute best-case scenario was that we were deliriously happy for a little while until I died, and he'd be left to mourn me. He wouldn't be able to make another bond. Dragon shifters bonded for life. Me agreeing to be with him was dooming him to a lifetime of loneliness. I couldn't do that to him.

"Don't worry." Deacon tucked a strand of hair behind my ear. "I don't need you to say anything. I don't need you to do anything. I just needed to set the record straight. Now that you know the truth, I'll go get in the other bed and go to sleep. Tomorrow, we'll get back to work."

He got up from the bed, and I missed his warmth. I couldn't bear to look at him, to watch his perfectly sculpted body move about the room, clearing the dishes from the bed, knowing that if I let him, he'd spend the rest of my life loving me. I may be strong, but I wasn't that strong.

I got under the sheet and closed my eyes. A few minutes later, the light switched off, and for the first time since Alistair had disappeared, I slept in peace.

40

It felt strange to come to the enclave without glamour, especially now that the threat against me was more real, but we'd weighed out the risk and decided it was minimal. The Circle generally didn't bother much with the enclaves. We'd checked in with Sybil this morning and there had been no unexpected visitors and no calls to my phone. If the Circle wasn't hunting me at my home, they wouldn't be hunting me at the enclave.

We pulled into the parking lot of Bubbles and Brews at five minutes to eight. The morning had been remarkably comfortable. It took me a while to figure out why there wasn't any awkwardness between us. It was because nothing had changed. Deacon had always felt this way. He'd been living with this knowledge this whole time, so of course he was the same way around me as he always had been. That realization itself winded me.

Today we were all business. Part of what I loved about Deacon was that he knew our personal life could wait until our job was done. I didn't need to make time in my schedule for emotional labor with him. The work came first because the work involved innocent lives. This wasn't a desk job or some soulless pursuit of money. It was a mission in every sense of the word. When the mission was complete, we'd have time for our personal lives. They seemed so insignificant in the grand scheme of things.

As was often the case, having a large dinner only made me that much more ravenous in the morning. I looked forward to this meeting because if nothing else I would get a good meal out of it.

From Dorran's reputation, he didn't seem like the talkative type, but I did expect to get something of value. He wouldn't go to the trouble of contacting me if he didn't have a reason. I admitted to some curiosity about what such an ancient person would take the time to say to me. It was an added bonus that this conversation would take place against the backdrop of a delicious meal.

Bubbles and Brews wasn't too busy. We slid into a booth in the back that gave us a clear view of the door. Deacon and I sat side-by-side, leaving the space across from us for Dorran. For some reason, I'd expected him to already be here. His note had said eight o'clock, and in my world, that meant five till eight.

It might be proper etiquette to wait for him and order a small meal that allowed for easy conversation, but my stomach rumbled, and I didn't much care about etiquette. Deacon ordered a boring steak and eggs combo that only differed from the human variety in that the meat and eggs came from Elustrian animals.

I usually just had a cup of coffee. I rarely indulged, not liking a heavy breakfast weighing me down, but today, I didn't care. I wanted lots and lots of glorious carbs.

I ordered deep-fried French toast with an Elustrian berry medley and a stack of bacon. The bacon was made using pigs from Earth—nothing in Elustria really compared when it came to bacon—but the folks at Bubbles and Brews advertised that their pigs were enchanted to produce healthier bacon. I called bullshit, but I happily bought into the lie today.

Just after we placed our orders, the door opened. In walked a man wearing a long brown robe with a cowl over his head. He carried a tall staff with a gem in the top.

Dorran.

I checked the time. It was eight o'clock on the dot.

He walked right to us and slid into the booth.

"You should get out of the habit of being early to places." His voice was stronger than I'd expected from someone who appeared so old. "It's a terrible waste of time being early. It may not seem like a lot now, but five minutes early to every meeting over hundreds of years really adds up."

This was already the most interesting meeting I'd had in a long time. I didn't bother introducing us. It seemed superfluous. "We've ordered, in case you want something."

"Oh, they know me here."

That seemed to be the general consensus. People just knew Dorran. "It seems a lot of people know you. The Dragon Prince has met you. Why haven't I until now?"

I couldn't get a clear look at Dorran's face. His cowl was pulled too far forward. His dark brown skin faded into shadow, only standing out with its deep creases and wrinkles. His dark gray beard defied the odds. I would have expected it to be snowy white.

"We've always been on the same side. You fight to protect Earth and keep the Directorate from soiling this world the way they have Elustria. Up until now, there's been no need for me to see you."

"So what's change that you want to speak to me now?"

"That's a rather ignorant question coming from the Dragon Fae."

"Come now, Dorran. You're too old to believe in fairytales. You know what I am. You know who I work for." The truth was he knew far more about me than I did him, as was proved by how easily he found me.

"Good, good. It's good that you don't believe it all. As the humans say, don't believe your own press."

Between the long brown cloak and the mystical walking staff, he didn't seem like the type of person who would be talking about human PR.

Our food came out along with a bowl of soup for Dorran. I didn't recognize it from the menu.

"Deacon, you're awfully quiet," Dorran said between mouthfuls of soup.

I dug into my food, the warm carbs having the desired effect. It was nice to see Deacon in the hot seat for a change.

"Don't have much to say. Don't see the point in speaking otherwise," he said then took a bite of steak.

"I like you. I know people gravitate to the talkative ones, looking for a bit of entertainment, but trust me, that gets old. Nothing like the companionship of someone you can sit in silence with," Dorran said.

My mind went to last night, and I smothered the butterflies in my stomach with more carbs. I didn't like how much Dorran seemed to know us.

"How is it you were so easily able to find me? Was that message a threat? Letting me know that I can't hide?"

No one outside of the Circle and the fae court had come anywhere close to me in all my time on Earth, yet he'd found me in the most obscure of places. To be able to deliver a note to my car in a location where it had never been before meant he always knew where I was.

Dorran took a sip of soup and waved his hand. "No, no. I understand your concern, but don't worry. No one else could find you like I can. I don't even know where you were when you got my note. The bird didn't tell me, and I'm not inclined to ask."

"So all it takes for someone to find me is asking a bird to give me a message?" This was the opposite of comforting.

"You misunderstand. I've been here a long time now. The earth trusts me. I've built relationships and put in my time. While the birds themselves might not be old, I have known them for generations. The trees they fly in have been around for hundreds of years, and I know each of them. Earth is one giant network of interconnected life, and I am intimately familiar with it all."

All right, I was satisfied that no one else would be able to find me using the Bambi network. "So what is it you wanted to tell me? You didn't track me down just for some company over breakfast."

"You're right. I reached out to you because I wanted to show you this." Dorran waved for the shade we had spoken with last time to come to our table. He wouldn't recognize us. This was the first time we'd come to the enclave without glamour.

The shade came to our table with solemn respect. He bowed to Dorran then turned to us. He went to one knee and whispered, "Fealty to the Dragon Fae."

As he said the words, he looked up at me. His eyes flashed green and green scales momentarily appeared on his neck. Dragon scales. He stood, gave another bow, and went back to work.

"Okay." My mouth hung open for a beat, then I turned to Dorran. "That has got to stop happening. We're not gods. I'm barely a fully functioning adult."

"I won't argue with you," Dorran said. "I will only say that being a fully functioning adult has never been a prerequisite to being a hero or a leader. Though it would help if you pulled yourself together."

"What was it that happened with his eyes and skin?" Deacon asked.

"That's what I wanted to show you. You have followers here. The Dragon Fae plays an important part in the story of Earth, so it's important to me. I've been traveling around finding those who are loyal to you. When they make the oath to me as proxy, they get that enchantment. It's a way for us to recognize each other. The people here have been waiting. They know a time will come when they'll be called upon. This enclave is entirely loyal. It's become something of a Mecca for your followers. They don't take kindly to strangers, so most who aren't loyal have chosen to leave of their own accord."

I remembered back to the first time I brought Deacon here. In the park they'd been assembled and seemed wary of us. It made sense now.

"But I only just became the Dragon Fae."

"I knew it was coming, so I prepared. There've always been those who believed in the Dragon Fae more strongly than others. It hasn't been difficult to find believers."

"And what exactly do you expect? You presented me with these followers, so what would you have me direct them to do?"

Dorran chuckled. "You are wiser than you look. I can understand why you would think that. It is the right thought. I have no desire other than that Earth remain peaceful. And if not that, then at least that her problems be caused by humans and humans alone. Elustrians don't have the right to infect this planet."

As tables got done eating, they came to us. They each bowed their heads and murmured under their breath, their eyes and neck flashing green. Then they left. The unearned deference made me uncomfortable.

Like a lightning bolt, it hit me. I knew what I'd been missing this whole time.

Dorran grinned. "Ah, yes, you figured it out. Good. If you weren't so strung out on the nether, you would have figured it out earlier, but as the humans say, better late than never."

"What?" Deacon looked at me for an explanation.

I didn't know how Dorran could tell what I was thinking. "What we were missing earlier. Goffrey isn't the rival fae."

"How do you know?" Deacon asked.

My mind was still piecing it all together. "The deference. The fae around him didn't show the proper amount of respect to him. Then there's the fact that he's a man. The fae have almost always had queens, not kings. Like Drake said, all the ancient races have are their traditions and rituals. There is no way that Goffrey is leading an entire rival court."

"Very good," Dorran said.

"You knew?" I asked.

"I know everything that concerns Earth. Now let's get going." Dorran stood with his staff. "I can't wait to see their faces."

"Go where?"

"To Norway, of course, for you to confront Goffrey."

I hadn't thought that far ahead. I didn't know if merely confronting him would get me a favorable result. But it seemed prudent to follow Dorran. "You want to come?"

"Naturally," Dorran scoffed. "This is the most fun I've had in a long while."

41

Dorran took us right outside the entrance to the court in Norway. I saw the body of the assassin still lying on the ground. I wondered if the Circle didn't know yet that he was dead. It seemed a little long for him not to have checked in. Perhaps they had chosen to leave his body behind. I didn't know, and I didn't much care. As long as we were safe.

Dorran knocked on the rock face with his staff, and the gem glowed. It allowed us entrance, but this time we didn't go to the dark antechamber. Instead, we stood outside an ornate door. The hall we occupied was lit by large chandeliers. If I had to bet, I'd say the door led to the throne room.

Two fae stood guard outside the door. They didn't seem too perturbed at our entrance. Given the security and toll coin system, they likely expected that anyone who showed up was wanted.

To think Goffrey was just a decoy. No wonder he didn't look particularly concerned about his safety. He hadn't taken on this role to be safe. His job was to die if need be to protect the true rival.

Whoever the true rival was, it had to be someone important, someone they thought had a real chance to depose Malev. Otherwise, they wouldn't have gone to such lengths to protect her identity, and I felt sure now that it was a woman.

Even the toll coins had Goffrey's crest on them. Given the difficulty of learning what was on the toll coins, we had wrongly assumed that the magic around the coins was the security. The coins acted not just as tokens of safe entrance to trusted members of the court, they also acted as decoys themselves.

It was a brilliant plan, but I was embarrassed that I hadn't figured it out sooner. As Dorran said, if I hadn't been so strung out on the nether, I would have.

The nether. It still called to me. Even knowing how destructive it had become in my life, I wanted to be there now.

The door opened just wide enough to allow one person to exit the throne room. Goffrey appeared, and the door shut behind him before we could get a peek inside.

"You're back," Goffrey said to me, completely ignoring Dorran.

"Yes, I am. You said to come back today, and I'm here." I didn't know if it actually was the next day in Norway with the time difference. "Do you have an answer for me? Or was that just bullshit?"

That was the other thing that hadn't sat well with me. If Goffrey were the leader, he wouldn't need to think over whether to help me or not. He'd have a decision. He'd only put me off a day in order to speak with the real leader and come up with the next play.

"Has the actual leader of the rival court told you what answer to give me yet?" I asked.

Goffrey smiled good-naturedly. "What makes you think I'm not the real leader?"

"Chalk it up to you just not being regal enough, Goffrey. No one around you seems to notice or care that you're their esteemed leader, the one they're risking their lives for by setting up this rival court. You expect me to believe that you're standing against a fae so powerful that most don't even speak her name and yet no one around you shows basic respect and deference?"

"Part of the reason we are revolting against Malev is to break free from such stifling restrictions. We seek a more harmonious and equitable existence."

"Quit with the horseshit, Goffrey," Dorran said. "You're just butt sore that she figured you out. You're not quite the actor you think you are."

"You have no authority here," Goffrey said. I had to hand it to him, that was a pretty ballsy move, one I didn't think I'd make. The fae were arrogant—long life and power did that to them—but none of them were as long-lived as Dorran.

A stalagmite jutted out of the stone wall and shot as fast as an arrow across the hall, snagging Goffrey's shirt and pinning him to the opposite wall.

"Is that enough authority for you?" Dorran asked.

Sweat broke out on Goffrey's brow, and the color drained from his face. He pushed against the stalagmite without success. He even tried his magic against it. Hubris.

"Fine. Release me, and I'll take you in to see her. You all can be her problem. I agreed to lay down my life for her, not put up with this shit."

"Good boy," Dorran said, and the stalagmite retreated back into the wall.

Goffrey straightened his shirt and went back into the throne room, closing the door behind him.

"Why don't you shift?" Dorran asked Deacon.

The hall was big enough for it, as was the door leading to the throne room. I looked at Deacon. "Yes, why don't you?"

A smile spread across his face. It was rare that he had the chance to shift, and I would love to see him again. His dragon had a majesty that would fit in well with our surroundings. We'd make quite an entrance.

When he shifted, it was a tight fit. He couldn't spread his wings fully, but he could stretch them a little. It was better than nothing. He shook his head and I saw just how sharp and lethal his horns could be. I wanted to climb onto his back and go flying, but we had work to do. Plus, I didn't know how to get out of here.

"Impressive," Dorran said with admiration. It meant a lot coming from him. Seeing a dragon wouldn't be a novel experience for someone his age. "Much better fit for the Dragon Fae than Drake ever was."

I put my hand on Deacon's chest and stroked above his scar. "Agreed."

Goffrey emerged from the throne room. "She'll see you now."

The doors flung open, and the three of us walked down a blue carpet into the chamber. Once over the threshold, I saw a woman sitting on a throne at the far end of the room.

"You!"

42

From the moment I saw her, I knew she was familiar, but it took a second to place her. I'd seen her in the fae court. She'd stood right there with Malev, her right-hand woman.

"Yes, it's me. I'm surprised you recognize me. I didn't think you would." She stood from her throne, walked down the steps from her dais, and approached our party.

"I welcome the Dragon Fae and the Dragon Companion to my court." Then she sank into a deep curtsy and bowed her head.

Her throne room wasn't as full as Malev's, but there were still a few dozen people there, and they all saw her bow to me. I didn't think for one second that she did it for my benefit. There was something in this for her.

"Why don't we go somewhere private to speak?" She led the way to a small reception room. If she didn't want her court to see her bow, she wouldn't have done it. I didn't like being used in this political game.

Deacon shifted when we got to the room. The doorway was too small for him as a dragon. The reception room was decorated in pink and gold, down to the pink shag carpet. The furniture looked like it came out of Versailles. It was the only place I'd seen in this court that didn't look like a cave. Bubbly drinks were laid out on a table.

"Please, help yourselves," she offered as she grabbed one and sat on a pale pink chair trimmed in gold.

Not only were we full from breakfast, but neither Deacon nor I had a death wish, so the drinks remained untouched. We sat with Dorran across from her.

"Suit yourself. I don't blame you for not trusting me. First things first, allow me to introduce myself. My name is Cassalina Snowfort."

The name didn't mean anything to me. Sybil might recognize it. "You're close to Malev. I saw you at her court."

"Yes, I am high ranking in the court. My position at Malev's side doesn't allow me to get away as much as I'd like. I'm here today because Goffrey brought me your offer, and I knew I would have to address it in person. The fact that I'm here should tell you how important this meeting is to me."

"But you didn't even know we would come," Deacon said.

"You're right, I didn't know. But I thought it was important enough that I be here just in case, and since I traveled all this way, I figured I might as well take care of some other business. Like I said, it's not often that I can leave Malev's court. When I do, I aim to get as much done as I can."

I sat in awe of this woman. She seemed competent, and she had the nerve to stand side-by-side every day with the woman she was betraying.

"And what exactly is it you're doing here?" I asked her.

I didn't need to elaborate. She understood my meaning. "I have a legitimate claim to the fae throne. That's why Malev keeps me close. She thinks by doing so she neutralizes the threat I pose. For more than a hundred years I have played the part of friend and confidant, waiting for my moment."

"And yet you bowed to me."

"You're the Dragon Fae. Bowing to you gives me more power with the people. Besides, you won't be around for long. My ego is not so shortsighted as to stand against you."

She would outlive me by hundreds of years, and she knew it. Better to play me and get what she could. The Dragon Fae's popularity with the people outlasted her own lifetime. I wouldn't live to reap the rewards of the work I did, so Cassalina made sure she was in a position to reap what I could not.

I outlined my position. "If you want to align with me, you're going to have to give me something in return. I won't let you trade on the myth of the Dragon Fae without getting what I need."

"Yes. Your friend. I can tell you that he is being treated well." She sat back and took a drink of her bubbly pink beverage.

"I wouldn't call losing a hand 'well.'" Hatred stirred in me for this woman. She'd stood by while Alistair was captured, used as a hostage, and tortured. She may be turning against Malev, but she was cut from the same cloth. I was sick of the fae, their deceit and their games. I hated that I had to play nice with this one.

"You're right. I meant besides that," Cassalina said. "He's not being starved or beaten or anything like that. She pretty much leaves him alone. Taking his hand was the only act of violence done against him since he was captured. I'm sorry it happened. I wish I could've done something, but I can't expose myself. Not yet. I won't waste all the work I've put in up to this point."

Yes, I was sure that were she not busy overthrowing her friend, she would've popped down to Alistair's cell and freed him.

"How long do we have until Malev decides to perform another act of violence against him?" I asked through gritted teeth. There was no sense pretending. I didn't need to put on an act.

"I'm not sure she will. She has another plan that she's working on should you fail to bring her Goffrey's head. She and Meilin are in talks to depose you since you're not serving either of them."

"Lovely. So they're both working against each other except when it comes to stopping me."

"The enemy of my enemy and all that," Cassalina said.

"I want you to get Alistair out for me."

Cassalina laughed, a high tinkling sound that would be cute if it weren't so annoying. "That's not possible. I won't stand in your way, and I'll do what I can to help you, but I can't get him for you. She keeps pretty good tabs on me. If I'm in the fae realm, she knows where I am. She'd stop me before I got to him. Then we'd all be in a worse off position than we are now."

"So what can you do? Or were you just hoping I'd figure this all out on my own and then you'd take credit for helping me?"

"No, I do have a gift for you, a symbol of my hope that we might have a fruitful partnership." She wiggled her fingers, and a scroll appeared. She handed it to me. "This is a description of the magic keeping Alistair imprisoned. I can distract Malev long enough for you to free him if you can figure out how to beat that security."

This was more than I'd hoped for, but I wouldn't let her know that.

"Other than the skill to get to him, you'll need a fae to transport you to the fae realm, or at least you need to find a way to mimic a fae, someone Malev doesn't pay much attention to. They need to have access to the court, so they must be high fae. However, she'll take notice of someone close to her. If it's someone she ignores, she won't notice where they're at. I can't help you with that. In fact, I must insist that you don't involve any members of my court."

"I can agree to that. How will I get word to you when we're ready to go?"

"You won't. I'll have one of my people monitoring the area around Alistair. When they notice that you're making your move, they'll let me know, and I'll keep Malev distracted. For your safety, it would be good for you to come in subtly. That way if she is in the area, I have time to get her away before she notices you're there."

"Understood. Thank you. This is helpful."

"What do I get in return?" Cassalina asked.

"You get my sincere thanks," I said with a smile.

"I need more than that."

"You're not getting more. You can have my thanks or you can be my enemy. Those are your options."

We both knew helping me had political upside for her. I gave her rebellion legitimacy simply by going against Malev myself. I didn't need to give her anything else, and I wasn't prepared to make any formal alliances.

"Then I guess I'll take it." She looked at the druid. "Dorran, it was nice seeing you again."

"And you, Cassalina. Nice to see the cycle of rebellion and betrayal is alive and well in the fae court."

Cassalina sneered at him. "You can leave now. I have much to do."

Dorran struck his staff on the floor and teleported the three of us back to the enclave.

43

The most important thing was figuring out how to get past all the enchantments and charms that were listed on the scroll. It wouldn't matter if we could get into the fae realm if we couldn't free Alistair once we were there.

Besides, we always had a last resort of having Sybil port us in. It would immediately alert Malev to our presence, and she'd probably overtake us before we could get to Alistair, but it was an option. Once we bypassed all of the security surrounding him, there wouldn't be anything preventing us from porting away. We just had to get to him.

Deacon and I sat with Dorran in the gazebo at the park. People bowed their heads to us as they passed, but they kept their distance. Dorran felt the enclave was one the safest places for us.

"Do any of these look familiar to you?" I asked Dorran. I didn't know if he had any familiarity with fae magic, but Deacon and I had nothing to go on.

He read through the list on the scroll and whistled. "Fae magic isn't my specialty. I personally don't care for the stuff. It uses and mimics nature, twisting it into dark purposes. It's an abomination to what I stand for. I don't know any specifics, but I can tell by looking at this that you're going to need blood magic to get past it."

Of course. I should've expected that. Malev wouldn't make it easy for anyone to help us rescue Alistair. Blood magic required sacrifice, a sacrifice that was too great to rescue someone you didn't know.

"Do you know if I have enough fae blood in me to do blood magic on myself?"

"Nadiya," Deacon said, his tone sharp. "You can't."

"We don't know that. If I can, I will."

Dorran shook his head. "I don't know how much fae blood you have, and I don't know how much it takes to do this kind of blood magic. Even if you did, I don't think you could be adept enough to make it work. Blood magic is a complicated business."

I looked at Deacon. "How much fae blood do I have?"

"What?" He plastered a dumb look on his face.

"Don't pull that with me. You're the best sniffer I've ever met. You can tell how much fae magic I have."

He sighed. "You don't have much. Hardly any at all. Just enough to qualify as the Dragon Fae."

I trusted he told me the truth. I didn't feel very fae. The Origin would know, but she'd made it clear she didn't want to talk to me again.

"So how do we find someone who can use blood magic to help us?" The type of person who could do what we needed wouldn't be a savory character. "What about the shade?" I asked Dorran. "You seemed to know him."

He looked over the list again and nodded. "He might be able to help. If he can't, I might know someone else. If you'll allow me to keep a copy of the scroll, I can see what we can come up with."

If I had to, I could ask Gordon to look into it, but that could be too risky. Sybil might know something that could help, but it wasn't likely. She wouldn't have ever learned blood magic. She spent her entire life working as the Oracle, studying the prophecy, preparing the way for the Dragon Fae. That didn't leave time to master high-level fae magic.

"Make a copy for us, and then you take the original." There might be something on the original that could help him and the shade.

Dorran duplicated the scroll and handed us the copy. "I'll go get started on it with him now. What's your next move?"

I looked at Deacon, and I knew he had the same thought I did. Deacon nodded, and I turned back to Dorran.

"Drake offered to ask some of the high fae he knew for help. I turned him down at the time, not thinking it was worth the risk. It wasn't then, but it is now. We know more about the situation. He might know someone who can get us inside."

"The Dragon Prince? That young pup is full of piss and vinegar. Good luck with him."

"Thanks. We've come to something of an understanding." Who knew how long this newfound peace with Drake would last.

"If you need me, leave word at Bubbles and Brews." He tapped his staff once and disappeared.

"So we're going to the Syndicate compound?" Deacon asked.

"Yes, I think it's our best option."

"I agree. I'm just wondering how we're going to get there. Should we take that stylish rental car or do you want to port?" Deacon asked with a grin.

"Ugh. That thing is horrible. The pain of teleporting us there with the cuff on is less than the pain of driving that car, but I don't want to bother with coming back for it." I walked in the direction of the Bubbles and Brews parking lot, and Deacon followed. "I guess I'll just have to see how fast I can push her."

Turned out compact cars could go faster than I thought.

44

In the courtyard of the Syndicate compound, two dragons sparred. They screeched and roared as they locked horns in the sky. Their talons slashed at their sensitive underbellies. As shifters, they'd be able to heal quickly, so there wasn't any real risk of permanent damage.

While the compound was large by human standards, it was relatively small for dragon shifters. I imagined spending so much time cooped up together required the opportunity to blow off some steam. Twenty or so bystanders stood in their human forms cheering, clapping, and whistling for their favorite.

Drake noticed our arrival and came to greet us. "And to what do I owe this pleasure?" He looked back up at the sky and clapped while he cheered one of the dragons.

"Shouldn't you stay neutral?" I asked.

"No. Kayla's been a handful these last few weeks, and we've all been waiting for Celia to put her in her place."

I assumed Celia was higher in the hierarchy. Dragon shifters lived by strict pack law.

"So what can I help you with?" Drake asked.

Deacon and I told him everything that had happened since we last spoke.

"You have to stay here. I won't take no for an answer," Drake said.

It never occurred to me when I left my apartment that I should stay at the Syndicate compound. "No, we're fine where we are."

"You're the Dragon Fae. You're not going to hide in some hotel under an alias. My honor cannot remain intact if I allow that as long as I've sworn fealty to you."

Wow, he was really laying it on thick with the whole macho chivalry thing.

"I agree with him," Deacon said.

That I did not expect. We had a tenuous peace with Drake, but I didn't think that meant Deacon would be comfortable in such close quarters with him. "Are you sure?"

"Yes," Deacon said. "This is the safest place for you. It's the responsibility of the dragons to protect you. We can't deprive them of that."

If he felt so strongly about it, why hadn't he brought it up last night? I thought back to his insistence that we share a room. Real smooth, Deacon. I couldn't blame him. I'd enjoyed the time alone as well.

"Fine, I won't argue with both of you."

Drake pressed his victory. "You should also bring the Oracle and your little dragon pet too. I can put one of my shifters on your neighbor. They'll be better at looking out for magic, and they can do more should a threat appear. I'll protect this Harry Harmon as if he were a member of my clan."

"Thank you." Drake's kindness did overwhelm me a little. It would be nice to have Pint safe with me. I worried about him getting into trouble by taking on an enemy should one appear. He wouldn't back down.

"As for the other thing," Drake said. "I have just the fae to ask to get you inside. A man by the name of Farawyn. He's a member of the court but completely devoid of ambition. He prioritizes the arts over magic and politics. But if all you need him for is to get inside the fae realm without anyone noticing, I'm pretty sure he's your man. He can also do any basic magic you might need."

"As long as you're certain it won't get back to Malev," I said. "If she gets wind of this, it's done before we even start."

"Like I said, he's not very political. I don't think he's particularly loyal to Malev, but he's one of the more involved high fae that we mate with. He comes and visits his brood, likes to play with them, takes an interest in their upbringing, a real standup guy. He wouldn't put them at risk for anything."

The picture of a fae playing with a baby dragon shifter was too adorable. I'd always known they mated with the dragon shifters, but I'd never thought of all that entailed.

"So you don't think he'd know much about blood magic?" I asked.

Drake laughed. "My guess is he'd blanch just at the mention of blood magic. For that, you'll need someone else. I'll send one of my shifters over to your place now to get Sybil. She can take a look at the scroll, see if there's anything she knows."

It felt like we were so close, yet we still didn't have anything concrete. Multiple things had to come together for this to work. And the worst part was there wasn't anything else I could do.

The words of the Origin flashed in my memory. She'd told me to rely on my community. She hadn't said how difficult it would be.

"In the meantime, you can get settled in." Drake called one of the women over. "This is Riya. She'll show you to the guest rooms."

The first time I walked through the door of Drake's home, I would have never guessed that I would one day return as a guest.

45

On the way to the guest rooms, my stomach growled, so Riya showed us the kitchen and dining room. Drake had a full-time chef, and Syndicate members fully staffed the kitchen.

After Deacon and I settled into our side-by-side rooms, we grabbed some lunch. Drake also had an extensive library, and after our meal, I fully intended to scour it for any information on blood magic. I needed at least a basic understanding of it if I was going to pull this off.

"Stop it," Deacon said as we finished our meal.

"What?" I asked. We had eaten in silence. Like Dorran said, nothing was better than comfortable companionship that didn't require words.

"You're thinking about doing something. I can tell. What you need to do is relax and prepare mentally for the mission ahead."

"I was thinking about going to the library and looking for books on blood magic. I could take one back to my room and do a little bit of light reading before bed tonight."

"Uh-huh." Deacon's tone was skeptical.

I didn't know how to explain to him that I had to keep myself occupied to distract from the headache and nausea from the nether.

A shifter appeared in the doorway and cut our conversation short. "Excuse me, but the infantas would like to see you, sir."

Deacon's head whipped up, and he stared at the man. Shock filled his eyes. "The infantas?"

"Yes, sir. They're in the upstairs living room," the shifter said.

Deacon stood. "I can find it, thank you."

The shifter bowed his head and left.

Deacon turned me. "Will you come with me? I'd really like you to meet them."

I stood, because of course I would go with Deacon anywhere. "Who are they?"

"My sisters." He paused, as if relishing the sound of the word in his mouth. "It's been ages since I've seen them. Part of my exile was to keep them safe. They always loved me, doted on me as a child. When our father died, I didn't want them suffering backlash from Drake. I hadn't expected to ever see them again."

I couldn't imagine what Deacon felt right now. "I'd be honored to meet them."

On our way upstairs, Deacon fidgeted. His eyes looked worried, like he didn't know what kind of reception he would get. I wondered if he asked me to come with him for moral support more than anything.

"I thought you would have seen them when you stayed here before."

Brief confusion crossed Deacon's face. "Oh, no, I wasn't staying here before. Not really. I camped just outside the compound. I didn't want to risk any conflict."

I supposed he'd spent most of his life camping in one form or another. Since the anointing, things had changed. Before, Drake had held out hope that he'd be the Dragon Companion. Now the time for conflict was done. Deacon still looked nervous, though he didn't have any reason to be.

"They're going to love you," I told him. How could they not? And if they didn't, I would shut the whole thing down.

Deacon nodded in acknowledgment of what I said, but he had a distracted look, like he hadn't fully processed it. We went upstairs and turned a corner down a hallway, and there was the living room.

A dozen women sat around talking. About half of them held babies or toddlers. When Deacon and I appeared, the first one to spot us squealed and jumped up.

"Deacon!" The first woman crashed into him with a hug. Then the rest followed suit, pushing me out of the way. One of the women even handed me her baby so she could join in the group hug.

It was the first time I'd ever held a baby. The little guy was cute and chubby, but I had no clue what to do with him. I did my best to imitate people on TV in the way I held him. He was a good sport about it, even blowing bubbles when I cooed at him. After that, I was out of ideas.

My discomfort must've shown on my face, because one of the other women noticed. "Let me take him from you. I'm Korine, by the way. How are you?"

"I'm fine, thank you. I'm Nadiya."

Korine laughed. "I know who you are."

The women were backing up from Deacon enough that I could see him again. He had misty eyes as he tried to make sure he hugged every woman present. The joy in the room overwhelmed me.

For these women, Deacon was the only brother they had aside from Drake. In order to ascend to the throne, Drake had killed his other brothers. Deacon had been spared only because he was a bastard and stayed out of court politics. He never made any claim of legitimacy, so he hadn't been a threat to Drake.

The women resumed their seats. Deacon sat between two of them on the sofa, and he looked happier than I'd ever seen him. It pained me to realize that he'd been forced to give up his family.

I sat in a chair across the room from him, and he caught my eye. "Everyone, I want you to meet Nadiya."

The women went around the room introducing themselves to me. I tried to give them each my attention, but I kept getting distracted by the sheer joy that radiated from Deacon. He drank in the sight of each of them. Given the way they treated him, I could imagine they spoiled him rotten when he was a kid. Especially if he'd been as cute as the babies I saw in the room.

"It's wonderful to meet you all," I said when they finished. I felt awkward, like an intruder in the moment. Luckily, they didn't seem to pay me much mind after the introductions.

"We were all so proud when we found out you were to be the Dragon Companion," Korine said.

"We were hurt that we weren't invited to your bonding ceremony," another sister, Jayla, said.

Deacon shifted uncomfortably. "We haven't bonded."

I could tell the admission embarrassed him, and I felt guilty about it. At least it didn't appear to be common knowledge.

"We would've invited you to the anointing had we known ahead of time that it was going to happen," I said as a peace offering and a diversion.

"Yes, from what we've gathered, the entire thing was quite rushed," Pauline, another sister, said.

"It was. Although we've known Deacon was to be my companion for quite some time. At least the Oracle did. I didn't know any of this until recently."

While I spoke, Deacon got the attention of one of the toddlers. He made funny faces until the child giggled. Then he held out his hands, and the little girl went toddling into them. He picked her up and bounced her on his knee, totally engrossed with her. It was hard to believe that this man was the giant dragon who soared above Norway a day ago.

"Tell me everything," Deacon said, looking around the room. "So much has changed."

"Not everything," Jayla said. "Cressida still gossips a mile a minute. Helena still irritates Drake for sheer entertainment because she knows no matter how mad he gets, he'll never do anything about it.

Korine is still like a mother to all of us, as you can tell. We've just gotten older, fatter, and we've all got little ones clinging to us now."

"What have you been up to?" Cressida asked. "You're the one who's changed. You left here in exile, and you returned as the Dragon Companion. I bet you have stories to tell. We heard how you helped defeat Marguerite Drothcar."

Deacon told the story of defeating Marguerite. This whole scene fascinated me. I'd never had a large family, so this dynamic was completely foreign to me. I liked how the entire room felt cozy despite its size.

When Deacon got done with that story, the women started to tell him more of what had happened in his absence. When one woman would laugh, the rest of the room would join in. When another recounted the difficult loss of a child, everyone teared up.

Children crawled and toddled around, going from woman to woman, sucking up all the attention they could get. I'd only ever thought of the Syndicate in political terms, but this was a family. I imagined the other clans that made up the Syndicate were much the same.

I wanted this for Deacon. He needed their support. Someday in the not-too-distant future I would die, and it would be these women who would support him. They didn't know it, but they already had my thanks.

The only family I'd ever had outside of Alistair was Harry. I knew Harry had extended family, but they didn't often visit. He'd been pretty alone since his husband died. When "Freddie" showed up, he'd been thrilled.

That was still a problem that needed to be dealt with. I had to make sure that no matter what happened with Alistair's rescue mission, Harry stayed safe.

As I had been so lovingly reminded by Deacon, there wasn't much for me to do other than wait. This seemed like the perfect time to take care of the Freddie situation. I needed to find out if the real

Freddie was still alive, and if so, what kind of presence the fae had with him.

Best-case scenario they hadn't put anyone on the real Freddie. Harry didn't have enough contact with his extended family to notice that there were two Freddies. Why would he call to make sure the Freddie visiting him was the real one? It didn't make sense. Worst-case scenario they had killed the real Freddie. Most likely they were holding him hostage.

Deacon deserved this time alone with his family, and I felt like an intruder anyway. While he was engrossed in a story from one of his sisters, I quietly slipped out.

On my way downstairs, I could hear laughter echoing from the living room, and it brought a smile to my face. Coming here had been the right thing to do.

46

I pulled out my burner phone and called Trevor. If I wanted to find Freddie, I needed help. I didn't realize until the third ring that he was likely asleep.

I was about to hang up and do an Internet search when Trevor's groggy voice came on the line. "Hello?"

"Hey, Trevor, it's me."

He perked up. "Are you okay? It's good to hear from you."

"Yeah, I'm actually doing really well. I'm somewhere safe. I was calling because I need your help finding someone."

"Okay, give me a second." I could hear him moving around, getting to his computer. "All right, who is it?"

"I have a friend, Harry Harmon. He's a retiree and widower. He has a nephew named Freddie. I don't know if he has the same last name or not. I need Freddie's address."

"All right, do you have any other information on Harry to give me? A phone number or address?"

I gave him both. "Can you give me a call back on this number when you get something?"

"Sure thing. It probably won't take long." Trevor hung up, and I headed to the library to see if I could find any books on blood magic.

The library was quite large for a private home. It was done in all dark woods and leather with a masculine feel to it. For some reason, it made me think Drake spent a lot of time here.

There were several chairs and tables strewn about, and at the farthest one sat Sybil. When she saw me, she jumped up and ran to give me a hug.

"I was wondering when I'd see you," she said.

"How long have you been here? Is Pint here too?" I asked. I had thought Sybil would seek me out as soon as she arrived.

"Not too long. Pint is off playing with some of the children. I think he's happy to finally be around other dragons."

I imagined he was. He never mentioned missing dragons, but that was just how Pint was. He didn't dwell on things he couldn't change. It must be great for him to really revel in being a dragon here. With me, he always had to hide, make sure humans never saw him, pretend he was a lizard. Having the companionship of dragon shifters would be good for him.

"So what are you doing in here?" I asked.

"Drake got me up to speed. I was just looking over a copy of the security you can expect around Alistair. I'm afraid I'm not much help. I don't know anything about blood magic other than that it requires blood and suffering." Her face fell, as if disappointed in herself for not having knowledge that there was no earthly reason for her to possess.

"Don't worry about it. We have other people working on it."

"I just want to be useful."

"Believe me, I understand the feeling." Every moment I was here and Alistair was still captive weighed on me. "You want to come help me with something?"

"Yes, please." She looked relieved to have something to do.

"I want to find Freddie. I need to know what Malev is doing with him. Once she realizes we've taken Alistair or if we get caught trying to free him, it's likely she'll kill Freddie and Mr. Harmon. Did Drake leave one of his shifters back at your place?"

Sybil nodded. "Yeah, he has two rotating shifts. They're good. They'll make sure Freddie doesn't do anything to hurt Harry."

I hadn't doubted Drake, but I couldn't expect other people to take Harry's safety as seriously as I did. "Good. When Deacon and I make the rescue attempt, we need whoever's on duty to kill Freddie. We can't do it too soon because then we risk tipping off Malev if she can't get a hold of him. Before all this happens, we need to find the real Freddie. If he's being held hostage, we need to take out his captor."

"What if that tips off Malev?"

I'd thought about that, but I didn't think it would. "Malev's concerned with using Harry to control me, to exert pressure. If she has someone on Freddie, I doubt they keep in regular contact. She couldn't care less what happens to him. Her only concern is Harry because that's the only person I care about. I think it's an acceptable risk."

My phone rang, and I answered on the first ring. I knew it would be Trevor. No one else who wasn't here had this number. "That was fast."

"It wasn't too difficult. Freddie's a single guy living by himself outside of Albuquerque, New Mexico. I'll text you the address."

"Thanks, I really appreciate it. You just saved a person's life." I liked letting him know how important his work was.

"Really?"

"Really."

"Damn." I could hear the smile in his voice. "Just doing my job."

I laughed. "Yep. That's what this is all about. Hopefully I'll see you soon."

"Stay safe." Trevor hung up.

I looked at Sybil. "We're going to New Mexico. You mind porting us?"

"Not at all."

I wrote a note to Deacon explaining what Sybil and I were doing and left it for him. If everything went well, we might even be back before he noticed my absence.

With Sybil, I wouldn't need to perform magic unless it was an emergency. So there was no way for Deacon to know what was going on. I wanted him to simply enjoy this time with his family.

We looked up the address online and got a street view of the area. Sybil found a good spot where we could port in and likely avoid detection. She grabbed my hand, and in an instant, we were there.

We were in an alley across the street and a few houses down from Freddie's. We didn't want to get too close and alert anyone to our presence. As soon as we left the alley and got to the main road, I stopped. A horribly sweet rose scent filled the air. It had to be fae.

"There's someone with him."

The fae presence was good news. It meant Freddie was alive. There was no need to have someone babysit a corpse.

"So how do you want to do it?" Sybil asked.

We had to take him by surprise and neutralize him before he could port away. "I need you to incapacitate the fae until I can void him."

"But we have to sneak up on him. I don't know how to get you close without tipping him off."

I could smell the fae from this distance but knew Sybil couldn't, and he couldn't smell Sybil. My heightened senses from the anointing were at work. "We just need something to prevent him from porting."

"I can do sensory deprivation. It's unlikely he'd be able to collect his thoughts enough to port right away."

Sybil liked performing sensory deprivation on people. She had the tiniest sadistic streak when it came to that.

"Do you think you can port us inside and then perform sensory deprivation before he has a chance to port away?"

Sybil looked at the house, picturing its layout. She nodded. "Yes. I don't need to see him to do it. I just need to be able to focus on him and his magic. It won't be as good as what I did to that human in St. Louis. The fae will likely be able to fend off the attack, but it will at least keep him from porting right away. How much time do you need?"

"Hardly any at all. I just need to void him, and then we can take our time."

"I think we can manage that."

"Alright then, whenever you're ready." We walked back to the alley where we were less likely to be seen disappearing into thin air. The neighborhood was a quiet collection of small homes with sandy yards. Most people were probably at work, so there wasn't much risk.

I placed one hand in Sybil's and the other around the hilt of my void blade. I wouldn't unsheathe it until we were in the house. I didn't want to risk accidentally nicking either one of us when we ported. The void blade didn't work on intention. If it drew blood, it voided the victim.

Sybil took a deep breath. "One, two, three."

We were in the living room of the house, just in front of the window we'd seen from across the street. A lamp crashed to the floor as the fae stood up and moved frantically about, confused by his lack of senses.

Already I could see that he was regaining his vision, so I drew my blade and crossed the few feet to him. I plunged my dagger in his shoulder and forced him to the ground. He let out a scream, too distracted by the physical pain to realize that he no longer had magic.

"You can release him now," I told Sybil.

His eyes focused on me. I gave the dagger a push, and he winced in pain.

"Now, what happens next is up to you. I need some information. If you give it to me, I'll have mercy on you. Understand?"

"Get the fuck off me," he sneered. "I'm not going to tell you shit. Just you wait until you pull that dagger out of my shoulder."

He obviously had too much adrenaline running through him to realize that he didn't have magic.

"Sybil, would you care to make him more compliant?"

Using her magic, she levitated a shard of glass from the shattered lamp over to his face and slowly slid it down his cheek, drawing blood. It really freaked me out seeing this side of Sybil, the way she was so adept at causing pain and fear when she needed to. When she'd drawn a thin line of blood all the way down his face, she took his sight again. I could tell by the way his eyes lost focus.

"Ooh, it's like doing it to a human now," Sybil said. Without his magic, he couldn't put up the defenses that made it harder for her to perform this type of magic on a fae.

"Where's Freddie?" I asked.

Sybil set the shard of glass down on his cheek again.

"He's in the bedroom," the fae said with a strained voice.

"Have you hurt him?"

"No, I just keep him asleep, that's all."

"And when do you check-in?"

He started to shake his head, but it pushed the glass into his cheek. "I don't. I'm just supposed to stay here and keep him asleep until told otherwise."

"So you have no clue how long you'll be here?"

"No idea. That's the truth."

I stood up and pulled my void blade from his shoulder. I wiped it off on his clothes and sheathed it. "Keep him restrained while I go check out his story," I told Sybil.

In the one bedroom I found Freddie asleep in his bed. He looked exactly like the fae version. Logically, I knew he would, but it was still weird to see. There was hardly any magic on him from what I could smell, enough to be consistent with the fae's story that he was simply keeping him asleep. I was satisfied that Freddie would be okay.

I went back to the living room. "All right, your story checks out."

"So you're going to let me go? Are you going to give me my sight back?"

I nodded to Sybil, and his eyes focused. He scrambled up, cradling his shoulder.

I wanted to take his hand as payment for Alistair's. I wanted to do horrible things to him, but I wasn't in this for revenge, only justice.

The fae had a confused expression on his face and looked around as if he'd misplaced something. "What did you do to me? My magic…"

"It's gone."

"You said if I told you what you wanted, you'd have mercy on me."

"You're right, and I'll fulfill my end of the bargain. Sybil, restrain him." The fae went still, and I walked behind him. With one quick motion, I snapped his neck, and he crumbled to the ground.

"You let him off easy," Sybil said.

She'd expected me to exact revenge on him for what happened to Alistair. "It's not his fault. He didn't take Alistair, Malev did. Can you dispose of his body? Then I want to check on Freddie, make sure that if we leave him here he'll wake up eventually."

Sybil nodded and disintegrated the body. The spell she did removed all of his organic material, so that meant even his blood in the carpet. The only sign of a struggle was the shattered lamp.

Back in the bedroom, Sybil looked over Freddie. "It's freaky how much they look the same."

"I know. Do you think it's fine to leave him here, or do we need to do something to make sure he'll snap out of this? There's not much magic on him from what I can smell."

"In that case, I think it's fine to leave him," Sybil said.

Harry hardly ever heard from his family, so it wasn't likely if we left him here that Freddie would call his uncle. I doubted the fae would've told him anything about what was going on, if he even knew the full story himself. Freddie would wake up very confused.

I walked to the kitchen and opened the fridge. He had half a case of beer, and I grabbed it. I opened each can and emptied them down the sink.

"What are you doing?" Sybil asked.

"I don't want him to wonder too much about what happened. I want him to wake up and simply think he has a really bad hangover."

Once I'd emptied all the cans, I took them to his room and dumped them on the floor by the bed. I could look through his phone and computer, see if he had a girlfriend, make it look like she'd broken up with him and he'd drowned his sorrows, but I didn't think anything more was necessary. He'd likely wake up, see the empty beer cans, and come to the most logical conclusion: that for some reason he had gotten so drunk that he passed out.

"All right, our work here is done," I said and held out my hand to Sybil.

"This was fun. I like these girls-only missions. We should do them more often." She put her hand in mine and took us back to the Syndicate compound.

47

When I returned to the compound, I told Drake what we'd done. He agreed that as soon as Deacon and I left to rescue Alistair, he'd have one of his shifters take out the fake Freddie while trying to avoid upsetting Harry.

The rest of the day passed uneventfully. Deacon didn't like that I'd gone without him, but Sybil and I had returned before he even found my note. He couldn't really stay mad when I'd been with Sybil.

I spent my time learning what I could about blood magic from Drake's library. In order to do powerful blood magic, the blood used had to be potent. That meant that it had repeatedly suffered and been used for blood magic before. I didn't know how we were going to manage that. But Dorran sent word that he was working on it and not to worry.

That was all anyone ever told me anymore. We're working on it. Don't worry. But what else was I supposed to do? Alistair was Malev's prisoner, the Circle wanted me dead, and we had to mount a rescue mission in the fae realm without any idea of how to do it, but I wasn't supposed to worry? Okay.

By the next morning, I couldn't take it anymore. I shook with anticipation, nerves, and withdrawal from the nether. I couldn't sit around. There was one person who I could ask for help, one place that I could go to soothe my nerves.

Maybe this time in the nether would be different. After all, I could honestly tell the Origin that Deacon and I had spoken about bonding. We were one step closer. Didn't that count for something?

It wasn't like there was anything else for me to do. That had been made abundantly clear to me. At the same time, talking to the Origin was something only I could do. She had knowledge to give us, and it was up to me to get it.

That was all the justification I needed.

After breakfast, while Deacon was off getting reacquainted with people from his youth, I created a portal in my room and went to the temple.

The temple itself was a peaceful place. I liked that no one ever bothered me when I came here. For me, this place held only good memories. There weren't many places like that in my life.

The moon elf priestess noticed my arrival and gave me a little nod of acknowledgment. I knew when I was done she'd have a cup of water waiting for me.

I felt anxious as I walked to the pillar with the dragon eye. I didn't know what I'd do if I didn't get answers or some advice. I couldn't wait to tell the Origin that I'd done what she asked. I relied on my community. That's why I was here with time on my hands.

Perhaps she'd reward me with the key to getting Alistair back. Perhaps this entire thing had been a test, and only once I relinquished control to the people around me would she reveal the knowledge I needed to rescue Alistair. I would know soon.

I placed my palm on the cool dragon eye and the color drained from the world.

Gusts of wind blew around me, creating clouds of fallen leaves. The only sound I heard was the whooshing of the wind as it went past my ears. My head throbbed, like something was trying to break free. This had never happened before.

"I did what you asked. I'm using my community. Everyone's helping. All I have to do is wait for them."

Still the only sound I heard was wind.

"I know I haven't bonded yet, but we did talk about it. I'm pretty sure it's going to happen. I just need to know that I'm not going to hurt him. You have to understand that."

Still nothing.

Last time, when I'd wanted her to leave me alone, she couldn't keep quiet. Now that I needed her, she was nowhere to be found.

"I did it. I passed the test. I did what you asked of me. Now I just need a little bit of help. We have to use blood magic to get to Alistair. I don't know if we'll be able to pull it off. You have to know if there's some other way."

Still there was nothing. The wind stopped blowing. The air sat still. Instead of whooshing, I heard the pounding in my skull.

I grabbed my head between my hands, hoping pressure would ease the pain. It didn't.

I'd never felt anything like this. It was a pain so intense that I couldn't imagine ever being rid of it.

"Why won't you talk to me? Why won't you help me? I'm trying. I want to do the right thing. I can't let Alistair down. I can't be the Dragon Fae without him."

The silence somehow only intensified the pain in my head. I let out a scream. I didn't know what to do.

"Help me!"

The world spun. I closed my eyes against the pain. The nether crept into my mind and took hold. It clung to me, and when the strands of life pulled me back to the temporal realm, the nether ripped out those parts of my mind and kept them.

When I opened my eyes, I was sitting with my back against the pillar. The priestess stood aside with a cup of water. Was that really it? I took the cup and drank, but it did nothing to alleviate my pain.

For the first time I really understood what nether madness was. It literally kept part of my mind.

I handed the cup back to the priestess, and she stood back, giving me privacy but not completely leaving.

Why had the Origin forsaken me? Why had I been cursed with nether addiction? Deacon hadn't felt the urge to return after the anointing. This whole prophecy was a curse. It caused nothing but pain to everyone involved.

I let out a sob. I tried to hold it back, retain some of my dignity, but what was the point anymore? I succumbed to the sobs and let it all out.

For the first time, I really accepted that I was powerless. I had lied in the nether. I hadn't yielded to the help of those around me. I'd arrogantly thought that I could come here and get the answers and then run off and save Alistair. No one else would have to be involved. I wouldn't have to wait around feeling worthless any longer.

"Tsk, tsk, tsk, what have we here?"

I recognized that voice. I looked up and saw Jaygar standing over me.

"If you aren't the saddest looking Dragon Fae I've ever seen."

I smiled. "That is the general consensus."

"Come now, self-pity is beneath you."

I looked away. "You were right to doubt me."

"No, I didn't doubt you. I accepted you. I meant the oath I swore that day," he said, his voice deep with surety. "We all did."

I wanted to call him a fool, because that's how I saw it, but I wouldn't disrespect him that way. I wouldn't disrespect the acolytes who had witnessed my anointing then swore their allegiance to me. I didn't have the luxury of quitting.

Right now, all I cared about was rescuing Alistair. I loved him and needed him to be safe. But this was about so much more than that.

Alistair's capture was a symptom of a much larger problem: the instability in our world. There had long been conflict in Elustria, but now it bled over to Earth. Two rival fae courts fought each other. The Directorate and the fae both used Earth as a pawn in their games.

They would tear both Elustria and Earth apart in their quest for power.

And now the Circle was wading further into fae politics and conflict. The Dragon Fae came for this time, to bring peace, to fight for the people.

The Circle and Malev both wanted to depose me. The only way to keep that from happening was to get Alistair. It was the only way to take back the power and then fight for all the people who had sworn fealty to me.

When they had knelt and sworn an oath at this very temple, it had nothing to do with me. It had to do with hope in the Dragon Fae. Sybil had said I would need the memory of that day to get me through what lay ahead. She was right.

I couldn't let them down.

I had to keep fighting, get Alistair, and lead these people to a more peaceful time. I didn't know how, but it wasn't my job to know how. The Origin had said to rely on others, that this job was too big for one person to do alone.

I did what she said. I now needed to take it on faith that it would all work. The people at my anointing took it on faith. The people who had sworn loyalty to Dorran as my proxy took it on faith. The people who had shown me their mark of loyalty at the enclave took it on faith. How could I not do the same?

I surrounded myself with capable people. I needed to trust them to do their jobs the same way they trusted me to do mine. Jaygar was right, self-pity was beneath me. I moved to get up but was still shaky from the nether. Jaygar stepped forward and offered me his hand.

"The living aren't meant to go to the nether," he said as he pulled me to my feet.

So he knew. "Why are you here? I haven't seen you since the anointing."

"I heard that you had visited the nether multiple times. I decided to come and offer my assistance."

"Oh?" I had a feeling he meant more than assistance standing up.

"Yes. I thought you needed to be reminded of who you are. You won me over, and you won the people over. Now, have another cup of water."

This time when I drank it soothed my head a little, or maybe it was only wishful thinking. "Thank you."

"It's time for you to go back to Earth. You aren't supposed to be here yet."

I wondered what he meant by that, but I knew better than to ask. I created a portal to the compound and stepped through.

I sat down on the bed in my room. I could really use another cold glass of water. I just needed a minute to collect myself.

The door swung open, and Deacon stood there staring at me. I got up from the bed.

"I'm sorry, Deacon. I know I shouldn't have gone—"

"There's no time. Cassalina sent word. We have to go today. Everyone's waiting for us." He turned and led the way to the dining room. As we approached, I could smell a variety of magics.

My people had come through.

48

"I've never had such an assembly of magic folk in my home," Drake said from his seat at the head of the table. We were quite the eclectic bunch. Dorran, the shade, Sybil, Deacon, me, and Farawyn.

I took over from Drake. "Thank you all for your help. It means a lot, especially when there's nothing in it for you other than my heartfelt thanks."

"Well, there's also sticking it to Malev," Dorran said.

It felt like everything was a game to him. When he lived as long as he had, it must be difficult to take things too seriously. His manner completely contradicted his appearance. I think he adopted the aura he did just to awe and impress people.

"Yes, well we can only stick it to her if you have a solution for us for battling past her enchantments," I said.

The shade pulled a handkerchief out of his pocket and unfolded it. In the middle sat a severed finger.

Sybil gasped.

"This is the finger of a high fae who practiced potent blood magic," the shade said.

"And where did you get this? Please tell me you didn't take some fae's finger for this mission." It really shouldn't matter to me, especially since anyone practicing blood magic wasn't on our side. Still, I didn't like getting innocents involved.

"Don't worry. This individual owed one of my colleagues a substantial sum of money. What you see is an attempt to collect a debt. It just so happens that we're benefiting from it."

I supposed that's what you got when you asked a shade for help.

"So we have the finger. What do we do with it?" Deacon asked.

"Aw!" The shade lifted a finger in the air. "I forgot. We were also able to extract from the fae instructions on how to get past the enchantments."

Dorran and the shade shared a glance at the word "extract," and I got the feeling that the debt collector in question was Dorran himself.

"And what's to keep this fae from going to Malev? She'd reward such an informant well." I doubted shades were in the habit of thinking through all the repercussions of their actions.

"That won't be a problem," Dorran said. The finality with which he said it silenced any follow-up.

"I can get us into the fae realm," Farawyn said. "But I think we should practice first, know exactly what we're going to do once we get there. I'm not very fast on my feet, so the more prepared we are, the better."

"All right, but we don't have much time," Deacon said. "Cassalina passed word through Goffrey that we need to act soon. She also got me a copy of Malev's imprint. I've practiced with it a few times, and I think I can pull it off."

We had an awful lot of moving parts that had to work in harmony and not a lot of time to perfect our rhythm. "All right, let's run it through and see how we do."

I was glad to finally be doing something. We were one successful run-through away from getting Alistair back.

49

*D*eacon and I stood with Farawyn going over our last minute checks. We had one chance to get this right. If we screwed it up, none of us would come back alive.

As much as I didn't want him to back out, I had to ask one last time, "Farawyn, are you sure you want to go through with this?"

"I'm positive." He nodded. "My family are dragon shifters as well as high fae. If I have to choose between the Dragon Fae and the fae queen, my choice is clear."

Our run-through had gone well. I liked Farawyn. He was nice and mild-mannered, not the type of person you'd expect to attempt a jail-break. Not only would he be getting us inside the fae realm, he'd be lending us his magic.

I tapped my pocket to assure myself the severed fae finger was still there. If I lost it, we were doomed. Then I felt at the small of my back for my void blade. It sat secure, ready for use, though I didn't expect to use it.

We had to avoid a confrontation with Malev at all costs. There was no plan that would give us victory if we faced her. I couldn't be quick enough with my blade to best her in her own realm. Still, I liked the security of it at my back.

"Remember," Deacon said, "if you get hurt, let me heal you. It's better that we stop for the few minutes it'll take than to get sloppy because of pain. And under no circumstances can you let your blood touch the ground. It'll alert Malev to our presence. So if either of you get cut, let me know immediately, and I'll seal the wound."

Farawyn and I nodded our understanding, then I took over giving instructions. "It's going to feel like time is moving faster than it is. We need to think slow. Mistakes are more expensive than time."

Farawyn sighed. "We've been through all this. We're as prepared as we're going to be. It's time we leave."

It was just the three of us in a room in Drake's house. We hadn't wanted the distraction of anyone else around for goodbyes and well wishes. We needed to stay focused.

Farawyn took us right to the stairway that led to Alistair. Our mission was laid out in front of us in five phases. We just had to take them one at a time.

The three of us stayed close as we began our descent. We didn't know exactly how it worked for Malev, but we did know that she was connected to every aspect of the fae realm. If we strayed too far from Farawyn, there was a chance she'd detect us. We weren't sure, but we weren't willing to take the chance. Our run-through had been mainly spent practicing our movements close together.

I pulled the finger out of my pocket and unwrapped the handkerchief that held it. We would have to use some of the blood to counteract the different enchantments and charms. Malev had designed this entire prison to respond to her and her alone. Anyone who wanted to overcome that limitation would have to resort to blood magic.

Farawyn, Deacon, and I each held out a palm, and I rubbed the end of the finger across each of them, smearing some blood. Then we pressed our palms against each other and recited the incantation in our minds. Pain ripped through me and Deacon from the cuff, but we'd prepared for this.

An orb of yellow light encircled us. It pushed back the enchantment on the earthen walls that was meant to choke off magic. To keep the orb in place, we had to keep our palms touching. Deacon arranged himself so that he was the one going downstairs backward. We took it slowly, one step at a time.

So far, so good.

The stone staircase took us deeper and deeper into the damp earth. This part was easy. Still, I smiled encouragement at Farawyn. We needed to celebrate our victory at making it this far. Our little successes here would propel us forward.

A few seconds later, Deacon held up his hand, and we stopped. This was the sign that he saw our next obstacle.

When Sybil and I had come here with Malev, fireflies provided light as we got deeper down the stairs. However, the scroll Cassalina provided revealed that light was not the fireflies' main function. They allowed Malev and her guests to pass freely but would attack anyone else. There was only one spell that could kill them, and we had to perform it while maintaining our yellow orb of protection.

I held up the fae finger again and Farawyn and Deacon presented their palms for the blood. I swiped both of their palms and then handed the finger to Deacon so he could do mine. After he was done, he handed it back. When I grabbed for it, it slipped, tumbling through my fingers down the dark expanse below.

"Shit."

We all froze. If we didn't find the finger, we wouldn't be able to proceed past the next obstacles. One problem at a time though.

I signaled for the others to join their palms with mine. Once we had a connection, we performed the spell. This time, we created an electric blue ball of light that crackled through the air and sent it out down the stairwell. We held our breath as we listened.

Zap. Zipt. Zzzp.

It worked. The electric light consumed the fireflies.

We didn't need to maintain our connection to keep the blue light going, we just had to maintain our yellow protection orb. I nodded to Deacon, and he started back down the stairs.

We followed the blue light until it stopped zapping and fizzled out. A few steps later, Deacon held up his hand again.

We had reached the end of the stairs. They landed on an ancient tree trunk. According to the scroll, without Malev here, it would incinerate us. We needed the finger to counteract it. Deacon searched the landing, but it was too dark. The light from our protective bubble didn't extend far enough.

Without warning, Deacon breathed fire. For a moment, the entire landing was lit. I spotted the finger and reached out my hand, levitating it to me. The pain from the cuff was nothing compared to being incinerated alive.

The finger firmly in hand, we proceeded with the spell. This one required all three of us to hold onto the finger and squeeze out a few drops of blood onto the landing while we recited the spell in our minds.

After three drops of blood, a film covered the trunk. It worked.

Deacon lightly touched his foot to the landing, and seeing that it didn't burn, he placed his full weight on it. He turned back to us and nodded. We proceeded onto the landing.

Once we were all off the stairs, they disappeared and sconces on the wall lit with green flames, providing light. For a brief moment, I felt trapped as I had when Malev brought me and Sybil down here.

"All right, we should be fine to release the yellow light," I said. According to the scroll, once the stairs disappeared, the enchantment from the walls would no longer have any effect. We released our hands and nothing happened.

This next part would be the hardest so far. Deacon and I needed to mimic Malev's magic.

"Take a deep breath," Deacon said. "We've got this. You concentrate on revealing the doorway and let me handle mimicking her imprint. I'll do it exactly like we did in practice."

This was the trickiest part because Deacon had never actually met Malev. All he had to work off of was the imprint Cassalina provided.

In practice, it had felt like hers from my memory, but we had a lot riding on the accuracy of Cassalina's intel.

I reached out my hand and touched the wall. Pain from the cuff covered me as Deacon mimicked Malev's imprint. Before I could get the doorway open, the ground shook.

Farawyn screamed behind us. We turned to see hundreds of bugs crawling out of the tree trunk. They attacked Farawyn, probably because he made the most noise.

Deacon blew fire, but it was tricky since he didn't want to burn Farawyn. I used my magic to sweep away the bugs then incinerate them. It was no use. They just kept coming.

"Farawyn, you have to calm down." It was easier said than done. There weren't many people who could keep their wits about them while hundreds of bugs crawled up their body.

Farawyn's screaming stopped, but he still breathed heavily. "Keep going. We can't stop them. Maybe they'll go away when you get the doorway open."

This wasn't in the scroll. It seemed that Deacon mimicking Malev's imprint was what triggered it. Perhaps Malev could sense her magic being used elsewhere in the fae realm. If so, she knew we were here, and we didn't have much time.

"She knows," Farawyn said. "I can fight them off. Just keep going. We can't let this all be for nothing."

Deacon and I turned back to the wall, and I tried to block out Farawyn's breathing. I shook my hand and tried again. The ground shook as soon as Deacon activated Malev's imprint, but we worked through it. I focused on the magic in my hand, urging the wall to life.

Flowers blossomed and green vines grew out of the wall. They rolled back, revealing a doorway. This was it. We were to the final stage.

I turned around to see Farawyn fighting off the bugs. He'd found a spell that worked well for him, but there was no end in sight.

"We just have to get through the doorway," Deacon said. "Stay focused."

I nodded and turned away from Farawyn. This would use the last of the finger. If it didn't work, we'd be stuck here with no way out.

I held the finger in one hand and reached my other hand to Deacon. He grabbed onto me and extended his other hand to Farawyn. He took hold of Deacon while using his free hand to fight off the bugs.

This was it. My one chance. Deacon continued to mimic Malev's imprint, and I took the finger in my hand and squeezed it as hard as I could, obliterating it as I thrust my fist through the doorway.

There was resistance, but I pushed against it. It was like pushing against a heavy wall, but the wall gave way. Slowly. Inch by inch. We pushed through until we emerged on the other side.

"Nadiya?"

Alistair's voice was the sweetest sound in the world. He came running toward us, cradling the stump where his hand had been.

"What are you doing here?" he asked.

"What does is it look like we're doing? We're saving you. Now hurry up." I gathered him, Deacon, and Farawyn in a circle. My magic was exhausted from breaking through the doorway. "Farawyn, can you get us out of here?"

The walls around us shook and crumbled with Malev's ire.

"Close your eyes," Farawyn said.

I obliged, and when I opened them, we were back in Drake's house.

50

The room was filled with people waiting for our return. We were swarmed as soon as we appeared.

"Don't worry, Alistair, we have your hand. We can try to reattach it," I told him. In the bright light of the room, he looked even weaker than he had in the fae realm.

One of the shifters tasked with keeping Alistair's hand alive approached. They had the adjacent room set up to start reattaching it. The shifter didn't even bother trying to escort Alistair. He simply lifted him up and carried him away.

Sybil crashed into me. "Are you okay?"

"Yes, I'm fine. Someone needs to tend to Farawyn." I looked behind Sybil and saw that he was already being escorted out of the room.

"I knew you'd do it," Sybil said. The amazing thing was, I believed her. Her enthusiasm and belief carried our little group.

Pint landed on my shoulder and licked the side of my face. "I'm glad to have you back."

He only cared about Alistair because I did. Pint had been jealous of him in the past, the way he was jealous of most people who had my attention.

Drake approached. "Congratulations. You got him home safely. This was a success."

"Thank you. What about the fake Freddie? Was he killed?"

"I haven't gotten word yet, but the order was given. I have no reason to doubt that it was carried out. I'll let you know as soon as I hear."

"Come rest," Deacon said as he put his arm around me.

I didn't want to rest. This wasn't over, not yet. We had Alistair back, but I needed to stay with him, see him through this. I wanted to be there when his hand was reattached, and if it couldn't be, I wanted to be there to lighten his burden.

I shook my head. "No, I won't be able to. I want to see Alistair."

I walked out of the room with Deacon and Sybil following. The hallway was lined with dragon shifters. When they saw me, they let out a cheer that rippled down the hall and through the house. I wanted to ignore it, go see Alistair, but I couldn't. I wasn't Nadiya right now. I was the Dragon Fae. These people had helped me, and they expected me to be their leader.

I raised my hand and waved. "Thank you. We couldn't have done this without you."

Another cheer erupted. I gave them a smile then turned and entered the operating room.

It was a large space, probably used as a meeting area on a normal day. The shifters, Dorran, and a priestess from the temple all worked to reattach Alistair's hand. He lay on a bed that had been brought into the room especially for this purpose.

I went to him and knelt at the side of the bed, taking his good hand in mine and kissing it. I'd never shown so much affection toward him, but I couldn't help myself, not when I'd thought I'd lost him forever. "I'm sorry it took us so long."

"What are you talking about?" Alistair said. "You were amazing."

He seemed so frail, so different from the last time I'd seen him. "Did she starve you?"

"No. I tried to eat as little as possible. I could tell the food was doing something to me. It kept me docile, and each bite I took made me feel hungrier. It was a balancing act. I knew I needed to eat to keep myself alive, but I also knew that the hunger I felt was an illusion from the food itself."

He shook his head, as if to rid himself of the memory. This was the type of magic the fae were known for. Trickery and deceit. Mind games. "I can't believe you were able to keep my hand alive."

"That was all Deacon and the dragon shifters. We had to try. I don't know if they'll be able to get it working again."

"This is already more than I'd hoped for," Alistair said. He grimaced at something they did to his hand. "If the pain's anything to go by, I'll get full use back." He chuckled without humor.

Drake was in the room watching over everything that happened. I asked him, "Has food been ordered?"

"Yes, it should be here shortly."

I turned back to Alistair. "You're in for a real treat. Drake has a great chef."

Alistair smiled. "Look at you. I was shocked when I heard that you'd announced yourself. I'll never forget where I was in Elustria when I heard the news. I wish I could've been with you. I was so proud."

"It was a stupid move," I said. "Impetuous, impulsive, definitely not the way I was trained to behave."

"You've never behaved the way you were trained to," Alistair said. "I wish I could've been there for the anointing."

"Me too," I said. Alistair had been the one to believe in me from the beginning. Which reminded me, "I met an old friend of yours. Gordon."

"Really? Did the Circle assign you to him?"

"Yes"

"Good. You couldn't have been assigned to a better handler."

"I don't know what will happen with us and the Circle now."

"It doesn't really matter," Alistair said. "This has never been about the Circle. The Circle was simply a tool for finding you. You're not meant to work for them."

"Well that's good, because I'm pretty sure I'm fired after this." I smiled, and Alistair chuckled. For a moment it felt like it was just the two of us again.

Alistair sobered suddenly. "I'm sorry. She got your address from me. I tried to fight her off, but she invaded my mind. I tried to resist." Guilt covered his face.

"Don't worry about it. Of course you couldn't help it." The last thing he needed to worry about was the past. "It all worked out, didn't it?"

Distraction arrived in the form of food: a broth.

"Here," the chef said. "We need to start him off on something light. If he can keep this down, we'll move on to something more substantial."

I nodded and let go of Alistair's hand to take the broth. But when I let go, my hands started to shake. Deacon noticed. He knew the source and came to my rescue.

"Here, let me take that," he said. I stood, and Deacon took over my spot and fed the broth to Alistair.

Drake came over when the chef had left. "I just got word. The fake Freddie is dead. Harry slept through it. As far as I know, he's still asleep."

"Thanks," I said. It seemed so inadequate, but I didn't know what else to say.

"Of course," Drake said.

"Sybil?" I asked. She came over to me from Alistair's bedside. "I need you to go home and check on Harry. I don't want him to wake up and be scared when Freddie's not there. Make sure he's all right, and take care of him if you can," I said.

I held her gaze for a moment. I didn't ask her to, but I silently hoped she'd perform mind magic on him to erase the memory of the last few days.

"I understand," Sybil said. "I'll take care of it." She ported away immediately.

I sat in a chair at Alistair's bedside, and Pint rested in my lap. I had to clasp my hands together to keep them from shaking. My white-knuckled grip did not escape Deacon's notice. It didn't matter though. It was over. We were safe, and Alistair was back. I could deal with everything else later.

Alistair kept the broth down without a problem. The work on his hand finished, and it would be a waiting game to see how much functionality returned. Magic could do incredible things, but it couldn't work miracles, and sometimes it took time.

The priestess made a potion for Alistair to restore his strength and help him heal. After he took it, he was able to eat a large meal. Then he fell asleep with the aid of another potion.

I couldn't leave him, so I just watched his breathing. My legs fidgeted, and I squirmed in my chair. Pint sat steadfastly in my lap, unperturbed by the movement.

"Why don't you get some rest?" Deacon asked. "I'll stay here and watch him for you. I promise."

"I know you will, but I can't. I'm too high strung to sleep even if I wanted to."

My phone rang, and I hurried to answer it so it wouldn't wake Alistair.

"Hi, Sybil. How's Harry?"

"I took care of him. He won't remember a thing."

"Thank you," I said.

"No problem. I want to let you know that Gordon called. He left a message for you. He says Meilin knows what happened. She's pissed."

"Of course she is. We expected that."

"Yeah, but this is different. I think she's going to come after you."

I knew this moment had to come. The Dragon Fae couldn't work as a Circle operative. It didn't make sense. "So I guess I'm a free agent then."

"Gordon also said congratulations. He sounded happy you were successful."

I made a note to pass that on to Alistair when he woke.

"Is there anything you want me to bring back with me?" Sybil asked. "Harry's fixing some food right now. I was going to eat with him and then come back."

"I can't think of anything that I need."

"All right then. I'll see you soon." Sybil hung up.

Dorran came in to give me an update. "Alistair should wake up soon, and he'll be really hungry when he does. That potion is pretty powerful. A bunch of us are going to Bubbles and Brews tonight to celebrate. It would mean a lot if you came."

I didn't feel like celebrating. All I wanted was to keep everyone I loved close and safe. But that wasn't realistic.

"I'll be there," I said.

"Are you sure?" Deacon asked.

"Yes, I'm sure."

"Good," Dorran said. "A lot of people have believed in you for a long time. They need this." He left the room.

Deacon sat in a chair beside me and took my hand in his. I'd gotten my shaking under control through sheer force of will.

"Are you going to tell me what happened in the nether?" Deacon asked.

"Nothing. The Origin abandoned me."

Deacon looked at me and raised his eyebrows. "I thought you said she wouldn't leave you alone last time."

"Yep. When I didn't want her, there she was. When I needed her, she forsook me. Jaygar was there afterward. He had some words of encouragement."

"I'm just glad this is all over," Deacon said with heavy relief. "I guess it's naïve to hope for a little bit of peace."

I laughed. "That's what I hoped for the other day sitting on Sybil's sofa watching TV with you. So yeah, don't get your hopes up for peace."

Deacon grinned. "We'll have to finish that show some time."

I returned his smile. "It's a date."

Bubbles and Brews vibrated with music and excitement. Everyone had at least one drink in their hand, some people two.

"To the Dragon Fae!" Farawyn cheered.

The entire bar answered, "To the Dragon Fae!"

I raised my glass in acknowledgment of their cheer but quickly lowered it. I wondered if they could see how badly the liquid in my glass shook. I couldn't control the trembling anymore.

Next to me, Alistair sat at the bar with a drink and a smile on his face talking to Sybil. He'd wanted to hear everything about the anointing and what had happened while he was captured. His newly attached hand rested on the bar.

I felt like my skin was peeling off my body. I only had to get through tonight. All I had to do was put on a smile and pretend for one night. Once the celebration was over, I could get some sleep, and I'd feel better in the morning.

"A pixie sparkle for the lady," Deacon told the bartender as he sidled up next to me.

I laughed, and it was strained even to my ears. That was the same drink I'd ordered at the enclave bar in Norway.

"I have it on good authority that you like these," Deacon said. "Don't worry though, I wouldn't dream of making assumptions about your character based on your drink preference."

"Ha ha, very funny." Even with all the noise around us, I could hear the shaking in my voice.

Deacon put down his drink and peered at me intently. "What's wrong?"

"Nothing." That wouldn't have convinced anyone.

"It's the nether, isn't it?" Deacon asked.

"Don't worry about it. It'll pass. Enjoy the night." I raised my glass and took a drink before the shaking could get the better of me.

"All right, I'm taking you home." Deacon pushed our drinks back and moved to help me up. Alistair turned at the motion.

"What's wrong?" He looked between me and Deacon.

"Nothing," Deacon said. "I'm just going to take her home. She needs some rest."

I silently thanked him for covering for me. I didn't want Alistair to realize that I'd become addicted to the nether. I couldn't stand the thought of losing his respect.

"Oh, okay then. You've earned it," Alistair said with a smile and a tip of his glass.

"Thanks," I said. "Enjoy your night." I forced a smile, but I could tell it didn't fool him. He narrowed his eyes at me and stood from his barstool. "Don't worry about me. Seriously, stay here and enjoy your drinks." I turned toward the entrance and took a few shaky steps.

The door opened.

I couldn't believe my eyes. "Julien?"

My ex-fiancé stared at me from the doorway.

The world tilted, and the last thing I felt before passing out was Deacon lifting me into his arms.

ABOUT THE AUTHOR

Caethes's writing is influenced by her observations of this imperfect world and the flawed characters who inhabit it. She enjoys playing RPGs and making up complex backstories for her avatar and the characters she encounters. Caethes has lived in seven states and is always looking for the next place to call home with her husband and dogs. She currently resides in Florida where she's often found at theme parks when she's not writing.

Join her Facebook reader group:
CaethesFaron.com/fbgroup
Contact her:
CaethesFaron.com/contact
Visit her site:
CaethesFaron.com